EXIT 9

Praise for *Sick*, the first Project Eden thriller:

"*Sick* didn't just hook me. It hit me with a devastating upper-cut on every primal level—as a parent, a father, and a human being." — Blake Crouch, author of *Run*

"*Sick* is a gem of an outbreak story that unfolds like a thriller movie and never lets up, all the way to the last page. Absolutely my favorite kind of story!" — John Maberry, *New York Times* bestselling author

"*Sick* not only grabs you by the throat, but by the heart and gut as well, and by the time you finish you feel as if you've just taken a runaway train through dangerous territory. Buy this book now. You won't regret it."—Robert Browne, author of *The Paradise Prophecy*

"Like a fever, *Sick* makes you sweat and keeps you up all night, wondering what the hell is happening. It'll make your heart race like someone shot you with an EpiPen. You think Battles was badass before? He just cranked it up to 500 joules. CLEAR!"—PopCultureNerd.com

"*Sick* is Brett Battles at his best, a thriller that also chills, with a secret at its core that's almost too scary to be contained within the covers of a book." — Tim Hallinan, author of the Edgar-nominated *The Queen of Patpong*

ALSO BY BRETT BATTLES

Short Stories
PERFECT GENTLEMAN

For Younger Readers
THE TROUBLE FAMILY CHRONICLES
HERE COMES MR. TROUBLE
YOU'RE IN BIG, MR. TROUBLE (Late 2012)

EXIT 9

by

Brett Battles

A PROJECT EDEN THRILLER

Book 2

What Has Come Before

IT HAS BEEN nearly eight months since humanity was rocked with the news of the Sage Flu outbreak in the Mojave Desert of California. The strain was particularly deadly, seeming to kill everyone who became infected. But before it could turn into an even larger problem, it mysteriously lost its potency and disappeared.

The world breathed a collective sigh of relief. They talked of remaining vigilant, but in most people's minds, mankind had dodged a bullet.

If only they'd known the truth, that this was merely a test performed by a group dedicated to giving the human race a restart, and that when this group moved out of the testing phase, things could become much, much worse.

There was, however, a band of people who did know the truth, who had dedicated themselves to trying to keep this horrific plan from becoming reality. But in the months since the test outbreak in the desert, they had made far too little progress.

Unfortunately for them, and for all of humanity, the ones behind the plan had not been experiencing the same problem. They'd been busy.

Very busy.

1

I.D. MINUS 41 DAYS

"This just came in."

Matt Hamilton took the piece of paper from the communications specialist and looked at the message.

MO KO EB PT TI HU JN RN MU ER UG YS UC ZR JZ
CZ CN EN TS LV NA HS CG GU HC DV DO MO JN OB HN
GU PH OM UI BC WF CU OF SR HP OV JG GJ TL OK YS XT
KV XD ML CA

"Have you decoded it?" he asked.

An uneasy nod.

"What?"

"It's from Heron."

Heron. Their deepest mole, tasked with only one job so as to preserve his cover. A fail-safe.

A second sheet of paper containing the translation was held out.

It's a go. Sometime in the next seven weeks. Project Eden calls it Implementation Day.

Best location BB n of sixty-six. Sci fac.

The paper slipped from Matt's hands and fell to the floor. "Dear God."

2

I.D. MINUS 27 DAYS

"THE COLD WAS unrelenting, its fierce bite intensified by the wind that sliced across the ice and snow. How anyone could ever choose to live above the Arctic Circle, Sawyer would never understand. Sure, the work done in most of the research stations that had been built this far north was important, but damn, the weather was brutal.

Of course, it didn't help that he and Napoli were not ensconced inside a building, sucking down hot coffee, and being warmed by heated air. Instead, they were lying prone on top of a ridge, under the near constant night sky of the approaching Arctic winter, as they observed the Brule Institute Outpost.

This was the fourth installation they'd checked in the last eleven days—one in northern Greenland, and the other two on individual islands in a winding line stretching into Canada. Their current location was Yanok Island, an otherwise uninhabited piece of rock roughly five miles in diameter.

Sawyer and Napoli had been there for twenty-two hours, arriving on a modified, cold-weather fishing boat. They had anchored in a cliff-ringed bay on the side of the island opposite the station. They climbed to the top with the help of an old land slide, and not too far from there they had found a cutout in a small hill—not quite a cave, more an overhang that had kept most of the ground underneath clear from snow. Using tarps and some other gear they'd brought along, they walled it off, and created a heated shelter, complete with two cots, a hot plate, and a two-way, encrypted radio.

So far, the only report they'd sent in was similar to the ones they'd been transmitting since their assignment began: *No sign of unusual activity.*

"Number seven just came outside," Napoli said, looking through their tripod-mounted, night-vision binoculars. Over the course of their observations, they had given a number to each person from the outpost they'd seen, identifying them by some unique aspect of their gear—patches, color, type of boots.

Sawyer lifted his head a fraction of an inch as if he could see the man as easily as Napoli had, but at this distance in the darkness he had a hard time even identifying the main door.

Napoli moved the binoculars. "He's heading up to the Gazebo."

Like the numbers they'd given the people, they'd developed a shorthand to describe the facility. The Gazebo was a circular outbuilding, considerably smaller than the main structure. According to the specs they'd been given prior to arriving on the island, it served as the station's warehouse.

Within the same group of papers was a description of the outpost's purpose. The Brule Institute was a scientific research organization loosely associated with the University of Heidelberg in Germany. Their goal here was the same as those of most of the other places Sawyer and Napoli had checked—monitoring the effects of global warming on the arctic ice pack.

Napoli leaned back and rubbed his eyes. "He's inside now."

"You want me to take over for a while?" Sawyer asked.

"No. I'm still good." Napoli looked back through the binoculars. "Could use one of those energy bars, though. As long as it's not frozen solid."

"I'm only here to serve you," Sawyer said.

"Well, you're doing a lousy job."

With a sneer that couldn't be seen under his mask, Sawyer crawled over to the pack to his left to grab a bar for his partner. As he opened the bag, he heard a thud. He looked back. Napoli and the binoculars were both lying in the snow.

"Nap?" he asked.

When there was no response, he moved back over.

"Hey, what have you been doing? Drinking on the job?"

Napoli was a bit of a clown sometimes, and Sawyer figured his friend was making a joke about the monotony of their assignment.

"Ha, ha. Funny," he said, and pushed Napoli in the shoulder.

His friend's head rolled to the side, and Sawyer saw the bullet hole just above Napoli's left eye.

Immediately, he grabbed his gun, rolled to the left, then did a rapid, three-sixty scan of the area. About thirty yards away, two shadowy figures were running up the slope, the nearest pointing a rifle at Sawyer.

"On your feet! Hands in the air!" the man commanded.

Sawyer's gun was in his hand by his hip. He made a slight adjustment to the barrel and pulled the trigger, knowing the bullet would find its mark. Without waiting for confirmation, he switched his aim to the farther man, and shot again. This one was trickier, the distance and angle both having to be compensated for, but he'd trained for moments like this. It was why he had been selected. Survival of at least one of his team was paramount to their mission.

Even as the nearer man was falling to the snow, the second bullet ripped through the side of his friend's head.

Staying low, Sawyer checked the area again, his gun tracking with his gaze. He detected no movement. He grunted to his feet, grabbed the pack, and looked back at his friend one more time, knowing he'd have to leave him there. "Sorry, Nap."

He hurried across the ice and snow to a shallow valley a quarter of a mile away. Parked there out of sight was the specially outfitted motorcycle he and Napoli had ridden across the island on.

He swung his leg over the seat, started it up, and took off along the same path in the snow they'd created on previous trips.

Though they observed no vehicles at the outpost, he knew there had to be some. Snowmobiles, most likely, perhaps even a larger snowcat that could carry more than a couple people. Whatever they had, he was certain they would be coming after him.

There was no question in his mind who these people were. This was not some academic research station, or even a disguised military facility. If it were either of those, Napoli would have still been alive. No, this was something else entirely. This was what he and Napoli had been sent to find.

He now had one job, and one job only. A job he *must* fulfill: get back to the radio and let the others know.

He weaved through several hills, then up onto a wide, flat section that he knew ran for about a mile. Unlike earlier, though, when he reached it, he found himself in a dense cloud that hung tightly to the ground. If it weren't for their earlier tracks, he would have had to stop and wait until visibility increased. As it was, his eyes strained to keep the tracks in sight.

At the end of the plain, the road dipped down again, below cloud level. Immediately, he increased his speed, the snow flying up from under his metal-spiked tires and filling the air behind him. Their camp wasn't far now, just a few more minutes at most. The question running through his mind was: should he just grab the radio and make for the boat? Or should he report in first, then get off the island?

Go for the boat. That made the most sense. Once he was surrounded by the sea, it would be harder for them to get to him. At that point, he could radio in without fear of being interrupted.

As he sped toward the overhang, he carefully examined the surrounding area for signs that anyone else might be around. There was no way to know how he and Napoli had been discovered, but one of the possibilities was that the people from the outpost had run across their camp. Thankfully, everything looked as it had when the two of them headed out several hours earlier.

He parked the bike next to the entrance, and ran inside. He headed straight for the radio. It was the only important thing. He stuffed it into its carrying case, returned to the bike, and took off again.

When he finally reached the top of the path that led down to the bay, he stopped. He didn't even consider riding the bike down. That would be a great way to accidentally kill himself. He ditched the bike, and moved as quickly as he could down the makeshift trail. He could see the boat now, rocking on the water. There was something else, too. Even in the short time they'd been on the island, the bay was starting to ice over. Another couple of days and the boat would have been caught in it.

When he reached the bottom, he headed straight for the small Zodiac he and Napoli had used to reach the shore. The craft was right where they'd left it, lashed down and secured to the ground by metal pylons hammered into the ice.

Sawyer quickly undid the rope, and manhandled the boat as far out onto the ice as he dared. He climbed inside, and used one of the emergency oars to shove the Zodiac along until the ice cracked underneath and the boat splashed into the water. He started up the motor and dropped the propeller into the sea. Ignoring the freezing spray from the waves, he twisted the handle, giving the engine more power, and aimed for the boat.

Every few seconds, he glanced back at the shore, sure he would see half a dozen men with rifles preparing to shoot at him, but the beach and cliffs remained empty. He was going to make it. Once on the boat, he'd kick on the modified dual engines that would have done many tugboats proud, and he'd be miles away in no time.

He brought the Zodiac around to the rear, lifted his pack and the radio onto the aft deck, then climbed aboard. With no time to bring the Zodiac on after him, he secured it to a cleat, giving it enough line so that he could tow it without it getting in the way of the motors.

Once he finished, he grabbed the bags and raced into the cabin, heading straight for the controls. He turned the key and pushed the button to start the engines.

Nothing.

He tried again. Not even a sound.

Had the batteries died? Had water gotten into the fuel line and frozen?

Both he and Napoli had been given crash courses on the ins and outs of all the systems on the boat, so they could take care of any problems themselves. Growing up on a farm surrounded by complex equipment, understanding the boat and its workings had come easily for Sawyer. For Napoli, it had been more of a struggle.

Angry and annoyed, Sawyer turned to head out to the access panels on the deck.

"Your engines are fine," a voice said behind him.

Sawyer reached for his gun.

"Not a good idea. You'll be dead before you lift it an inch."

Sawyer held his hand above the gun's grip for a second longer, then, reluctantly, he let his hand drop to his side. He couldn't allow himself to be killed. Not yet anyway.

Slowly he turned back around.

Standing in the cabin, just to the side of the stairs that led to the living quarters below, was a middle-aged man with close-cropped hair and steely eyes. Behind him at the top of the stairs was a younger man pointing a gun at Sawyer.

"Which one are you?" the middle-aged man asked. "Napoli or Sawyer?"

Sawyer kept his face neutral, hiding his surprise at hearing the names.

"You're probably Sawyer, aren't you? Yes, Sawyer. Napoli was shorter, if I'm not mistaken. Sorry we had to kill him, but it was either him or you. He just happened to be in the wrong spot." The man smiled. "Mr. Sawyer, we need your help."

"Too bad."

"Spirited. Nice. But I was only being polite. We're going to get your help whether you give it freely or not."

Were there more men below? Or was it just the two? If so, Sawyer thought he had at least an even shot at taking them out.

"Son," the man said. "It would be better for you if you just cooperated. Trust me, you don't want to go through what will be done to you if you don't. Let's save a lot of time, huh? All we need you to do is give us your confirmation code words."

This time it was harder for Sawyer to keep his expression from cracking. "I don't know what you're talking about."

Confirmation codes? Jesus, how did they even know about that?

The codes were an ever-changing set of phrases used to authenticate the user's identity.

"I respect that. A lot more than if you had just given them over, that's for sure," the man said. "Unfortunately for you, respect is about all I can give you. You need to tell us, or we start ripping you apart. Simple as that."

Sawyer's eye twitched. "I'm not telling you anything."

The man stared at him. "That's disappointing."

The boat rocked upward as a particularly large swell passed underneath.

There was no other time. It was now or die.

Sawyer shot a hand out, grabbed the handle of his backpack,

and flung it at the man with the gun. Just as it hit him, the guy pulled his trigger, but the barrel had been jerked upward, so the bullet went harmlessly through the ceiling of the cabin. The man with the gun tumbled backward down the stairs.

Sawyer pulled out his pistol and aimed it at the older one.

"I told you I didn't want to talk," he said.

The man looked as calm as he had a moment earlier. "And I told you you're going to talk no matter what."

The window behind Sawyer shattered. Before he could even turn, he was hit in the back twice, not by bullets, but by what felt like spikes or—

With a sudden jolt, he lost all control of his body and fell to the ground, his muscles contracting randomly, out of his control.

He had two coherent thoughts before he finally passed out.

The first: *I need to tell the Ranch that I found Bluebird.*

The second: *That's never going to happen.*

DR. NORRIS TOLD Major Ross it would take no more than an hour to extract the information from the man named Sawyer. It actually took almost three, but this didn't surprise the major. He had seen the determination and drive in the man's eyes as they talked in the cabin on the boat.

No, Sawyer was never going to be easy, but he was always going to lose.

Codes in hand, Major Ross walked down the hall to the room where Sawyer's radio had been set up. The proper frequency had already been tuned in. Now it was just a matter of making the call.

He handed the list to Olsen, who was seated in front of the microphone. It had been determined he had the voice that matched Sawyer's the most.

The major pointed at the appropriate code. "You ready?"

Olsen looked at the list, then back at the script that had been written for him. He jotted in the code at the appropriate place. "Ready now, sir."

The major nodded.

Olsen leaned into the mic.

3

MUMBAI, INDIA

"HURRY! HURRY!" AYUSH yelled from the truck.

Sanjay ran down the street as fast as he could.

Ayush was leaning out the open back, one hand gripping the side of the vehicle, the other held out toward his cousin. "Faster!"

It was Sanjay's own fault that he was late. It had been the carambola. It wasn't that he particularly liked star fruit, but he couldn't avoid stopping at the stall selling it, the stall Kusum's family owned. He'd stayed only long enough to see if she was there. If she had been, Sanjay probably wouldn't have even been in time to see the truck pull away, but the only people working that morning were Kusum's mother and sister, so he'd continued on his way.

Now he was angry with himself. Ayush had promised to help him get a job today with a European company that was looking for workers. Sanjay should have avoided the market completely. There were so many different routes he could have taken, three of which were shorter than the one he'd chosen. But Kusum…he just wanted ed to see her, that's all.

"Sanjay! Come on! You can run faster!"

Sanjay tucked his head down, and concentrated all his energy into his legs. With a burst of speed, he shot forward, and came within a foot of grabbing his cousin's hand before the truck accelerated out of reach. He slowed, knowing he'd missed his chance.

"Tomorrow," Ayush yelled as the truck grew more distant. "Don't be late!"

"I won't be," Sanjay said in a near whisper, too winded to yell back, as he moved to the side of the road and watched the truck dwindle to nothing.

What an idiot he'd been. An actual *job* with a European company. According to Ayush, they were paying more per day than Sanjay usually made in a week. If he had a job like that, maybe he could convince Kusum's parents he was worthy of their daughter.

Tomorrow, Ayush had called out. So there was still a chance. Sanjay wouldn't be late next time. He couldn't be. He'd force himself to avoid the fruit stall, and be waiting at the corner *before* Ayush arrived.

Tomorrow, he, too, would become an employee of Pishon Chem, but until then, perhaps a piece of star fruit wouldn't be such a bad idea.

---

13 MILES NORTHWEST OF
SAN JOSE, COSTA RICA

ERNESTO RIOS TRIED to move as little as possible. It was a skill he had perfected in the nine years he'd owned the garage on the road between the port in Puntarenas, on Costa Rica's Pacific coast, and San Jose. He had long ago discovered that if he found the exact right position in the airstream of his electric fan, he could almost pretend the humidity didn't affect him.

That wasn't true, of course. The tropical humidity affected everyone. There was just no way around it. But there, in his little office when he had no pressing jobs to finish, he did his best to try.

Of course there was something he should be working on today—the old Ford a customer had given him in lieu of payment. Ernesto had promised his wife he'd get it running and let her use it. So far, he hadn't been able to even turn the engine over.

Later, he thought as he closed his eyes. For now, perhaps a little nap wouldn't be a bad idea. Just a few minutes.

A…few…

An air horn blared.

Ernesto's eyes shot open as he sat up, dazed. He'd been so deep in a dream that for a second, he couldn't figure out where he was.

The air horn sounded again.

He jumped up, realizing what it was this time, and circled out into the main part of the garage. Just beyond the single large door stood two men. Parked behind them was a cargo truck with a third man sitting at the wheel. One of the men outside was dressed like a typical truck driver in jeans and dusty button-up shirt. The other man, though, was wearing a suit, and looked like the businessmen Ernesto would sometimes see on TV. The man's skin was fair, his light-colored hair neat and trim. A foreigner, Ernesto guessed.

"*Hola, señor*," the trucker said.

"*Hola*," Ernesto replied. "What can I do for you?"

"We've got a leak in our water hose. Need to get it fixed. Can you do that?"

"Sure. I can fix anything."

The trucker glanced at the man in the suit, then back at Ernesto. "Need to do it quick, though. We have to keep on schedule."

Ernesto shrugged. A busted hose wasn't that big of a deal. He could do it blindfolded. "Let me take a look."

As he stepped out of the garage, he saw that there were three more identical trucks pulled alongside the road, their engines idling. "You all together?"

"Just fix the leak," the suited man said in perfect Spanish.

This surprised Ernesto. Since the suited guy had seemed disinterested, he had assumed the man didn't speak his language. That was obviously not the case, so the garage owner would have to be careful what he said.

The man who'd been behind the wheel climbed out and had the hood open by the time Ernesto and the other two arrived. Ernesto stuck his head inside and checked around. Sure enough, one of the hoses was cracked near one end and no longer able to hold a tight seal. He didn't know if he had the exact same size, but he was sure there'd be something in back that would work.

As he stood up, he smiled and said, "Fifteen minutes."

"Do it in ten, and I'll pay you fifty dollars US," the foreigner said.

That was more than double what Ernesto would have charged. He walked quickly back to the garage, grabbed the tools he would need, and went in search of a replacement pipe. He found three in his supply room that were about the right size. One of them would work for sure.

He replaced the hose with a minute to spare, and pocketed the fifty-dollar bill the suited man gave him. Standing in front of his garage, Ernesto watched as the four trucks pulled out in unison and continued their eastward journey.

For a fleeting moment, he wondered what they were hauling, but then a drop of sweat ran down the side of his face and all thoughts of the trucks were replaced by images of the fan and the chair in his office.

Half a minute later, he was again perfecting the art of not moving.

THE PORT OF FREMANTLE
WESTERN AUSTRALIA

THE MARY RAE arrived just before dawn, and was guided to the dock of the small harbor at the mouth of the Swan River. There, at exactly 8:30 a.m., the process of removing shipping containers full of food and clothing and other items commenced.

John Palmer's interest was only in the group of twenty-five containers his company had been hired to pick up. They'd first be taken to his warehouse in Perth, then, at a date yet unknown to him, trucked to specific locations throughout Western Australia. His understanding was that this was part of an expansion plan by a Dutch retailer. Apparently, an American competitor was planning a similar expansion, so the Dutch were hoping to get in first and gain a foothold prior to the other company's arrival.

The details didn't really matter. For Palmer, it was getting the business that was important. The years of global stagnation had been hard on his company. He'd had to release some good people, and even sell one of his distribution centers. But this was a big job. Not only were there the twenty-five containers today, but at least another hundred were on their way over in the next two weeks. Beyond that, his new client had indicated that similar shipments would continue on a monthly basis if everything went according to their business plan.

He sure as hell hoped it did. Palmer Transport & Shipping wouldn't be totally out of the woods, but the steady business would help. With any luck, other companies would also be expanding into the west.

By two p.m., all twenty-five containers had arrived at his warehouse and were being offloaded by his men.

As instructed, he called his contact at Hidde-Kel Holdings, the parent company of the retail chain.

"Mr. Vanduffel, John Palmer in Perth."

"John, good to hear from you. How are you?" Mr. Vanduffel spoke English well enough to almost but not quite hide his Dutch accent.

"I'm well, thanks. You?"

"Very good. Thank you."

Without even thinking about it, Palmer began doodling on the pad of paper next to his phone. It was an old habit, an outlet for the frustrated teenage artist still buried deep inside him. "Just wanted to let you know that your first shipment's arrived, and at this very moment is being safely stored away in my warehouse."

"Excellent news. How does everything look? Any sign of damage?"

"Checked the containers myself and they all look fine on the outside. Do you want us to open them up and do an inspection?"

Mr. Vanduffel paused as if considering the idea. "No, I don't think that will be necessary. But thank you for offering."

"Not a problem. If you change your mind, happy to do it."

"Thank you. I should have the distribution plan worked out in the next day or so, and will send it to you then. My hope is to have the containers that arrived today already on their way to the different sites before the next shipment comes in."

"That would be great but no worries. I have the room if that doesn't work out."

"Good to know. Thank you again. We appreciate your efficiency. Have a good day."

"You, too."

Palmer snickered at the drawing he created, a rendering of what he thought Mr. Vanduffel looked like. Not half bad, either, though the mustache he'd given him was a little cartoony for his taste. He tossed the drawing in the trash, and walked back out to the warehouse floor. He was happy to see that over half the containers were already stacked in place.

Yes, he thought. Things *were* getting better. He could feel it. The worst was behind them.

Next year would be great.

S. B. KELLER MEMORIAL LIBRARY
HAWKINS UNIVERSITY
ST. LOUIS, MISSOURI

JEANNIE SAUNDERS SHUT her book. "Okay, I'm done."

Corey Wilson smiled, but kept his eyes on his laptop's screen. "You finished all five chapters?"

"Four."

"Thought you had to do five."

From the corner of his eye, he could see her scowl. "I've read enough for today. Come on. Let's go get something to eat."

This time he did look up. "Don't know if you noticed, but, unlike you, I haven't finished yet."

"That paper's not even due until the end of the semester," she argued.

"Because it's a *research* paper. Meaning I've gotta do a lot of research first before I write it."

"Ugh!" She leaned back in her chair. "What am I supposed to do? Just sit here and wait?"

"Go get something to eat."

"How much longer are you going to be here?"

"At least another couple of hours."

"Come on, Corey. I'm hungry."

"Go. I'm not stopping you.

The scowl reappeared. "Fine." She stood up. "Want me to bring you back something?"

"Banana?"

She came around the table, leaned down, and gave him a kiss. "You'd better still be working when I come back."

As she walked away, he returned his attention to his computer. The research paper he was working on was for a class called Business of Agriculture 523. Ag business also happened to be the emphasis of the MBA he was working on. The assignment was to pick out a particular agriculture-associated company and do a detailed analysis of their business model, strengths, and weaknesses. Corey had chosen Varni Gen-Sym, a seed company specializing in genetically enhanced produce. The reason he went with Varni was because it was the same company that had been providing seeds to his uncle's farm for the last several years.

What he hadn't expected was to find that the company was basically boring. There was no real meat to sink his teeth into. Not only was it a family-run business that only sold seeds, but it didn't even develop its own product. Instead, it licensed its seed designs from others, and had no research arm of its own. Even its profit was steady but unremarkable.

He'd decided that morning he was going to look around and see if he could find something more interesting. The big problem was, the obvious companies had already been snatched up by his classmates. He needed to find something different, perhaps a little unusual, a company no one else would have even thought to claim.

So far he'd come up with a couple of different possibilities. Top on that list was Komai Produce. It was a regional company in the Pacific Northwest, so not well known to the students of Hawkins University. What Corey liked about Komai was that it was considerably more diverse than Varni. It had started off as a produce distributor, but had since entered several other areas including produce display, where it had a division that created consumer-friendly bins and storage units that kept produce fresh by means of micro-temperature control and automated misters.

Corey particularly liked the fact Komai was expanding while a lot of other organizations were holding pat. That afternoon he was working his way through articles about the company, starting with the earliest he could find and moving forward.

The story he'd been reading when Jeannie interrupted him was from six months earlier. He finished that, then moved on to the next one, but after only a few paragraphs he looked up, frustrated. Turned out Komai had been purchased outright five months earlier by a company called Hidde-Kel Holdings.

That was a bummer. He'd really liked the small-guy-against-the-world aspect, and was far less interested in recounting the successes of a larger conglomerate.

Having already spent so much time on Komai, he read some more, wanting to understand the original owners' motivation for selling. Though the details were kept private, it appeared as though the three friends who started Komai had come out of the deal considerably wealthier than they had ever expected. They had created a good company so Corey wasn't particularly surprised. He noted one odd thing, though. None of the three founders was asked to stay on beyond the date of final purchase. Wasn't that pretty standard practice, to ensure stability and continuity for an organization as it moved forward? Apparently Hidde-Kel had decided it was unnecessary in this case.

Maybe there was something here of interest after all—what happens to a regional food business after it's purchased by a larger company.

Yeah, that might work.

In fact, the more he thought about it, the more he liked the idea. He could even get a little bit into the parent company and show why the two were a good fit—or not. This could be a huge paper if he wasn't careful, but that thought didn't scare him at all. It was more like a challenge.

The Effects of Hidde-Kel Holdings on Komai Produce. A no-brainer title.

He didn't need to look any further. This was it. This was what he wanted to do. Sure, it was a slight spin on the assignment, but it wouldn't take much to talk Professor Nesbitt into okaying it.

With renewed enthusiasm, he hit the Web. First up, find out more about Hidde-Kel and see what else they might be into.

4

"MATT HAMILTON RAISED the Taurus OSS, sighted down the barrel, and pulled the trigger—once, twice, three times. The first shot nearly ripped the target in half. The following two finished it off.

If not for the ear protection he was wearing, the roar of the pistol in the enclosed firing range would have temporarily deafened him. As it was, the muffled pop was still enough to cause his aging ears to ring.

He took aim again, this time imagining where the target had been, and sent off three more shots in rapid succession. It wasn't quite as satisfying when there was nothing there to hit.

He pushed the retrieval button and the remnants of the target rushed toward him. So far, he'd already gone through fifteen of them and an entire box of ammo. It was the only thing he could think of doing to keep himself from going crazy. The concentration down the sight, the power of the gun, the smell of the powder—each took his mind away, and kept him from wondering what was going on.

He clipped in a new target and hit the button again, sending the paper flying back toward the other end of the range. He raised the .45, and imagined the flight his bullet would take.

"Matt!" a distant voice called out.

He pulled the trigger, and watched unmoving as his shot hit the imaginary foe in the bridge of his nose. He held his position for a moment longer, then lowered his gun and turned. Standing just outside his shooting stall was Rich Paxton.

Matt raised a hopeful eyebrow. "They check in?"

Pax shook his head. "No."

That made it seventy-two hours since their missing scout team had last made contact. Matt had been trying not to assume the worst, but he couldn't avoid it now. The irony, of course, was that this could very well mean the team had discovered what it had been sent out to find.

He closed his eyes for a second. Yes, they were fighting a war, and yes, people were going to die doing things he sent them out to do, but he didn't have to be okay with it.

He removed the mag from the Taurus, emptied the chamber, then put the gun and the unused ammunition on a shelf along the back wall.

Nodding to his friend, he said, "Let's go."

He followed Pax into the corridor and down to the Bunker's communications room, ignoring as he always did the pain in his bad knee.

Sometimes it was hard to remember they were over thirty feet below the basement level of the Lodge—the Ranch's main building. At that moment, though, Matt was keenly aware of it, feeling every inch of dirt pressing down on him.

The year that was finally coming to an end had not been a good one. First there had been the Sage Flu outbreak in California during the spring, a planned attack meant to test a particularly vicious viral strain. There was no question in Matt's mind that the people of Project Eden—the people he and his meager group of like-minded individuals were trying to stop—considered the test a success. Even at conservative estimates, when the virus was in its deadly phase, its mortality rate was near 99.8%. Unleashed on a worldwide scale, it would mean the deaths of seven billion people, and unleashing it on the world was exactly what the Project had in mind.

Not long after the outbreak scattered, reports came in from all over the globe. The few warehouses and depots owned and operated by the Project that Matt's people had been able to identify were being stocked with food, medical supplies, weapons, and pretty much anything else the Project would need to survive the apocalypse it was planning on causing. These were just the tip of the iceberg, he knew. There had to be more, hundreds, maybe over a thousand.

Matt and his people, taking a cue from the French in World War II, had started referring to themselves as the resistance. They'd been trying for years to get a better handle on the Project, and to figure out a way to stop it before the organization carried out its plans. Sometimes it felt like Matt and his team were getting close, that they *would* be able to stop the horror before it happened. But that had just been a dream.

The Project had been going on for decades, and now had people entrenched in governments and businesses and organizations all over the globe, in position to obstruct any potential threat to their plans. In the last six months, the resistance had been falling farther and farther behind, and then, three weeks earlier, the message had come in from Heron, the only operative they still had within Project Eden. They didn't have years to stop the coming genocide. They didn't even have months. Seven weeks, the message had said. Tops. Which meant no more than four now.

The Project was calling it Implementation Day.

Such a sterile name for such a horrific plan.

The Bunker's communications room had become the de facto command center for the resistance. There were nearly two dozen people there when Matt and Pax arrived. While a handful was manning the actual communication terminals used to keep in contact with field teams, most were gathered in the far corner near the conference table.

Rachel Hamilton, Matt's sister, was the only one sitting down. The others were looking at a map of the Arctic Circle pinned to the wall.

Out of habit, Matt glanced at the row of monitors that had been set up on a table nearby. Five were playing feeds from the major cable news networks: CNN, MSNBC, FOX, PCN, and BBC. At the moment, the reports seemed to be the typical crap that had no relation to anything important. If Heron's message was right, though, that would change soon.

As Matt walked up, the others moved to the side so he could approach the map. Black Xs marked the current locations of the different scout teams that had been sent north. Each team had been given a list of ten to fifteen research stations and outposts to check. This had been the final part of Heron's message, an arrow pointing in the direction of Bluebird, Project Eden's main facility where all the decisions were supposedly made.

Best location BB n of sixty-six. Sci fac.

Best location for Bluebird, north of the sixty-sixth parallel. Science facility.

The sixty-sixth parallel was basically the location of the Arctic Circle, minus a few degrees. Though sparsely populated, there were a considerable amount of scientific outposts north of the imaginary line. If the information was correct, one would be Bluebird. The problem was, which one?

Five teams had been sent out, each designated by a color: orange, green, purple, yellow, and brown. Lines were drawn from location to location, indicating the path a particular team was taking. Those places already checked and cleared were circled in black. So far the tally was twenty-seven. Those that had been checked but with inconclusive findings were circled in blue. There were only two of these. Once Bluebird was found, it would be circled in red.

The missing team's color was yellow. Matt retraced its progress from where the team had started along the northern edge of Greenland, then across the Lincoln Sea to Ellesmere Island in northern Canada, Axel Heiberg Island, Yanok Island, Amund Ringnes Island, Ellef Ringnes Island, and then nothing.

"The weather's pretty rough up there right now," Leon Owens said. "Could be they got caught in a storm."

That had definitely been a chance they'd taken, sending their teams out as winter was approaching, but given the deadline, they couldn't very well just wait until spring. At first they'd been aided by a mild fall that seemed to affect the entire Northern Hemisphere. Matt had hoped that would continue, but always knew it was unlikely.

He touched the X on Ellef Ringnes Island. This was where the team's last transmission had originated from. The outpost they had checked there was a relatively new facility constructed only a few miles away from a permanent automated weather station that had been on the island for years. Was it possible that the facility was Bluebird? Had they, perhaps, hidden their identity enough so that yellow team had reported the location as checked and cleared, then been eliminated by the Project? Or had the team made it to its next destination, only to be captured or killed soon after arrival?

Matt followed the line to what yellow team's next stop would have been. Lougheed Island. By the schedule, the scouts should have arrived there two days ago, right around the time they stopped reporting in. So could that be where Bluebird was?

It just didn't feel right. It was too…easy.

"Josh?" Rachel called out. "Can you play the yellow team's last message for me again?"

Josh was one of the people manning the communication terminals. "Sure," he said.

Matt glanced at his sister. He could tell something was bugging her and she was trying to work it out. He refrained from asking her what she was thinking, though, knowing from experience it was better to just let her go.

The room was wired so that communications could either be heard over headphones worn by the people at the terminals, or on a speaker system that broadcasted the voices to the whole room.

After a few seconds, a voice fighting through static said over the speakers, "Yellow calling Bravo Four. Yellow calling Bravo Four." Bravo Four was the code name for the Ranch.

"Bravo Four. Go, Yellow." The new voice was crisp and clear. Matt recognized it as belonging to Gary Atkins, a member of the communications team.

"Lake hunter. Repeat, lake hunter."

There was a pause as Gary no doubt was checking the list of codes to make sure yellow team had used the correct one. Each was used only once, and in a specific order.

"Roger, Yellow. Quiet night." That would be the return code.

"Status, Y6 clear. Proceeding to Y7." Ellef Ringnes clear. Proceeding to Lougheed Island.

"Roger, Yellow. Y6 clear. Proceeding to Y7. Good luck."

"Thanks, Bravo Four. Yellow out."

The recording cut off.

"Play it again," Rachel said.

The message once more filled the room, but whatever Rachel had noticed, Matt had yet to pick up.

When it was through, she said, "Play the reports from the last four stops."

They listened as the yellow team reported in from two different locations on Amund Ringnes Island, one on Yanok Island, and one on Axel Heiberg Island. Each report was basically the same: target checked and cleared, moving on.

When they finished, Matt couldn't help but ask, "What is it?"

Rachel frowned and shook her head. "I...I don't know. I thought I had something, but..."

"What?"

Again, she shook her head. "Nothing, I guess."

He knew that was a lie. Whatever it was, she was still mulling it over. But that was her way. Once she had it figured out, *if* she ever did, she'd share it with him.

He looked back at the map. "We can't ignore the fact that they might have found Bluebird. We're going to have to divert one of the other teams to check this out. Leon, correct me if I'm wrong, but it looks like brown team is almost done with its route."

Leon nodded. "They're due to report in this evening. Once they've done that, they're freed up."

"Good. Send them to Lougheed. Let's find out what happened to our people."

"Will do."

Leon and the others returned to their desks, leaving Matt and Pax standing at the map.

"And if it is Bluebird?" Pax said.

Matt knew exactly what his old friend was asking. It was something he'd also been giving a lot of thought to. "It'll be time to bring him in."

5

I.D. MINUS 14 DAYS

BROWN TEAM LEADER Gagnon looked out the window from his seat behind the controls of the seaplane at the circle of light on the choppy ocean below. Wright, his partner, sat in the seat behind him, operating the wireless remote that controlled the spotlight attached to the bottom of the plane.

Since the previous afternoon, they'd been searching for any sign of yellow team. They would have started sooner, but a severe storm had passed through the area, grounding them for over forty-eight hours.

The real miracle, if one wanted to call it that, was that the sea hadn't completely iced over yet. That was global warming for you, Gagnon thought. Even this close to winter, there were still ice-free parts of the Arctic Ocean that had never been that way at this time of year in the past.

"Anything?" he asked.

"Just water."

It was all that Gagnon had seen, too. "Let's move on to the next sector."

He straightened out the plane, and headed for the next grid coordinates.

They were both acutely aware that it could have been the middle of summer with twenty-four-hour daylight, and they might still not spot any wreckage if something *had* happened to the yellow team's boat. A rogue wave could have swamped the vessel and taken the whole thing down, or the rough seas could have broken everything into tiny bits and spread it far and wide so that there'd be nothing to draw attention. The fact that it was less than two weeks shy of winter, and the only light they had to cover the hundreds of square miles below them was a small spotlight, made the task seem impossible.

Two more hours, Gagnon decided. If nothing turned up, they'd call it a night and radio the Ranch to see if they should continue the search tomorrow or pack it in.

THE ISLAND WAS small, found on only the most detailed of maps. At its widest, it was only a quarter-mile across. It was, in the most generous terms, a rocky, ice-covered piece of nothing.

Five hours earlier, two men, a camouflage shelter, and the equipment they would need for their assignment had been flown in. At the time of their drop-off, they'd been unsure how long they were going to have to stay, but at most, it would be no more than two nights, and it was quite possible they'd be sleeping in their own beds back at Bluebird that very evening.

Ten miles away, a Project boat, looking very much like a fishing vessel slowly making its way back to port somewhere to the south, was scanning the skies with a compact yet powerful radar system. The information it collected was transmitted real-time via satellite to a handheld device that was part of the equipment the two men had brought with them.

For nearly an hour, they had been watching a blip weave back and forth across the screen, slowly growing closer to the island. It was getting late, though, so at some point the plane would undoubtedly break off and head back to the small village several hundred miles away that its occupants had been using as a base. If that happened, the men would definitely be spending the night.

"We could try it now," the junior of the two suggested.

Without looking away from the screen, the other man shook his head. "Not yet." It was important that this worked so he didn't want to risk any mistakes.

Over the next thirty minutes, the plane continued to move closer. Finally, when it was within two miles, the man in charge looked up.

"Now," he said.

The younger man picked up a second device, a tablet computer synced in to a localized network they'd set up when they first arrived. The man brought up the appropriate screen, and pressed the appropriate button.

Ten seconds later, on the other side of the island, a radio beacon went live.

––––––––

BOWOP-BOWOP.

The signal came in bursts of two, each set separated by a second of silence. It was so faint at first that it didn't even register with Gagnon or Wright. When it finally did, the pilot looked over at the radio, surprised.

The receiver had been tuned to the frequency that would be utilized by the yellow team's emergency beacons, but since the searchers had started the day before, they'd picked up only silence. They assumed any beacons were either at the bottom of the sea or no longer working.

Gagnon turned up the volume.

Bowop-bowop.

Bowop-bowop.

"Is that them?" Wright asked.

Gagnon looked at the radio. "It's the right frequency."

"Which way is it coming from?"

"I'm not sure yet."

Gagnon banked the plane to the south to see if the signal strength would grow, but instead it diminished to almost nothing. When he turned back in the other direction, its intensity increased for a minute or two, then started to fade again. He brought the plane around once more, heading back to the point where the signal had been strongest. From there, it would have to be coming from somewhere off to one side or the other, but which one?

"You see anything out there?"

Wright was moving the light around. "No."

As they neared the height of the signal, Gagnon mentally flipped a coin, then turned the plane east. Instead of fading this time, the signal got even stronger.

After a few seconds, Wright said, "Is that an island up ahead?"

Gagnon studied the ocean ahead of them. Sure enough, about a mile away, there was the tiny silhouette of a rocky hill sticking out of the water.

"Maybe they're just stranded there," Wright suggested, unable to keep the hope out of his voice.

Gagnon wasn't quite ready to jump for joy yet. "Let's find the signal first."

As they flew closer, it was clear the signal was indeed coming from the island, specifically the northwest side. As soon as they were within range, Wright fired up the spotlight and aimed it at the tiny piece of land. At first all they saw were just rocks and a few patches of snow and ice. No sign that anyone had ever been there. But then, as the northwest edge came into view, they found what they were looking for.

Both of them stared silently at the debris caught in the circle of light. It was piled haphazardly on the beach. Not even close to a full boat's worth, but enough for them to know that whatever vessel it had belonged to was unlikely to still be afloat. Wright panned the light over everything, then held it steady on one point as they flew by.

"There it is," he said.

He didn't have to elaborate. Gagnon had seen it, too. An empty life vest, stuck in the middle of the debris. The light near the top was blinking weakly in the night, at almost the same rhythm as the message of distress coming from the radio beacon buried somewhere inside the vest.

"Do you see them anywhere?"

"No. Go by again."

In the end, they made four passes of the wreckage, and two complete circles around the island, but there was no sign of anyone, alive or dead.

"I don't like it," Gagnon said.

"What do you mean?"

Gagnon frowned. "Just enough wreckage to prove that something happened to the boat, with a life vest that still has an active emergency beacon conveniently washing ashore where it could easily be found? Does that seem likely to you?"

Wright was silent for a moment. "It *could* happen. The current could have washed it up."

Gagnon stared back at his partner. "Did you look at the water? There weren't a lot of waves on that beach. If there were, that stuff would be even more broken up than it is. I'll bet you the current runs right past that end of the island."

Wright looked out the window again. "You're right. It does feel wrong."

Gagnon took one last glimpse of the wreckage, and turned the plane back toward the small village where they were staying. Once the course was set, he picked up the satellite radio and called the Ranch.

"Bravo Four," a voice at the Ranch answered.

"This is Brown," Gagnon said.

"Go ahead, Brown."

"Blair House," he said, using the active code.

"Wanda June."

Satisfied he was indeed speaking with the Ranch, Gagnon said, "Wreckage found. No apparent survivors."

Momentary silence on the other end. "Please confirm. No apparent survivors."

"Roger, Bravo Four. No survivors."

"Any idea what happened?"

"Rough seas, maybe. A storm. It's pretty rough out there. I'd say this is an unfortunate accident."

Another pause. "Confirming."

"Roger, Bravo Four. That's what it is."

"Roger, Brown. Get some rest. Will touch base in the morning with new assignment."

"Will do, Bravo Four. Out."

———————

"THEY'RE LEAVING," THE senior man said into the encrypted radio.

"You think they will be back?" Major Ross asked. He'd been patched in from Bluebird.

"No, sir. They're returning to the outpost, then will be getting a new assignment in the morning. I think it worked."

"Good. Return to base."

———————

PAX KNOCKED ON the door of Matt's office.

"Come in," Matt called out.

Upon entering, Pax found Rachel and Matt in the more casual sitting area in the front end of the room. "Sorry, but you wanted to see this."

"Brown team found something?" Rachel asked.

Pax nodded grimly. "Yeah, but there's more."

He handed over a transcript of the conversation that had just come in. Rachel and Matt read it at the same time. Their first reaction was to the news that by all appearances, yellow team was dead. Their second was to the hidden message contained within brown team's words.

"'An unfortunate accident,'" Rachel read. She looked up. "That means…"

"…yellow team found Bluebird," her brother finished.

6

THE DIRECTOR OF Preparation tapped the lever another half inch toward Hot. Within a second, steam began to rise from the water washing over him. While Bluebird was always kept at a warm, comfortable level, the frigid view outside often made him feel like he was freezing. Other than avoiding the windows, the best remedy was always a hot shower. He took at least two a day, sometimes three. Though the official allotment was one, that didn't apply to him—like most of the other facility rules.

He was just starting to feel thawed out when the soft *bong* of his doorbell sounded in the other room. There was a time when he could have afforded to ignore it, but not now, not when they were this close to activation.

He turned off the water, and stuck his head out of the narrow stall. "One moment!"

He toweled off quickly, pulled on his slacks and shirt, then flipped on the monitor next to the door. His visitor was Carl Herlin, one of his aides.

The DOP opened the door. "Yes?"

"Sorry to disturb you, sir, but Major Ross wanted me to tell you they have the information, and that he would be in the map room if you're looking for him."

"Tell him I'll be there in a moment."

He shut the door without waiting for a response, finished getting dressed, and headed out.

Technically, the map room was called Conference Room B. It

received its unofficial name from the table that dominated the space. Using touch controls on either side, a map of any location on the planet in any format could be projected onto the tabletop from underneath. With another selection of the controls, the user could draw whatever they wanted on top of the map—lines, words, circles—and the resulting image could be saved and printed out.

Ross was leaning over the table when the DOP stepped inside. He instantly straightened up.

"Good evening, Director."

The DOP walked up to the table. "I hear you have some news."

"We think we've been able to pinpoint Bravo Four's location, and by the size of it, I would guess that it's their main headquarters. May I show you?"

The DOP dipped his head, and Ross touched the controls. On the table, a map of an area that encompassed parts of Idaho, Montana, Wyoming, Utah, and Colorado appeared.

"Their return messages have been coming from here." Ross touched a button, and a red circle appeared in the western portion of Montana, less than a hundred miles from the Canadian border.

Ross zoomed in on the map, then switched to a satellite view. The circle was in a wide valley with mountains blocking off the western end, and rolling hills to the north and south. Trees and meadows took turns filling the valley, but from the height the image was taken, the DOP could see no roads.

Ross removed the dot and pushed in again, focusing on an area near the center. Suddenly, several things came into view at once. There *were* roads, though none appeared paved. The more interesting item, though, was the large building right in the middle of where the dot had been.

The magnification increased one more level.

Large was not right, the DOP realized. Huge was more accurate. This was no mountain mansion. This would have been a big building in any city in the state. And yet, the only way to get there was by dirt road.

"Look at this," Ross said.

He was pointing at a spot that had to be a mile or two from the building. At first, the DOP didn't see anything important about it, but when Ross moved his finger back and forth in a line, it became clear.

A runway. Either covered with grass or painted to look that way.

Was this really it? Had they found it?

If so, he and the other Directors were going to be very, very happy.

It was, he knew, not a discovery that was necessary for their success. The people who lived there would all die just as quickly as those on the rest of the planet once KV-27a was released. If he could help it, though, that wasn't the kind of death he wanted for them. He wanted a more direct hand in what they would suffer. He wanted them to scream in pain, then beg and plead for their lives. These were the gnats who had been dogging Project Eden for years, never enough to throw things off, but causing annoyances just the same.

Definitely unnecessary, but wholly satisfying.

"Excellent work," he said. "Come up with a plan on how we might best deal with them."

"Yes, sir."

7

I.D. MINUS 13 DAYS

ALGONA, IOWA

THE BALL FLEW past the boy's glove, hit the ground, and rolled across the sidewalk into the grass-lined drainage ditch that ran along the road.

"Should have dived for it," his father said.

The boy retrieved it, and threw it back. It hit his dad's glove with a wet slap. Muddy water sprayed out from the impact, hitting his father on the cheek.

"Sorry, Dad," the son said, laughing.

"I'll bet you are."

Across the street, their neighbor Charlie Newcomb had just come out of his house. "Your boy's got quite a spitball, Adam."

"He does, doesn't he?" the boy's father replied as he tossed the ball back to his son.

"Hear we might be getting some snow this weekend," Charlie called out. "You guys need anything, you just let us know."

"Thanks."

Charlie gave him a wave, then got into his car.

"Snow. That'll be cool," the boy said.

His dad smiled knowingly. "Tell me what you think in a couple months."

They had moved to Algona, Iowa, just before the school year began. The man had taken a job teaching math and P.E. at Algona High School. In addition to his son, he also had a daughter, currently inside the house and, no doubt, lost in a book. She'd become quite a reader in the last several months, exhibiting a growing interest in vampires and ghosts and worlds that existed beyond the one she lived in. He wasn't sure if that was good or not. He knew a lot of other girls liked the same thing, but most of them hadn't lost their mother recently or had their lives completely upended. His fear was that the books were keeping her from facing reality and accepting it, but he couldn't bring himself to question her on it. Maybe escaping reality for a thirteen-year-old wasn't a bad thing.

As far as the people in town knew, Adam Cooper was a widower who'd moved with his family to Algona from Florida. "Too many memories back there," he'd say when asked, though he seldom was. The people of Algona were too polite to push the issue.

The boy, known to his classmates as Scott, had made the adjustment quickly. He was doing well in school and had lots of friends. Mary, as the man's daughter was called, was not faring as well. Her grades were fine, but she was withdrawn socially. There were a few girls she'd hang out with now and then, but for the most part, when she wasn't in school, she was in her room reading.

At some point, he would have to do something about it. Just…not yet.

After they threw the ball around for a bit more, the father said, "Getting a little too cold for me, buddy. How about some lunch?"

The boy nodded. "Grilled cheese?"

"If that's what you want. Last one in has to cook."

They raced to the front door, the boy getting there a split second before his dad did.

"You're it," the boy declared.

"Two out of three?"

"No way."

They removed their shoes in the mudroom, and entered the toasty confines of their small house.

"Sweetie," the man said, raising his voice so his daughter could hear him. "I'm making grilled cheese. You want one?"

No answer.

"Honey, grilled cheese?"

Still nothing.

He looked at his son. "Go see if your sister wants one."

The boy rolled his eyes. "She's just going to yell at me."

"She's not."

"She is."

"Just go ask her."

The man walked into the kitchen, washed his hands, and pulled out the fixings for lunch. As the cast-iron skillet warmed on the grill, he began buttering the bread. He was only halfway through the second slice when the doorbell rang.

"I'll get it!" his son called out.

By the time the man had wiped his hands on a kitchen towel and walked into the living room, his son had the door open.

"Is your dad home?" a male voice asked from the porch.

"Just a second." The boy turned toward the kitchen, then stopped when he saw his father approaching. "He wants to talk to you, Dad."

"Thanks, buddy."

As he reached the door, he gave his son's hair a tousle and looked outside.

There were two men on the porch. He had never seen one of them before, but the other he had—once, on the night he'd escaped certain death from a cell in the Mojave Desert.

His one-time rescuer nodded in mutual recognition. "Afternoon, Captain Ash."

———

DANIEL ASH, ALIAS Adam Cooper, let the men wait in his living room while he finished making lunch for his children.

Once the sandwiches were ready, he gave one to his son, Brandon, and poured him a glass of milk. "Treat today. You can eat it in my room and watch TV."

"You just don't want me to hear what you're going to talk about," Brandon said.

"Smart boy. Now go, or I won't even let you turn the TV on."

He carried the other sandwich into Josie's room, and set them on her nightstand.

Without looking up from her book, she said, "Thanks, Dad."

"No crumbs in the bed, okay?"

"Ugh. Disgusting."

He wasn't sure if she was referring to what she was reading or the idea of crumbs in her bed. "You want something to drink?"

"No. I'm fine."

"I'll come get your plate in a bit."

Back in the living room, he motioned for the two men to follow him into the kitchen. It was farthest from the bedrooms, and
provided the most privacy.

"We're sorry to bother you like this, Captain," the one he knew
said. "Pax sent us."

"You can call me Ash. I'm not in the army anymore."
Technically, that might not be true. If the army knew he was still
alive, and not, as they believed, dead from an intentional car crash
and subsequent fire in Nevada not long after the Sage Flu outbreak
had passed, then he would probably still be considered part of the
service. Long enough, at least, to be court-martialed and sentenced
to death for what they erroneously believed to be his part in the
spreading of the disease. "I don't know your names, though."

The first man said, "I'm Tom. Tom Browne. I hope you understand why I couldn't tell you that before."

Ash did, but said nothing.

"Pat Solomon," the other man told him.

"All right, gentlemen, what is it you want?"

Browne cleared his throat. "Matt and Pax would like you to
come to the Ranch for a meeting."

"A meeting."

"Yes."

Ash looked from one man to the other. "What kind of meeting?"

"I don't know all the details. I just know it's important."

"You don't have any details? Nothing to convince me to
come?"

Browne hesitated, then said, "Pax said to tell you the depots
have been filled."

The words hung in the air.

The depots. These were buildings spread all around the world
so that the Project would thrive while civilization collapsed around
it. Ash had seen one of the facilities in person that previous summer, had been inside its then-empty storerooms.

Probably a good thing it's not full yet, Chloe White had said to him
at the time. *Humanity's got a little more time until the plug gets pulled, I*

guess.

If Browne wasn't lying, time was about to run out.

"Can I get either of you something to drink?" Ash asked. "Water, milk, a beer?"

"We're fine," Browne said.

"Suit yourself."

Ash walked over to the refrigerator and opened the door.

He had been dreading this moment, knowing someday it would come. It wasn't so much that he realized because of the help he'd been given to save his children, he would eventually be asked to return the favor. What he dreaded was what it actually meant—that the Project was really going to try and restart humanity by culling it down to all but the necessary numbers needed to begin again. It was a potential reality he couldn't justify no matter how many ways he thought about it. And it certainly wasn't a reality he ever wanted his children to see. Brandon and Josie had inherited Ash's immunity to KV-27a. The flu would never kill them, only all their friends and neighbors. His kids had already lost their mother. He knew he would do whatever he could so that his children wouldn't lose everyone else, too.

As much as he wanted to grab one of the beers, he picked up a bottle of water instead and cracked it open.

"When do they want me?"

"Now."

There was a noise behind them. A footstep.

"When do they want you where?" Josie asked. She stood into the kitchen doorway, staring at her father.

Ash opened his mouth, intending to tell her to go back to her room, but he caught himself at the last second. "They want me to go back to the Ranch for a meeting."

Her eyes narrowed. "About what?"

"I don't know the specifics."

"But you have an idea, right?"

"I can guess, but it would only be that."

"What about Brandon and me?"

"If I go to the Ranch, you're coming with me." He didn't look at the two men to see what their reaction might be. It was a non-negotiable point.

"Just a meeting and then we come back?"

His first instinct was to just say, "Yes," but Josie wasn't a child anymore. Neither, for that matter, was Brandon. Not after what they had been through. So he told the truth. "I don't know."

A hint of worry entered her eyes. "This is about what you told us might happen, isn't it? About the flu? And the other people?"

"Yes," he said.

She fell silent.

"Should we go?" Ash asked her.

She chewed on her lower lip for a moment. "Do we have a choice?"

"There's always a choice."

"That's not what I meant."

———————

Calls were made and explanations were given. An ill father in New York. An unexpected trip so that Adam Cooper's children could see their grandfather for the last time. He'd call when he had a better idea of their return, and was told there was no rush. Family always came first.

Two hours later, the Ash family was eighty miles away at a small regional airport. There, they boarded the Ranch's private jet for the flight west.

As they lifted off, Ash glanced out the window and couldn't help but think that he and his kids would never be back there again.

8

THE FIRST SIGN of trouble was what appeared to be a faulty sensor along the southern portion of the security fence. The fence was a quarter of a mile away from the house simply known as the Bluff, the affected area reachable only by foot.

A squad of three men was dispatched to make sure it wasn't something more serious, and to fix the problem if possible.

The Bluff was on the western side of the Sierra Nevada Mountains in California, surrounded by pine trees and magnificent vistas. There were times during the summer when the nearby road was almost bumper-to-bumper with people from the lowlands out for an afternoon of communing with nature. Now, with the official start of winter quickly approaching, there were days when fewer than a dozen cars would drive by.

For that reason alone, it should have been surprising that a car had stopped at the Bluff's front gate. Only this wasn't the first time this particular car had done so. Lancer, the watch officer manning the security monitors, had witnessed the two previous stops himself.

As with the other trips, the same young couple climbed out of the car. Grabbing the woman's hand, the man kissed her as he pulled her over to the gate. Then, as if reading off the same script they had played out nearly half a dozen times before, they looked beyond the metal pipe-framed gate and down the dirt road on the other side before climbing over.

Lancer selected the call button for his boss. "Adam and Eve

are back, Mr. Briley."

"You've got to be kidding me," Briley said. "Send someone out again. Have whoever it is tell them next time we call the sheriff."

"Yes, sir."

For the past few visits, the Bluff had sent out the resident team to scare off the couple. The hope was that it might make them find some other place to fulfill their craving for a little outdoor sex.

The watch officer selected a different button. "Resident team, you're up. Adam and Eve are back, and they're waiting just for you."

There was a chuckle in the reply. "Sullivan and Rawlings on the way."

Sullivan and Rawlings would be dressed in civilian clothes as if they were out for a walk. They'd have Boomer with them, a beautiful black lab that could be friendly and playful one second, deadly the next.

Lancer watched the intruding couple as they came down the road for about thirty feet, then, as they'd done each time before, turn into the woods. He smiled. With any luck, Sullivan and Rawlings might get a little show.

"What's going on?" Murphy asked. He was working containment surveillance at a terminal two stations down.

"Our exhibitionists are back," Lancer said.

Murphy stood and walked over. "I've heard about them, but haven't seen them yet."

"Well, you can't see them now. They're off the road."

"Damn. Seriously?"

"Yep. Went off right there." The watch officer pointed between two trees on the right side of the screen.

"Couldn't you just pan the inside gate camera over?"

The inside camera was mounted in a tree forty feet down the road from the entrance. "I'm not supposed to move it off the gate."

"Come on. Just for a moment."

"I can't, and you know it."

"Fine," Murphy huffed, then brightened. "Maybe they'll make a run for it before they can get dressed."

"Fifty bucks says they don't."

"How about twenty?"

Lancer laughed. "Okay. Twenty."

Together, the two men watched the monitor. After a minute, Sullivan and Rawlings appeared at the far end of the road.

"Talk us in," Sullivan said over the radio.

"Forward another sixty feet, then go left," Lancer instructed.

Sullivan and Rawlings did exactly as told. They, too, disappeared off screen.

"Come on," Murphy said under his breath. "Come on."

"Not going to happen," Lancer told him.

"Don't be a downer, man."

The road remained empty, reinforcing the watch officer's belief that they weren't going to witness any streaking. He was about to tell Murphy to get his cash ready when Sullivan staggered into the frame and collapsed onto the road.

"What the hell?" Lancer said.

He started to reach forward to call in backup when something pricked his neck and Murphy said softly in his ear, "Sorry."

With a suddenness that was almost more shocking than the condition itself, the watch officer realized he was paralyzed, unable to move even a finger.

He could hear the others in the communications room going about their business. On the screen in front of him, he could see the young couple dragging Sullivan back off the road. He wanted to yell. He wanted to reach out to his keyboard and type in the three-character combination that would raise the alarm. More than anything, he wanted to slam his fist into the side of Murphy's head.

"It will all be over soon." Murphy patted him on the cheek, then removed the watch officer's headset. Into the mic, he said, "Resident team's having a hard time locating our visitors. Suggest dispatching second team to help in the search." A pause. "It's Murphy. Lancer's on a bathroom break…okay, great, thanks." He put the headset down in front of the computer. As soon as two more men appeared on the monitor, heading out to assist Sullivan and Rawlings, he walked back toward his own station.

Lancer concentrated on his hands, willing them to move, but they remained frozen in place. How long was this going to last? At some point the paralysis had to wear off, right? *For God's sake, someone please notice that there's something wrong! Look! At! Me!*

"Want to show you something." Murphy was back at his side.

The traitor set an inch-thick, square-zippered case on the desk. Lancer immediately recognized it as the case Murphy kept his personal headphones in, something he'd brought with him every day. Murphy unzipped it, and opened it up. The headphones inside were no mere earbuds. These were state of the art, and probably cost at least a couple hundred dollars. They had foam padding on each side that fit over the ears, and were connected via a horseshoe-shaped band that could extend or contract depending on the size of the user's head.

What? Was Murphy going to blast Lancer with music?

Then Murphy did something unexpected. He first peeled back the leather covering the padding on one side. Underneath wasn't padding at all. It looked more like a thin plastic bag that had been rolled so that it would fit snuggly into the space.

"Cute, huh?" Murphy said.

He stretched the plastic out.

Not a bag, a…lightweight mask, with a small circular opening where the mouth would be.

Murphy disassembled the other padded earpiece, this time removing a plastic oval ring, then the speaker itself. He mounted the speaker in the ring, and attached the ring to the opening in the mask, closing it off.

"This is the best part," he said.

From the headband he removed three thin flat containers. Each seemed to be divided in the middle, with a clear liquid on both sides.

"Can I use this?" he asked, reaching for Lancer's coffee mug. "Thanks."

He seemed to glance around, and Lancer heard him dump the remaining coffee on the floor before setting the mug back on the desk. He wiped the interior with a tissue, then poured in the contents from one side of one of the containers.

"I promised you it wouldn't be long."

He donned the plastic mask. Lancer immediately saw it for what it was—a gas mask.

No! No! The scream in his head wanted nothing more than to pass his lips, but his vocal cords didn't even quiver.

Murphy opened the second side—
No!
—and dumped it into the mug.

OLIVIA SILVA LAY on the bed of her cell, her eyes closed. She'd been this way for over an hour, and most observers would have thought she was asleep.

They would have been wrong.

She was in a meditative state, one that allowed her to conserve her energy while maintaining complete awareness of her surroundings. She floated on a sea of nothing—recharging and refreshing her mind.

But most of all, preparing.

When the alarm beyond her cell door went off, she opened her eyes.

THE GASEOUS NEUROTOXIN created by the chemicals Murphy had combined was cloudless, lethal, and, in the enclosed space of the control room, extremely fast-acting. It worked so quickly, in fact, that the two guards who were inside the control room hadn't even had time to know something was wrong before they fell to the ground, dead.

As pleased as he was with the results, Murphy's initial concern was that the sudden deaths would be noticed by the guards on the other side of the glass wall, but as his contact had predicted, unless someone had collapsed right next to the wall, the other would never notice. Most of those in the control room were sitting behind larger monitors, and were already hard to see.

Murphy returned to his own station, and accessed the controls to the Bluff's numerous security systems. He couldn't take them all off-line. That would trigger the master alarm, and seal everyone inside until reinforcements arrived. What he *could* do was set up a rolling blackout of the zones across the property, timed to match the progress of the assault team as they approached the house, and make it look like a systems test. He slotted the thumb drive into his terminal and uploaded the program that would trigger the progression.

Once the program was ready to run, he tuned to the radio frequency the assault team was using.

"Control down," he said. "Beginning blackout sequence on my mark. Mark." He clicked the switch, starting the program.

He then switched to the terminal in the back row that controlled the detention cells. The woman who'd been manning the station was slumped forward, dead like the others. Murphy pushed her to the floor and took her chair. Removing a second thumb drive, he mounted it in the appropriate port, and used the program it contained to bypass the security alerts and disable the automatic locking feature on the door leading into the detention wing. Though the monitors would still indicate the door was locked, it wouldn't be.

He brought up a view of cell number eleven. The Silva woman was lying down, apparently asleep.

Not for long.

He triggered the switch that unlocked her door, and accessed the alarm controls, hovering the cursor over the one for the detention wing.

Now it was time for part two.

Chaos.

———

TAYLOR HAD BEEN stationed at the entrance to the detention wing for nearly seven hours. One more and he would be done for the night. So far, besides the guards who had either been starting or finishing duty on the block, no one had gone through the door in the clear Plexiglas wall that separated the arrival area from the detention cells. That wasn't unusual. There were only twenty cells here, and only five were being used.

These were the most important prisoners taken by the resistance, members of the Project who were deemed both dangerous and potentially useful. Normally, the only time someone passed through the security door would be to question one of the prisoners, or deliver the meals. It was, without a doubt, a boring job, but one he and his fellow guards knew was important.

At the moment, though, his mind wasn't on the prisoners or the potential death of billions. He was thinking about the beer waiting for him upstairs and the basketball game that was already recording on the receiver in his room.

Bwhap—bwhap—bwhap.

He jerked as the alarm sounded, swiveled to the left, and checked the computer monitor. As it was supposed to do, the detention wing door had locked down. He glanced through the Plexi wall at the guards on the block. They were taking their assigned positions in front of the occupied cells.

Per procedure, he checked his weapon, and repositioned in front of the elevator that led up from the subterranean detention area to the main building of the Bluff. If the doors opened, he and the two guards who would be joining him from the control room would deal with whoever might step out.

Bwhap—bwhap—bwhap.

He guessed it was probably just another false alarm. They'd had them a few times before. Real problems, on the other hand, never occurred at the Bluff.

Bwhap—bwhap—bwhap.

The persistent alarm was loud enough that he didn't hear the door to the control room open behind him, but even if he did, he would have only thought it was the other guards heading his way.

Unfortunately for Taylor, he would have been wrong.

IT WAS AMAZING how easy it was. Murphy's contact had said it *would* be, had told him the resistance would never suspect the attack to come from within. Under the man's guidance, Murphy had practiced everything over and over until each move was automatic, natural.

He had watched the guard stationed at the door to the detention area check the status of the door, then head over to the elevators. As soon as the man was in position, Murphy exited the control room.

Holding a second container of the dueling liquids, he walked toward the guard.

TAYLOR FINALLY HEARD the footsteps when they were

only a few feet away. Since the lights beside the elevator door indicated the car was still at the top, he looked back, but instead of seeing one of the expected guards, it was a member of the monitoring crew.

Murphy? Maybe. It was hard to tell because the guy was wearing something on his face.

"Where are the others?" Taylor asked.

"Not coming." Murphy's voice was distorted by the thing over his mouth.

"What are you talking about?"

As he spoke, Taylor began to sense that something wasn't right, but he was already too late. Murphy was flinging something at the floor by Taylor's feet.

Taylor raised his gun. "Don't move."

"No problem," Murphy replied.

"What was that? What did you…"

Taylor suddenly felt like he was losing his balance, the world around him becoming a blurry, vibrating mess. The next thing he knew, Murphy was holding on to him, gently lowering him to the floor.

"Don't fight it," Murphy said. "You're not going to win."

Taylor stared at the other man, trying to see him clearly. "What…wha…"

The rest of the question was lost forever as he took his last breath.

————

THE YOUNG COUPLE known as Adam and Eve had been joined by six others. The assault group moved in as soon as Murphy radioed. Within ninety seconds, all eight were standing at the front door of the Bluff.

There should be only four more guards in the main house, none currently expecting any trouble. The four who had come looking for them had all been permanently eliminated, as had the three who had been sent out to check the problem with the fence.

"Like we drilled," the woman—Karie—instructed as they reached the front door.

Gleason unlocked the door with the keys he'd taken from one

of the guards, and pushed it open. No gunshots. No feet pounding toward the entrance. No voices shouting at them.

Quietly, they slipped inside. Within three minutes, the four remaining guards were all accounted for and dealt with. The team reassembled in the lobby where Karie, after a quick look at the map of the house's layout, said, "This way."

———————

JANICE HUMPHREY had been asleep in her room upstairs. It was early, but she was suffering from a cold. That was the only reason she was at the Bluff at all. She and her husband, Michael, had been called to the Ranch for a meeting, but Michael had insisted she stay and he would fill her in later.

So, drugged up with cold medicine, she had slept the afternoon away, and was surprised when she finally woke to see that it was starting to get dark outside. She was just grabbing a tissue when her door opened, and Robert Lieber, one of the Bluff's security officers, ran inside.

"Out the window," he said quickly.

"What?" she asked, thinking she wasn't hearing correctly.

"There are hostiles in the house!"

She stumbled off the bed. "How did that happen?"

"I don't know, but we don't have time to talk about it. Ma'am, you need to go out the window and hide on the roof. They won't look for you there."

Even with a head slowed by a cold, Janice got his message. She ran over to the dormer window and threw it open. A cold blast of air hit her in the face. All she had on were the sweats she'd been sleeping in. They weren't going to be enough.

Lieber seemed to sense this, too. He ripped the top cover off the bed and shoved it at her. "Take this. Now go, hurry!"

The roof outside Janice and Michael's room had a gentle slope, but losing her balance was a very real possibility in her condition. If she did, the only thing that would stop her descent was the ground. She held the window frame tightly as she climbed out into the growing twilight.

"Try to get above the window. They won't look there," Lieber suggested. "But once you're settled, don't move around."

"Aren't you coming with me?"

"My job is to try to stop them." He pushed the rest of the bedspread out the window after her.

"They'll kill you! It's not worth it."

"Please," he said. "Go."

Then she understood. It wasn't the Bluff he was trying to protect. It was her. The bedroom had obviously been occupied. The intruders would have to find someone there.

"Go!" he repeated.

With a sense of helplessness, she did as he told her, working her way above the dormer, then lying against the roof.

Lieber, no doubt to mask the cold air in the room, left the window partially open. Because of this, she could hear the door to her room open, and the gunshots that followed. A moment later, the window opened all the way again. From her vantage point, she could see the back of someone's head looking out. As much as she hoped it was Leiber, she knew it wasn't. He would have called to her, let her know it was okay.

After several seconds, the window shut all the way, and the light in her room went out.

———

BWHAP—BWHAP—BWHAP.

The detention area was the trickiest part. As simple as it would have been to toss the remaining container of toxin through the door, the cells were not airtight, so there was a very good chance the detainees would have been killed, too. Four of them wouldn't have mattered, but if the fifth had died, it would have defeated the entire purpose of the mission. For that reason, the detention area was going to be up to the strike team.

Murphy glanced through the Plexiglas wall to the other side. Of the five guards, four were standing in front of their assigned cells, their eyes forward. The guard closest to the wall, though, was looking in Murphy's direction, clearly confused. Murphy's job now was to sell that this was only a medical emergency, not some forerunner to something more disastrous.

He knelt beside the dead guard, pretending first to take his pulse, then talk to him. Out of the corner of his eye, he could see the lights for the elevator indicate it was moving down. When the car was approximately ten seconds from arriving, Murphy jumped up and ran over to the phone at the guard's desk near the door. As he'd hoped, the curious guard's gaze followed him, so the man did not see the elevator doors open.

Murphy, on the other hand, was positioned perfectly, and saw with more than a little relief that it was the strike team, not Bluff security. Three canisters billowing smoke slid into the room. Within seconds, everything on Murphy's side of the Plexiglas wall was hidden.

Murphy held his position as the others made their way to him. In addition to the gas masks they were all wearing, each had a pair of thermal goggles that allowed them to see heat signatures through the smoke. As he knew she would be, Karie was in the lead.

"Any problems?" she asked.

"None. You?"

"All secured. Door unlocked?"

He nodded.

Karie and four members of her team positioned themselves in the smoke a few feet from the door. A sixth man stood next to the handle.

"Everyone ready?" Karie asked.

The men standing with her raised their guns, each pointing at a different target they could see with their special gear. Karie lifted her own pistol.

"On three. One. Two. Three."

As she spoke the last word, the man at the door pulled it open, and the five holding guns opened fire.

"Hold," Karie said three seconds later, but it was unnecessary. None of them had had to take more than two shots. The guards, unable to see the shooters because of the smoke, had no idea they were being targeted.

With Karie still leading, Murphy and the strike team entered the detention area, the last through shutting the door to keep the excess smoke from billowing in.

Karie pulled her goggles off and looked at Murphy. "Which one?"

"Over here. Number eleven." He led her to the door of cell

eleven. "It's open."

"Wait here," she told everyone, and pulled the door open.

———————

OLIVIA SAT ON the edge of her bed, watching the cell door. For the longest time it remained closed, but she was patient. She knew these kinds of things took time.

The question running through her mind was who, exactly, was coming. She knew for sure someone was. She'd been left a message telling her that much.

When she heard the guard standing outside her cell slam against the wall and slide to the floor, she allowed herself a smile, but when the door opened a moment later, her face was once more neutral.

The light from the outer area was brighter than it was in the cell, so at first all she could see was the silhouette of a woman. It wasn't until the door closed again that her visitor's face emerged from the darkness.

"Hello, Karie," Olivia said.

"Olivia." Karie took a few tentative steps into the room, then stopped. "Have…have they treated you well?"

"Three meals, a bed, TV when they're feeling nice. Well enough, I guess."

The women silently studied each other.

"So," Olivia said. "Who sent you? The directorate? Dr. Karp?"

"Dr. Karp is dead."

Olivia cocked her head. "When?"

"Last spring."

"NB7?"

Karie's brow furrowed slightly. "Yes. How did you know?"

Olivia shook her head like it wasn't important. So the help she gave Ash *had* worked. It would have been nice if someone had told her. "The directorate sent you, then."

"I'm…no longer with the Project." Karie gestured at the door behind her. "None of us are."

It wasn't often that Olivia could be surprised, but she was now. "So, you're here to…."

"Once you were gone, the Project lost its most important

voice. We all mourned your death. Some of us more than others. Then, a few months ago, word got around that you were still alive. We thought the directorate would immediately attempt a rescue, but they did nothing. There were several of us who found that unacceptable, and decided to do something on our own." She held out her hand. "So we've come to get you out. After that, whatever you want to do, we'll follow."

"You sure about that?"

"One hundred percent." There was no hesitation.

Olivia took Karie's hand and pulled herself up. "Then I guess it's time to go."

9

P<small>AX WAS WAITING</small> next to an old station wagon at the Ranch's private airfield when the jet carrying Ash and his kids rolled to a stop and the door opened. Ash zipped up his jacket and scooted his kids toward the exit.

"Hey, Uncle Pax," Brandon said as he bounded down the stairs. He was starting to grow out of the hugging phase, but allowed Pax to give him a hearty handshake.

"How ya doin', Brandon? Great to see you."

Josie was next.

"My God, girl. Your dad's going to have to lock you up soon to keep the boys away," Pax said as he gave her a hug.

She scoffed and shook her head, but her dad, who was following right behind her, knew she loved every word of it.

Pax held his hand out to Ash. "Good to see you, Captain."

"You, too."

Ash had tried for a while to get Pax out of the habit of calling him Captain, but it had been less than successful. Now Ash barely noticed.

Once Tom and Pat secured the luggage to the station wagon's roof rack, all six of them jammed inside.

As they rode to the Lodge, Ash asked, "How long do you think we're going to be here?"

Pax shook his head. "Oh, I don't know. That would be—"

"—a Matt question?" Ash finished for him. It was one of Pax's stock answers.

"If you knew that, why did you ask me?"

Ash shrugged. "I'm hoping one of these days you'll actually tell me something."

The older man looked over, his brow furrowed, and they both chuckled.

After a few seconds of quiet, Ash said, "Seriously, the kids have school, you know? I don't want them missing too much."

"Don't worry. Rachel's lined up someone who will make sure they don't fall behind."

"That doesn't sound like you're planning on this being a short stay."

"Didn't say that. A little help never hurts, no matter how much time's involved."

Pax was a master at playing the runaround game when he wanted to, so Ash decided it was best to wait until he saw Matt.

"I thought there'd be more snow," Brandon said.

Ash glanced outside. Here and there were patches of the dirty white stuff, but most of the ground was bare.

"It's a little late this year," Pax told him. "But don't worry, we're supposed to get some in the next day or two."

Brandon leaned forward. "Really? If we're still here, can we have a snowball fight?"

Pax scrunched up his face. "This time of year, snow's usually not wet enough to make a snowball."

"What do you mean, wet enough? It's frozen water."

"You'll see."

Soon the main part of the Ranch came into view. Closest and just to the left was the dormitory. It was two stories tall, with stone surrounding the bottom and pine above that. When Ash had stayed there the first time he was brought to the Ranch, he'd felt like he was the only one in the whole building. This time he could see half a dozen people outside near the main door, and more through windows of some of the rooms.

Beyond was the Lodge. It made the dorm look like an outhouse—five stories aboveground, and four below that Ash knew of. With a bit of snow still clinging to the shaded spots in the valleys of the massive roof, the Lodge looked even more like it should be sitting at the base of a ski run instead of here in the middle of…

Well, Ash still didn't know where the ranch actually was. Colorado or Wyoming was his best guess. The nearby mountains in the west looked very much like the Rockies, but every time he'd flown in or out of the Ranch, the automatic shades had been closed on the jet's windows during most of the flight.

As they pulled up to the Lodge, Rachel and the chef, Bobbie, came out to greet them.

"Look at you kids," Rachel said. "It's only been a few months and you're both at least an inch taller."

"You think so?" Brandon asked, hopeful.

"I'm sure of it." Rachel gave him a hug, then held her arms open for Josie, who, after a moment's hesitation, allowed Matt's sister to wrap her arms around her. "And how are you doing, Josie?"

"I'm fine." The response was automatic.

Rachel put a hand on each of the kids' shoulders. "Why don't you two go with Bobbie? She'll get some dinner for you."

"Pizza?" Brandon asked.

"If you want," Bobbie said.

Josie glanced warily at her father. "What about Dad?"

"We're going to go have a little talk, and he can join you later," Rachel told her. "Josie, if you want, you can go check out the library after you finish eating. We've got some new books I think you'll like."

Ash could tell his daughter saw through Rachel's attempt to distract her. Josie was smart, something Ash knew she must have inherited from her mother, because he'd never been that smart at her age. She had also grown up so much since that night at Barker Flats when their lives had changed that there were times when she was more adult than teenager. It killed Ash whenever he saw that. He wanted her to be a kid as long as she could and enjoy growing up, but in the back of his mind he knew that possibility had died with her mother, with Ellen.

For a moment, he was sure Josie would call Rachel out on the ploy, but she nodded and said, "Okay."

The whole group entered the Lodge, and Bobbie headed to the kitchen with the kids.

Once they were gone, Rachel said, "We're down in the Bunker."

THE ROOM ACROSS the hall from the communications center was set up with several rows of folding chairs all facing a large flat-screen TV hanging on the wall at one end. Standing just to the side of the monitor beside a small desk were Matt, Billy, and Michael Humphrey. Billy was the Ranch's doctor and all-around medical expert. Michael's duties were a little harder for Ash to pin down, as he seemed to be involved in several things. There was no one else present.

"Great," Matt said, as Ash and the others entered. He walked over and shook Ash's hand. "Glad you're here."

Ash exchanged quick greetings with Michael and Billy, then looked around at the thirty or so empty chairs in the room. "Is it just us, or are others coming?"

"This meeting's just us." Matt gestured at the front row. "Please, everyone, have a seat."

Matt remained standing while the others filled the chairs in the front row.

As soon as they were settled, he said, "Ash, everyone else here already knows this. I can tell you with certainty the day we've all been fearing will happen sometime in the next three weeks unless it can somehow be stopped."

The words weren't a surprise, given what Browne had said about the depots. The time frame was, though. Ash looked at Matt, hoping it was some kind of joke, but there was no humor in the man's eyes. *Three weeks?* Even after what Ash had seen, what he'd been through with his children, and living through the outbreak that killed his wife, he never really thought it would get to this, or even *could* get to this.

"How do you know that?" he asked.

"Did Tom tell you about the depots?"

Ash nodded.

"Without exception, at every depot we're aware of, our people have witnessed the arrival of truckload after truckload of supplies. This began about three months ago, and finished at all the locations three and a half weeks ago. It would be foolish not to think the same has happened at their other warehouses."

"That still doesn't mean they're going to do something in three weeks."

"That's true," Matt said. "But I'm not finished. Over the past four months, most of our people who were able to infiltrate the Project have been rooted out and killed. Prior to this, we had already learned that while the leadership of Project Eden doesn't share many details with its members, activity levels had been increasing, including the distribution of new instructions to various groups within the Project. We also know that in August, Project members were given an inoculation that they were told would ensure their being around to help restart humanity. Though we were unable to obtain a sample, we know it must have been a vaccine for KV-27a, something they undoubtedly developed from what they'd learned about the immunity you and your children have."

An image flashed through Ash's mind—his kids strapped to hospital beds with needles in their arms, surrounded by monitors and members of Project Eden. It was all his imagination, of course. He hadn't been there to see what was done to his children. He'd only arrived at the end, just before the late Dr. Karp was going to eliminate them.

"Undoubtedly, it is similar to the vaccine we were able to come up with and have been trying to spread. The problem is, our production capabilities are horribly inadequate, even for the population of a medium-sized city. When we're talking the world…" He shook his head.

Ash was aware of the vaccine they'd been making based on a sample of his own blood. In fact, once he'd been reunited with his kids and found out about the resistance's plan to develop it, he had offered more blood. What he hadn't known was that Matt was trying to get the result of that out as far and wide as possible. No matter how small a dent that might make, at least it was good news.

Matt pointed a remote control at the screen and clicked on a video file. For a moment the screen went black, then an image appeared that was all gray and white whipping around rapidly until it settled into what appeared to be a room shot from a high angle.

"Because of the low light, he had to use night vision. What you're looking at is a factory floor."

Ash could make that out now. The space was large, but unlike an assembly plant or machine shop, it appeared more like what he'd imagine a brewery would look. He could see at least a dozen large, covered tanks running down the center of the room, and there may have been more in the distance, out of range of the camera. Odder still were the people moving around the tanks. He was sure brewers didn't wear biohazard suits when making a batch of ale.

"What are they doing?" Ash asked.

"Exactly what you think. This is one of who-knows-how-many mass production sites for KV-27a."

"Do you know where it is?"

Matt shook his head. "No location was included."

"Have you tried to get in touch with your agent? We need to find this place."

Matt paused a moment. "Though the footage had been uploaded for over three weeks, it wasn't discovered until eight days ago. He obviously had to upload it in a hurry and had mistakenly put it in a folder that doesn't normally get checked."

"But you're trying to get to him now, aren't you?"

"A week before we even knew about the file, his body was found washed up on a beach near Veracruz, Mexico."

Ash closed his eyes, shocked by the man's death and frustrated by the lost opportunity.

"There's more," Matt said.

Ash reopened his eyes and focused on the screen.

The new shot was of a loading area where large drums that must have held at least fifty gallons each were being moved into shipping containers. If Matt was right, each must have been filled with the virus.

Matt stopped on an image of a loading dock where sealed shipping containers were being lowered onto big-rig trucks. He let it play for half a minute before turning it off.

"So we don't even know where they went from there?" Ash asked.

"Does it matter?" Billy said. "Out into the world. The only reason we know none of it has been released yet is because there have been no reports of outbreaks."

Ash thought about it for a moment, his face becoming more confused. "None of this explains where the three-week window comes in."

"You're right," Matt said. "It doesn't, but this does."

He pulled out a piece of paper and handed it to Ash. On it was a series of letters coupled together. Lower on the paper was what he guessed was the decoded version:

It's a go. Sometime in the next seven weeks. Project Eden calls it Implementation Day.

Best location BB n of sixty-six. Sci fac.

"That was sent four weeks ago by the only person we have left on the inside."

"Implementation Day?"

"That's what they're calling it."

"How confident are you that this time frame is right?"

"Our man's instructions were simple. The one and only time he was to contact us was if Project Eden moved into the active phase. Our confidence is one hundred percent."

Ash stared at the message for a second, then looked at the others. "We have to let someone know. It's the only way to stop it."

"And who would that be?" Billy asked, as if the question was the stupidest thing he'd ever heard.

"The government. The military. The media. There's got to be someone who'd do something."

Matt stepped in before Billy could respond. "You're probably right. There are good people in important positions who would try to step in and stop it. But they'd never get far. Your own experience should be proof of that. All the governments and military and media who could do anything are riddled with Project members in high positions who would do anything to protect the plan. The moment anyone tries to move against the Project, they'll be discredited or even killed." He paused. "I'm not just saying this because we think that's what will happen. We know it will because we *have* tried. Many times. And each time we did, people died and nothing changed. We've even cut together news reports ourselves and uploaded them to the Internet, but they get pulled down almost quicker than we can put them up."

Pax turned to Ash. "We're on our own. Just like we've always been."

"The last part of the message is perhaps the most valuable," Matt said. "It gives us a ray of hope."

Ash glanced at the paper again, and reread the last line. When he looked up, Matt touched the remote, and a map of the Arctic Circle appeared on the monitor.

"BB refers to Bluebird," Matt explained. "That's the name Project Eden uses for its main headquarters. N of sixty-six?" He touched a dotted line on the map. "North of the Arctic Circle, where there are dozens of science facilities—sci fac. Right after we received the message, we sent out several teams to the Arctic in search of the Project's headquarters."

The Arctic. It made a certain crazy sense to Ash. The isolation would provide not only a formidable natural defense against any rogue virus, but against man himself. And with technology these days, they could still maintain contact with their people throughout the world even in such harsh terrain.

"Did you find it?" he asked.

Rachel leaned forward. "We might have. One of our teams has gone missing. We sent another team to check on it. They found wreckage and a signal beacon, but no bodies."

"So it was an accident."

She shook her head. "The searchers believe that the debris was staged so we would *think* it was an accident. Looking back, there were also some irregularities in the last several contacts from the missing team. On the surface they could easily be explained away, but given what the searchers found, I think the real answer is something else." She shot a look at Matt. "I think those transmissions were faked by the Project. I think our team was discovered at an earlier stop."

"When they found Bluebird."

She hesitated, then nodded.

"Where?"

She stood up and walked over to the map. "We've narrowed it down to what we believe are the two best possibilities." She touched the screen. "Here on Ellef Ringnes Island, and here, on Yanok Island. After Ellef Ringnes, the inconsistencies become clearer."

She looked back at Ash. "Bluebird is where the orders to start will come from." She drew a circle with her finger that included both islands. "Somewhere in here is where it will all begin."

Matt nodded, his eyes also on Ash. "And that's what we want to talk to you about."

Ash had guessed as much.

"Let's be honest," Matt said. "At this point, our time is better spent using our resources to try and mitigate the damage. Stop the outbreak where we can, minimize the effects where we can't, and get out as much of our version of the vaccine as possible. The only actual way to stop their Implementation Day from even happening is to cut off the head, but that doesn't seem very doable given the location and time of year. Rachel, though, has successfully convinced us we need to at least give it a try. Logistically, it would make no sense to send a large detachment. First off, we need the manpower here, doing what they can to keep people alive. But, perhaps more importantly, the larger the team, the likelier its discovery before it even arrives."

"How many people were on your missing scout team?"

Rachel took a breath. "Two."

"Two," Ash said, looking between her and her brother. "So unless you're sending someone up there solo, there's a good chance any-sized team is going to be discovered."

"You're right. But there's no way I would send anyone up there alone."

Ash was quiet for a moment. "You want me on the team."

"We want you to lead the team," Matt said.

"*Lead* the team?"

"I'm sure if you think about it, you'll realize you're the best for the job," Matt said as if reading Ash's mind. "You have the training and experience. You've gone up against these people before in tight situations. If you say no, we'll understand, but, Ash…" He paused. "It would be a hell of a lot better if you said yes."

A thousand thoughts crowded Ash's mind, each vying for his attention. Foremost amongst them were his kids. How could he leave them?

Then again, given what he'd be trying to stop and keep them from experiencing, how could he stay?

"When?" he asked, his voice a whisper.

But before Matt or Rachel could answer, the door slammed open, and Jordan, one of Matt's top assistants, rushed in.

"The Bluff," he said. "We've lost contact!"

10

THEY RUSHED INTO the communications room, cramming around a computer station manned by a woman named Sarah.

"I've been trying to raise the Bluff, but I'm not getting anything at all," she said. "There's no connection. It's as if they turned everything off at their end."

"Try again," Michael said, his tone desperate. He had left his wife Janice at the Bluff before flying out to the meeting. She was supposed to have come with him, but an illness had kept her at home.

Sarah did as he asked. Once more there was no answer.

Michael looked at Matt. "Is the plane still here? I need to go. I need to get out there."

"Hold on, Michael. We'll get you there, but I want to make sure it's safe first."

"I don't *care* if it's safe! Janice needs me, so I need to get out there now!"

Rachel glanced quickly at Browne and Solomon. The two men immediately moved in beside Michael.

"Come on," Browne said. "We'll help you get ready."

"I *am* ready."

"Michael," Rachel said. "Just go with them."

"If I can't fly out right now, I need to be here so I know what's going on." His voice cracked as he spoke.

Rachel touched his arm. "You're no help to Janice if you can't focus and remain calm. Go with them. Get your bag, maybe change your clothes, and get something to eat. Just try to relax. In the meantime we'll get the plane ready."

Michael, eyes wide, seemed temporarily paralyzed, but then he seemed to get a grip on himself. With a nod, he let Browne and Solomon lead him from the room.

As soon as he was gone, Matt said, "Has anyone checked the Bluff's security feed? Is that still running, or did that get cut off, too?"

"Have it here, sir," a young guy three terminals away said.

Matt walked over, and everyone else followed.

"It cut off about ten minutes ago, sir. But something was definitely going on."

"Show me."

After the man clicked a few keys, surveillance footage from near the Bluff's front gate appeared on screen. "This is from sixteen minutes ago. Two intruders were spotted, a couple that Bluff security calls Adam and Eve. Apparently they've hopped the fence before and have been caught messing around on the property."

On the monitor, the young couple—Adam and Eve—ran playfully down the road before turning into the forest. The operator then skipped ahead forty-five seconds to when a security team appeared from the other direction. When the men reached the same point in the road, they turned after the couple.

"Do we have anything showing the woods?" Matt asked.

"No, sir. No one turned a camera in that direction."

"Why not?"

"I don't know." The operator said nothing for a moment, then pointed at the screen. "Here. This is the important part."

Suddenly one of the Bluff guards staggered into frame and collapsed on the road. A few moments later, the man and woman appeared, and dragged him back into the woods. Less than thirty seconds after that, the picture went dark.

"That's it?" Matt asked.

"Yes, sir."

"What about from inside?"

"All the footage inside was normal."

"Then perhaps the building is still safe."

"No way to know at the moment."

Matt looked at Pax. "Fire up the plane and get a team ready. I want you out there now."

"On it," Pax said, moving over to a phone on an empty desk.

"Billy, go grab what you think you'll need and meet out front." Matt looked at Ash. "Sorry, we'll have to continue this later."

"I'm going."

Matt cocked his head. "You sure?"

"I'm sure." Janice was one of the people who had saved Ash's life. He owed her and Michael at least this much. "I just need to let my kids know."

"Make it quick."

———————

ASH FOUND BRANDON in the kitchen, sitting at the long table eating dessert with Bobbie.

"Where's your sister?"

Brandon had just put a spoonful of chocolate ice cream in his mouth, so Bobbie said, "She's in the library."

Careful not to say too much, Ash told her, "You should check in with Pax."

Bobbie grew instantly alert. As Ash left the room, he heard her get out of her chair and head over to the phone.

The third-floor library was three times the size of the conference room downstairs. Floor-to-ceiling bookshelves lined all four walls, breaking only for the windows, door, and the large fireplace at one end. A rolling ladder attached to a rail allowed access to the upper shelves. There were two long tables with wooden chairs around them in one half of the room, and in the other, a lounge area with overstuffed chairs and sofas near the fireplace, where flames were working their way through a couple of thick logs.

He found Josie on one of the sofas, reading.

"Sweetie, I need to talk to you."

Without looking up from her book, she said, "You're leaving, aren't you?"

Of course she would guess that. "Just for the night."

"Where are you going?"

"California."

That caused her to look over. "California?" It was where they'd been living when the Sage Flu struck. Where her mother had died.

"Some friends need help."

He knew she was conflicted. It was written all over her. For months she'd been vacillating between acting like a disinterested teen and a rebellious youth, but neither fit her. She was too smart, too compassionate. Too old for her age.

"What…what happened?"

"Some others have tried to hurt them."

"And you're going to stop that?"

"If I can."

She considered this for a moment. "You'll be back tomorrow?"

"Yes."

"You promise?"

"Pinkie promise." He held out his little finger to her as he said it, like they'd done when she was younger.

She frowned as if that was only for little kids, but after a second wrapped her pinkie around his. A single shake, then a pull in opposite directions, breaking the link.

"You have to now," she said.

"I know."

———————

BRANDON WAS EASIER. When Ash returned to the kitchen, he simply told his son he was going to go help Matt and Pax with something, and that Bobbie would take care of him until he got back.

"Don't worry," Bobbie said. There was tension in her face that hadn't been there when Ash came through earlier. "We're going to have plenty of fun here. You ever ridden a horse, Brandon?"

Brandon lit up. "A horse? No."

"Maybe we'll go out for a ride tomorrow."

The phone on the wall rang, and Bobbie answered. She listened for a few seconds, then said to Ash, "Meet in the front common room in three minutes."

He nodded, and looked at his son. "Be good, okay?"

"I will, Dad. Have fun."

Ash gave his son a smile and a hug.

The common room was a large open area, two stories high, just inside the front door. There were two giant stone fireplaces on both sides of the room, each with logs blazing. More of the over-stuffed furniture was arranged into several small sitting areas. On the walls were two oversized paintings of the nearby mountains—one a winter scene, and one a summer.

Pax was the only one present when Ash arrived, but less than half a minute later, Michael, Browne, and Solomon arrived. They were followed seconds later by four men Ash had never met. Each had a hard edge to him, something Ash had seen a million times before. Former military, had to be.

Matt and Rachel arrived next. As much as they both wanted to come along, they would be staying at the Ranch. Though they said the reason was because someone had to stay and keep an eye on things, Ash guessed that if it weren't for Matt's bum knee, he, at least, would have come along.

"What are we waiting for?" Michael asked, anxious.

"Billy," Pax said.

Michael looked over at the staircase. "Somebody call him. See what's taking so long."

"I'm sure he's on the way," Pax said.

"I'm sure I'm on the way, too."

They all looked toward the voice. Billy was heading toward them from the hallway off to the left. Behind him were three other men, all carrying plastic cases containing what Ash guessed were medical supplies.

Pax stepped toward the door. "All right, everybody. Let's go."

Fourteen minutes later, they were in the air, heading west.

11

NAIROBI, KENYA

LAWRENCE MWERLA WAS having none of it. As a rising administrator within the Ministry of Public Health and Sanitation, he'd been chosen to oversee Project Eradication. The project was yet another in a series of attempts to wipe out the malaria-carrying mosquito population, something that had been attempted over and over for decades.

Like most of the others who tried, the organization behind the chemicals to be used in Project Eradication had been confident that their method would prove to be the one that finally did the job. Given Kenya's—for that matter, the world's—history with such attempts, Mwerla was dubious at best.

That didn't mean he wasn't hopeful. To rid his country of malaria would be a miracle. Nearly every fifth child born in the country died from the disease. An unacceptable loss in itself, but deaths weren't only limited to the young. Adults, too, were susceptible. That's why any chance to curb the disease had to be tried.

But now the project was delayed.

"This is not acceptable," he said to the representative from the Pishon Health Initiative. They were in the man's office at Pishon's temporary headquarters in Nairobi. "My government has already contributed significant amounts of money to facilitate Project Eradication. We have arranged for thousands of volunteers across the country, based, might I remind you, on a timetable *you* gave us when you brought the project to us. To change the date like this will necessitate further costs. We cannot afford to do this. We are not a rich country like yours."

Hans Lesser, the Pishon rep, leaned forward in his chair. "Mr. Mwerla, we understand your concerns. The date change, though, is unavoidable and necessary. To truly guarantee the success of Project Eradication, dosing needs to be coordinated across the continent. All the target countries will be participating on the same day."

"The same day? I do not see the importance of that. If our programs run a week or two apart or even a month, what difference could that make? I believe the timing is just a stunt you are doing for publicity."

"I guarantee you, publicity is not our aim. Whether you get it or not, we don't care. Ridding the planet of this deadly disease—*that* is our goal. According to our scientists, the best chance we have of doing that is by this coordinated effort. If need be, I can have one of them flown down here to give you a full technical briefing, but I'm hoping we can avoid that." He paused. "The delay is only a few days, but we have no desire for this to be a burden on you. I have spoken with our team in Amsterdam, and have been able to pull together additional funds to cover whatever cost overruns the Kenyan government might incur."

Mwerla calmed a bit. That was more than he'd been expecting. Still, there was much additional work that would need to be done because of this.

He stood up. "I will have to bring this up with the minister. He will have the final word."

Lesser rose to his feet. "Of course."

He held out his hand, and Mwerla reluctantly shook it.

As the Kenyan official turned for the door, Lesser said, "Please remember, Mr. Mwerla, what we're doing here is a good thing."

"Yes. I realize that." Mwerla nodded grimly. "Good afternoon."

HANS LESSER KEPT the smile on his face until the door shut behind the Kenyan. He then picked up the phone.

"Do it," he ordered, and hung up again.

In all likelihood, everything would have gone smoothly and Mwerla would have played along, but taking that chance was not something they had time for.

Within the next thirty minutes, Lawrence Mwerla would be the victim of a tragic car accident, and his second in command—someone considerably more accommodating to the Project—would take over.

There would be no more talk of the date change.

BUENOS AIRES, ARGENTINA

SCHOOL HAD COME to consume most of Patricia Mendes's time, and the long hikes through the city she used to take when she was younger were a luxury she could seldom afford anymore. But it wasn't just school that was taking up her time. It was also her boyfriend, Sergio. Make that *former* boyfriend.

Sergio was pig, He knew *nothing* about what it meant to be in a relationship. Her friends had tried to warn her, but she hadn't listened. She'd only gone down to the park a week earlier because she knew the latest thing they had told her was a lie. But instead of proving them wrong, she'd found Sergio right where her friends said he would be, hiding behind the old shack in the park with his tongue stuck inside Maria Blanco's mouth.

She felt like a fool, like she had no worth at all. How could he have done this to her? She had been a good girlfriend—never fighting with him, always agreeing to do whatever he wanted to do. She had even let him put his hand up her shirt once, though when he'd tried for her skirt, she had quickly put a stop to that.

Was that Maria's attraction? Did she let him touch her down there?

No. It's not Maria's fault, she told herself. *It's Sergio's.*

He was the one to blame.

Unable to focus on her homework in the days that followed, she had started walking through the city again, trying to work through the hurt and anger that had initially consumed her. On this particular afternoon, she had wandered into the old neighborhood where her family once lived. It was odd and yet comforting to be on the streets where she had played as a kid. Though she didn't recognize any of the people on the sidewalks, the buildings were all the same, as if time had not passed at all.

Soon, she reached the corner of a dead-end street, and suddenly recalled with vivid detail the old abandoned building that used to be at the end of it. She decided to see if it was still there. It had apparently once been a small factory, but for as long as her family had been in the area, it had stood empty. She and her brother Rodrigo would play in it sometimes, pretending it was a secret fort full of hidden passages and buried treasure.

When the building came into view, her heart sank a bit as she realized someone had reclaimed it. Though she could only see the top of the building, the roof over the front area had been replaced.

She approached cautiously, assuming the building would be occupied, but the closer she got, the less likely that seemed. The layout of the old factory was such that there was a wide room in front where the work would have been done, and a row of rooms that had probably been used for offices with their own corridor in the back. The improvements she noticed appeared to be limited to only the roof over the front room. The brick walls looked just as rundown as before. The only other change she could see was the few windows that used to let sunlight into the front room had been sealed up.

She scanned the area. No cars around and no sign that anyone was there.

Partly out of curiosity, and partly because it was keeping her mind on something other than Sergio, she slipped into the narrow space between the end of the building and the property wall, and made her way to the area in back. There was another change here. Several large rocks had been placed in front of the hole she had used when she was younger to get into the building. This only made Patricia all the more curious about what was inside.

She continued around the building, and smiled when she saw that the missing bricks at the top of the back corner had not been replaced. She climbed up the wall like she had before and lowered herself inside. The room she was in was tiny. She and Rodrigo had assumed it was once a closet. Long ago its door had been sealed up and separated from the rest of the building. That was probably why the people who'd blocked the other entrance had not felt it necessary to do anything about the hole at the top of the wall. But did that mean they hadn't discovered the other way in?

In the back corner of the room was a narrow wooden cabinet. One of its doors was jammed in place, but the other, a bit more resistant now than before, still opened. At the bottom, its presence mostly hidden by an empty shelf a foot above it, had been a hole in the wall. When Patricia knelt down to check, she saw that it was still there.

She crawled through. The other side came out under an old metal desk that had piles of junk all around it. She and her brother had put the desk there and piled the scraps around it as part of concealing the secret back entrance to their fort. Even if other kids had found it in the years since, they had left it that way, no doubt thinking it added to the allure of the place.

She moved out of the office and into the hallway. It was obvious the new owners had zero interest in the back part of the building. It was as ratty and dingy as ever. Each room she looked into seemed untouched from when she'd last been there.

Halfway down the hall, there was a passageway that led into the large front room, or would have if a new wall of bricks hadn't been erected in the middle of it.

She frowned at it, thinking. There had to be another way into the front room. At least someplace where she could just get a peek. She was really curious now.

Then she remembered the weapons room.

It wasn't *really* a weapons room, just what she and Rodrigo had called it. It was the old office where they stored anything that looked like a gun or a sword. It had a common wall with the main room, and as a result of one of Argentina's many earthquakes, that wall had shifted slightly, creating a crack near the top. Though she'd never examined it closely, she thought she might be able to at least glimpse into the other room. The problem was that it was four feet above the top of her head.

She scoured through the back half of the building for something she could use to boost herself up. In one of the offices, she found an old tabletop that she thought she could lean against the wall and use as a ladder. Not wanting the thing to slip out from under her, she piled several loose bricks along the bottom until she felt confident they would anchor the table in place.

Once everything was set, she put her hands against the wall, and carefully inched her way up until she reached the top. The table was actually longer than she'd needed, so she ended up having to hunch down to both see through the crack and avoid knocking her head against the ceiling.

She peered through the opening. It definitely went all the way through. The problem was, since there was very little light in the other room, she could barely see anything.

She slipped her fingers into the crack. If she could widen it just a little and let more of the light from her room filter through, she'd be able to see better. She worked at one of the boards that didn't seem to be holding on to anything, but it held stubbornly in place. Determined, she pulled harder.

"Come on," she said, trying to rock it back and forth.

With a sudden snap, it broke free and her hand flew backward, shifting her weight away from the wall. Without even thinking, she grabbed the opening with her other hand and pulled herself back, but she yanked too hard and the change in momentum caused her to slam into the wall. Gasping for air, she held on as tightly as she could with both hands so she wouldn't fall. After several seconds, her breathing started to return to normal. She glanced down, and saw that the table had slipped sideways to the ground. She would have to drop onto the uneven terrain.

Just as she was psyching herself up to do this, she heard a snap, and then something in the wall groaned. Her gaze shot upward toward the break in the wall, but before she could even see it again, there was a crack, then another and another.

A groan, this one loud and sustained. She pressed her cheek against the wall, knowing there was little else she could do. She felt a part of the wall begin to tilt away from her as the groan increased. Then, with a final ripping of wood, it crashed into the other room while leaving her still dangling above the ground.

Dust billowed up and engulfed her, but it was thin enough for her to see that the wall below her chest level was gone. At first she couldn't believe it, but it was right there in front of her—a good chunk of the wall was missing, and *she'd* done it.

She searched the ground, chose a spot where she could avoid twisting an ankle, and leaped toward it. As she stood once more, the only thought on her mind was to get the hell out of there. But then she caught a glimpse through the new hole into the other room.

What's that?

She walked over to the missing wall. There was something large on the other side, taking up a good portion of the room. The air was still filled with enough dust that it was hard to make out exactly what it was.

Her curiosity returning, she stepped through the break. The item was about ten feet in, and went left and right like a wall. In the low light it was hard to tell for sure, but it seemed to be blue in color, and appeared to be corrugated in wide strips. It didn't go all the way to the ceiling, though. Earlier, when she'd been peering through the crack, she must have looked right over the top of it.

She followed the wall to the left, because all the debris from the wall was to the right. The corrugated wall stopped about fifteen feet from the far end of the room. She turned the corner and saw that the new side was maybe only a fourth as wide as the long side had been. The moment she saw that a set of doors almost completely made up the short end, she knew what it was.

A shipping container.

In the middle of a walled-up, deserted building? That didn't make any sense.

The doors were locked by some kind of device that seemed to be mostly *inside* the container. There were also two red bands around each handle. If someone opened the doors, they would break. Weird, she initially thought, but then quickly revised that assessment. The bands were seals, weren't they? A way to *tell* if the doors had been opened or not.

She went all the way around, but found nothing else that could possibly explain what it was doing there.

Maybe her brother could figure it out. He was good at puzzles like this.

Carefully, she worked her way back out of the building. As she headed home, she didn't even give Sergio a thought. Her mind was completely on the shipping container, and on the millions of possible reasons it was inside the deserted building.

Their old fort really did have a treasure in it now.

12

THERE WERE TWO Suburbans waiting for the flight from the Ranch when it landed at the private airfield just west of the Sierra Nevada Mountains.

The men quickly transferred their gear—both lethal and medical—into the vehicles, then headed for the Bluff. Driving as fast as they could on the dark, winding roads, they cut what should have been at least an hour-long trip down to forty minutes.

In the event of an attack on the Bluff, protocol was to drive to a point half a mile away, then travel the rest of the way on foot via a subtly marked, seldom used path through the woods. Ideally, they would have had another team on the other side using a similar trail so they could come at the Bluff from both sides. But it would have taken at least another thirty minutes to send one of the Suburbans around that way, and Pax decided that was a delay they couldn't afford.

After everyone donned their comm gear, Pat Solomon took point and led them through the forest with Michael right behind him, pointing out the trail indicators. When they were within one hundred yards of the fence, they stopped and gathered in a tight circle.

Pax pulled an iPad out of his bag, and opened one of the custom applications that had been developed at the Ranch. He had explained to Ash on the flight out that he should be able to tap into the Bluff's security cameras once they were close enough.

Now his finger moved quickly over the screen, touching different points. Suddenly he froze.

"Holy shit," he whispered.

"What?" Michael asked, panic threatening to overtake him again.

"Two down in the front room. Another in the kitchen." Pax started tapping the screen again.

"What about Janice? Can you check our room?"

"There's no camera in there. You know that."

"There's one in the hall," Michael said, moving around so he could see the screen, too. "If the door's open, you should be able to see part of the way in."

Pax frowned, and tapped the screen. "This one?"

"No. The next one down."

Another tap.

"Yes. That's it," Michael said. He leaned in. "What is that…?"

Pax seemed to hesitate. "A leg. Looks male, though."

"Oh, God."

Even in the darkness, Ash could see Michael pale.

"Doesn't mean she's in there," Pax said. "The only way we're going to know is to check."

He looked back at the screen, accessed a few more cameras, and sucked in a quick breath.

"What is it?" Ash asked.

Pax turned the tablet so they could all see.

On the screen was a view of the detention level deep below the house. The angle was from above the elevator door toward the Plexiglas wall that separated the arrival area from the detention block. Remnants of smoke hung in the air on the arrival side, and on the ground close to the elevators, obscured but not hidden by the smoke, was a body. There was no way to tell for sure if the person was dead or alive, but based on the five bloody figures sprawled on the ground on the other side of the see-through partition, it was a fair guess that no one in either half would ever take a breath again.

Pax switched to a view of the control room—bodies slumped over terminals, unmoving, with another two or three on the floor.

"We need to treat this as a poisonous gas situation," Pax said.

"But the guards in the detention block look like they were shot," Ash pointed out.

Pax grimaced. "Yeah. That bothers me, but I didn't see any blood in the control room, and with that smoke, we've got to assume the worst."

One of the men Ash hadn't met until that night pulled his backpack off, and zipped it all the way open. Inside were enough gas masks for everyone, plus a few extras in case they found survivors. He passed them out.

"No one makes a move onto the detention floor until we run a check," Pax said. "I want to know what we're walking into first."

There was a chorus of "Yes, sir"s.

"Any signs of who did this?" Ash asked.

Pax shook his head. "Checked cameras throughout the house and all the way to the front gate and back. Nothing. But we should proceed as if they're still there. They have to know we'd come, so they could be waiting for us."

More nods.

Pax pointed at four of the men. "Do a sweep all the way up to the front gate and back. We'll wait at alpha position until you return."

"Yes, sir."

The men immediately headed out. Pax took a moment to report in to Matt at the Ranch, then he and the rest continued on toward the house.

Alpha position turned out to be a dense cluster of trees about a hundred and fifty yards from the house. Ash could sense Michael's growing anxiety as they hunkered down and waited for the others to return. Each minute would be an eternity to him. Ash had been in that position himself once, and he knew there was nothing any of them could do to lessen the stress.

Finally, the others reappeared.

"Seven bodies," one of the men reported. "All ours. Three back near the side fence. The other four near the front gate. No one else around."

Pax closed his eyes a moment, his worst fears no doubt realized.

"All right," he said. "You four cut through the woods and come at the house from the other side. Browne, Solomon, Ash, and I will close in from this side."

"What about me?" Michael said.

"You stay here with Billy."

"No way."

"You *will*, or we'll stop what we're doing and take you out of here right now."

Michael took several quick breaths. "She's my wife, Pax."

"Exactly why you're staying here. You're too wound up and you know it. You make a mistake in there and you could get the rest of us killed. So what'll it be?"

He stared at Michael.

"I'll...I'll wait here."

"Good." Pax looked over at Billy. "Shoot him if he tries to leave."

The doctor nodded. "You got it."

Hippocratic oath or not, Ash knew he would do it.

The two teams headed out in different directions. Ash and his group caught sight of the building in less than a minute. Despite the fact that lights were on in many of the rooms, there was a definite stillness blanketing the entire site.

Pax led them to within fifty feet of the porch then stopped. The front door was open, but there were no signs of movement inside.

"In position," one of the men on the other team reported over the comm.

"All right. We're moving in. You cover us," Pax said.

Staying low, Pax, Ash, Browne, and Solomon rushed the porch, their guns raised in front of them. Browne and Solomon passed through the door first, each pointing their weapon in a different direction.

"Clear," Browne announced.

"Clear," Solomon echoed.

Pax and Ash moved in.

The two men lying in the front room had multiple gunshot wounds, including one each to the back of their heads.

Pax said nothing, but the anger in his face was more than telling.

"Up or down?" Browne asked.

"The house first, then we'll go down," Pax ordered.

A sweep of the first floor revealed no one else, so they called in the other four men before heading upstairs, where they split up. Pax and Ash were the first to arrive outside Michael and Janice's room. The body they'd seen earlier on the floor inside was another one of the guards. They checked the closet and the en suite bath, but both were empty.

"Where the hell is she?" Ash asked.

Pax shook his head, just as confused.

They returned to the first floor and met up with the others. Since there was no sign of anyone else, Pax sent one of the men to go bring Billy and Michael in. "Make sure Michael knows she wasn't in the room, and we haven't found her yet."

JANICE HUDDLED AGAINST the roof of the house. She had no idea how long she'd been there. Weakened by her illness, she'd passed out at some point and woken to find that night had fully descended.

Her whole body shook from the cold. It was as if she could feel it all the way down to her bones. She needed to get back inside. She needed to get into the heat. Nighttime temperatures had been routinely dropping into the low twenties, and even occasionally the teens. If she stayed where she was, she'd die of exposure for sure.

But could she risk trying to go back inside yet? Were the others still there? She had no doubt the intruders were from the Project. Perhaps they were even attacking multiple locations, attempting to cripple the only organized opposition they faced.

Had they hit the Ranch, too? Was…was Michael okay?

Dear God, please see both of us through tonight.

She had to get closer to the window. She had to see if she could get inside. Even if the others were still around, perhaps there was someplace she could hide. Surely they had already checked the rooms. If she were able to, say, climb into her closet, chances were they would never know she was there.

You can do this.

She silently counted to three, pulled the blanket off her head, and crawled back down to the base of the dormer. She lay back, panting, the short distance having required most of her energy. She didn't even realize she'd closed her eyes.

Nor was she aware of losing consciousness again.

———

LEAVING TWO MEN behind to stand guard by the entrance, Pax led the others through the house to the secret elevator that went down to the detention level.

"Put your masks on now," he said as they entered the car. "When we get to the bottom, Browne, I want you to keep your finger next to the Close Door button, but don't push it until I say. The rest of you stay where you are while I run an air analysis."

As they descended, Pax attached a long cable to his iPad. On the other end was a device that looked almost like a wand. He handed the computer to Ash. Holding the wand with one hand, he coiled up the cable, finishing just as the car began to slow.

He moved to the front and looked at Browne. "Be ready."

The car came to a smooth stop. After a second's delay, the doors slid open.

They weren't even a foot apart when Pax tossed the wand into the arrival area, letting the cable play out as far as it could go.

As soon as it stopped moving, Pax said, "Close the door."

Brown hit the button, and the doors slid shut around the cable.

Pax took the tablet back from Ash and studied the screen for several seconds.

"Smoke looks like it was just there for cover," he said, his voice both muffled by the mask and coming clearly over the radio. "There's something else, though." He waited for a moment, his eyes on the screen. Then his nostrils flared. "Those bastards. Double LG."

"Double LG?" Ash said, surprised. Double LG was the nickname for a deadly nerve toxin that killed within seconds of contact. He'd never heard of anyone actually using it before.

"There're only trace amounts left," Pax said. "But keep the masks on. Got it?"

On Pax's command, Browne pushed the Open Door button.

The room beyond the elevator was unchanged from their brief preview a moment earlier. With Pax in the lead, they moved out of the elevator.

As they neared the body on the floor, Pax glanced at Billy. "Check him."

The doctor knelt beside the still form, while the others headed over to the Plexiglas wall. Where it met the outer wall was the control room, itself fronted by a glass wall. Though they'd already seen the dead men inside via the camera feed, it was still unnerving to see nearly a dozen people slumped over desks and lying on the floor, dead.

Pax tossed the sensor into the control room and read the results. "Same. Concentration's higher, but that's probably because the room's smaller." He looked up as Billy rejoined them. "Dead?"

Billy nodded.

Michael moved to the control room window. "I don't see her. I don't think she's in there."

"No, but a lot of others were," Billy said.

Michael whipped around, his eyes on fire. "You think I don't know that? I worked with these people every day! They were my *friends*! Excuse me if I'm also concerned about my wife!"

"Michael, calm down," Pax said. "Or I swear to God I will send you back upstairs right now."

"My fault," Billy said, sounding like he actually meant it. "Sorry, Michael. I didn't mean anything by it."

Michael did nothing for a moment, then gave Billy a curt nod.

For the third time, Pax did his trick with the sensor, this time throwing it into the detention block.

"It's clear," he announced. "Don't think they used any gas in there. But just to be safe, keep your masks on."

Ash had guessed as much. The intruders would have only come down here for one thing: the detainees.

While Billy and Solomon checked the downed guards to see if any of them was still alive, Pax asked Michael, "Which cells are occupied?"

Michael thought for a moment. "Three…five, seven, um, eight…and eleven."

Ash had assumed all were full, so he was surprised to learn that most of the twenty cells were empty.

One by one, they checked each. In the first four, the prisoners had all been shot through the head. The fifth cell, though, was empty. Ash didn't need anyone to tell him who had been held there. He'd once visited cell eleven himself.

Olivia Silva's.

"Son of a bitch," Pax said.

———————

IT WAS A noise that woke Janice. Not just any noise. Voices, indistinct and coming from the other side of the window.

She tried to peek inside, but couldn't do so without risking being seen, so she hung back.

Once they were gone, she waited five minutes just to be sure. Then, using more strength than she thought she had, she raised the window and crawled back inside.

At first she just lay on the floor as she let the warmth of the Bluff flow over her and attempt to thaw her out. After a while, though still cold, she felt like she could stand. Using the bed to help her, she rose to her feet. That's when she saw Robert. He was lying near the door, a drying pool of blood at his side. He could have saved himself, but had instead given his life to save her.

She knelt beside him, and brushed a strand of hair off his cheek. He was *so* young. How would she ever repay his sacrifice?

Out of the corner of her eye, she noticed something under her dresser. She leaned forward to take a better look. A pistol, probably the one Robert had been using. She picked it up and checked the mag. It was full.

Though hiding in the closet had been her initial plan, a new one had taken its place. She would find the intruders, and get a good look at them so she could identify them later. If she were really lucky, maybe she would find one alone, and take one life in payment for the many that she was sure had been lost that day.

Quickly she exchanged her sweats for more practical clothing, then checked to make sure no one was in the hallway.

Without waiting another moment, she slipped out of her room.

———————

THE MOOD IN the elevator was somber as the team headed back up to the house. Counting the four prisoners in their cells, thirty-two were dead, and two—Janice and Olivia—were the known missing.

Not only were the losses devastating, but the numbers themselves were a problem. There had been thirty-five people at the Bluff, not thirty-four. Someone else was also missing. To try figuring out who it was, Browne and Solomon had stayed below to ID the bodies.

As soon as the doors opened at the top, they all ripped off their masks and took in deep breaths of fresh, untainted air.

"I need to report in," Pax said as he pulled out his phone and walked away.

Ash and the others headed toward the front room.

It was clear to him what had happened. The Project had found out that Olivia was alive and had come for her. She had been one of their leading scientists before she was taken and her death faked. There must have been a need she filled that required her return to the fold. How had they found out, though? A leak here at the Bluff?

Perhaps the missing—

A gunshot rang out.

———————

MOVING AS SILENTLY as she could, Janice listened for intruders as she made her way toward the stairs that would take her to ground level. So far she had heard nothing, and had the distinct sense the others were no longer on the second floor.

She was just starting to think that maybe they'd pulled out altogether when a male voice drifted in her direction, and was answered a moment later by a second man. They seemed to be somewhere ahead of her.

The hallway she was in T-boned with another that ran parallel to the front of the house. She turned left, heading toward the stairs, and soon discovered where the voices were coming from.

The hallway stopped at the edge of the second-floor mezzanine. There was no one there. The speakers must have been in the room below, their voices drifting upward. The problem now was, if she stepped out onto the walkway, she'd easily be seen from the lower level. She scanned ahead, and realized maybe that wasn't correct. If she stayed low, she could use the railing as cover and get even closer to the stairs.

Not allowing any time to talk herself out of it, she dropped into a crouch and crept along the mezzanine until she was three feet short of the stairs. She peeked over the top rail. Standing together in the lower room were two men, both wearing black, with rifles slung over their shoulders.

Without warning her head began to swim. She reached out and grabbed the rail to keep from falling down.

"Did you hear that?" one of the men said. "Up by the stairs, I think."

They'd heard her.

"We need to check," the other one said.

"I'll go."

No! Oh, God, no! They knew she was here. Now they wouldn't stop until…

…until I'm dead, too.

She had to buy time, but the only way to do that was to let them know for sure she was there. Without looking, she pointed her gun into the room toward where she thought the others were, and pulled the trigger.

———————

ASH RAISED HIS gun, and looked back at Michael and Billy. "Stay here," he said.

Billy wasn't armed, so he didn't put up any protest, but Michael looked like he was about to.

"Stay. Here," Ash repeated.

Not waiting to see if Michael complied, he ran to the end of the hallway and scanned the front room beyond. He could see the two men they had left behind, pressed against the wall opposite the front door.

Ash quickly waved his hand to get their attention. One of the men looked over and pointed at the mezzanine above him. Ash nodded, then held up his hand, telling them to stay put.

He turned and ran back down the hallway.

When he reached Michael and Billy, he said, "Is there another way to the second floor?"

"One of them is still here?" Michael asked.

"Is there another way or not?"

Michael nodded. "I'll show you."

Moving fast, Michael took him into a room that was set up as an office, then out a door on the other side. This led into a narrow corridor that fed into the kitchen. At the back of the room, next to the pantry, was a closed door. Michael wrenched it open. Beyond was a staircase.

Ash pushed past Michael and raced up. Behind him he heard the other man's feet pounding the treads.

Instead of arguing with him, Ash looked back and said, "Stay just inside the stairwell in case they try to use it."

Michael nodded. "Okay."

Ash took off down the hallway. Having never been on this floor before, he let his instincts guide him. Ahead, the hallway bent to the left. He stopped just short of the turn and listened.

Silence.

Planning to move as quickly as he could to the far end, he stepped around the corner. He was instantly halted by the gun thrust in his face.

JANICE HEADED FOR the back stairs, hoping the intruders weren't guarding them, but as she neared the end of the corridor, she heard footsteps running in her direction down the intersecting hallway.

She leaned against the wall and raised her gun.

AT FIRST, THE only thing Ash could see was the barrel of the pistol. Forcing himself to look beyond it, he made eye contact with the person who wanted to kill him.

"Janice?" he said, surprised.

Her eyes narrowed, confused, but she didn't lower the weapon.

"Janice. It's Ash. We've been looking for you."

More confusion, the barrel wavering slightly.

"Please. We're not here to hurt you. Whoever did this is gone. We just flew out from the Ranch."

"The Ranch?"

He could see she was having a hard time understanding. She took a harder look at him.

"Ash?"

Whatever energy had been holding her up vanished. If Ash hadn't jumped forward when he did, she would have smacked her head on the floor.

13

BROWNE AND SOLOMON accompanied Ash, Pax, Billy, Michael, and Janice on the plane back to the Ranch. The other men stayed at the Bluff, securing it until the cleanup team arrived the next afternoon.

Janice had yet to regain consciousness since falling in the hallway. After a quick examination at the house, Billy determined that in addition to the flu, she was now also suffering from hypothermia, which would explain why she hadn't been killed with the others. Somehow she had been able to hide outside.

Matt was waiting for them when they landed back at the Ranch. He had Ash and Pax ride with him, while everyone else piled into the other waiting vehicles.

"It was indescribable," Pax said as Matt pulled away from the airstrip. "A goddamn massacre. I don't think anyone even had a chance."

"We ran the names of everyone you identified," Matt said. "The missing person is a man named Jeremy Murphy."

Pax shook his head. "I don't think I know him."

"He was one of the control room technicians."

"So was he involved?"

"He'd have been perfectly placed."

Everyone was silent for a moment, then Pax said, "If that's the case, I wonder if he did this of his own free will, or was he coerced?"

"It doesn't matter one way or the other," Matt said. "They're all still dead."

Silence once more.

After a little while, Ash said, "Olivia must be pretty damn important to them."

Matt frowned. "Maybe a few years ago, but I wouldn't have thought now. Whatever skills she had, they would have surely replaced them by this point."

"Could be a personal connection. Someone in the Project who just found out she was alive?"

"That would make more sense."

"Or," Ash said, having another thought, "what if she was just a byproduct? And the real goal was to disrupt your organization."

"Then they would have struck here."

"Has Murphy ever been here?"

"Yeah, but like most of the people we bring in, he doesn't know where *here* is."

"You should probably still get ready, because chances are they'll figure it out."

"That's already being taken care of." Matt glanced at him. "I'm afraid I need your answer now."

Ash's mind had been so absorbed with the events of the evening, it took him a few seconds to realize that Matt was talking about Bluebird. "You should have Pax lead the team. He did a pretty damn good job at the Bluff."

"Pax will be going, but he won't be leading. He'll be there to help and advise, but mainly to be my eyes and report back. I can't have you burdened with dealing with me, too. Once you go, you're the authority. I won't contradict any of your orders. I'll have too much down here to deal with."

"You're assuming we won't be successful, aren't you?" Ash asked.

Matt said nothing for several seconds, then nodded. "Yes."

The rest of the ride was in silence. When Matt pulled up in front of the Lodge and killed the engine, no one made a move to get out.

"You're asking me to leave my kids," Ash finally said. "To quite possibly sacrifice my life for something you think is not going to work anyway. Why in the hell should I do that?"

Matt looked at him. "Because if you *do* succeed, you're ensuring that the world your children know will still be here."

It was as if Matt had been echoing his own thoughts.

"Well?" Matt asked.

———————

ASH SAT DOWN on the edge of his daughter's bed, and gave her a shake. "Josie, I need to talk to you."

She groaned softly and turned on her side, her back to him.

"Josie, come on. Wake up."

He put a hand on her shoulder and pulled her back around. She twisted against the mattress, then her eyelids parted.

"Dad?"

"Hi, sweetie. We need to talk."

"What time is it?"

"Nearly four."

She looked at the window, then back at him. "In the morning?"

"Yeah."

Looking completely confused, she asked, "What do you want to talk about?"

He patted her on the leg and stood up. "Get dressed. I'll wait for you in the hall."

Once she joined him, he took her down to the kitchen where Bobbie had some hot chocolate waiting. The house was eerily quiet, in part due to the hour, but also because, as Matt had told him, most of the resistance personnel had shipped out not long after the destruction of the Bluff was discovered, so as not to be caught in any action that might have happened at the Ranch. Those remaining would be moving into the Bunker in the next few days, where they would remain, acting as communications hub, until it had all played out.

It took Ash an hour to fully explain everything to his daughter. He left nothing out, and answered all her questions as honestly and directly as possible.

She took it surprisingly well, but telling her the world might end in the next few weeks wasn't the hardest part.

He took a sip of his now lukewarm cocoa. "There's a chance

we might be able to stop it. It's not a good chance, but we have to try."

"What is it?" she asked warily.

"We think we know where the Project's headquarters are located. If we can get to those in charge before anything happens, we might be able to stop it."

"Where?"

She was talking around the real question she wanted to ask, and he knew it.

"About three thousand miles north of here."

She contorted her face. "You mean the North Pole?"

He couldn't help but let out a quick laugh. "No, not that far, but close. On one of the islands in northern Canada."

"Oh." She stared down at her mug, lost in thought.

He waited patiently for a minute, then two. Finally he said, "They want me to go."

"I know," she whispered. "When?"

"As soon as possible, but it will probably take a few days to get everything together."

She stared at her hot chocolate again.

"I won't go if you don't want me to," he said.

Quiet again, then, "I don't want you to."

"Okay. Then I won't." He raised his mug to his lips.

"But, Dad?"

He moved the cup away an inch. "Yeah?"

"You have to go."

"No, sweetie. I don't have to. I told you, if you said no I wouldn't go, so I won't."

"No. That's not what I mean. I don't want you to go, but I know you *have* to."

She chewed on her bottom lip, trying not to cry.

He looked her, his chest tightening. "Sweetie, I *don't* have to. They'll still send a team. I just won't be on it."

Eyes full of tears, she said, "You have to, Dad. You're the one who can make it happen. You found Brandon and me. You saved us. Now you need to save everyone else."

As she started to cry, he moved around the table and knelt beside her, wrapping his arms around her. In that moment, she reminded him of his late wife more than ever, nearly bringing him to tears, too.

"You have to go, Dad," she whispered in his ear between sobs. "You have to."

14

MUMBAI, INDIA

SANJAY COULD NOT believe his luck. Not only had he been given a job the day he'd finally accompanied Ayush to the Pishon Chem offices, but after he took the test they gave him, he'd been given the position of supervisor, responsible for operations in his home neighborhood and several more surrounding it. Ultimately, over one hundred others would work directly for him.

Ayush had done even better. He was given the title of Coordinating Officer, and worked over the group of supervisors in charge of nearly half of Mumbai. Which made him Sanjay's boss.

Though the project they'd been hired for was a temporary one, the people at Pishon Chem made it clear that if they did their jobs well, some of the supervisors and coordinating officers would be kept on permanently. And the money they were paying! It was even better than he had hoped.

Tomorrow was going to be a big day. For the first time, the sweepers—the title of those working under the supervisors—would be practicing with the spray machines. The managers from Pishon Chem wanted everyone to be completely familiar with the equipment. When the day finally came for dispensing the miracle spray, the sweepers would need to move quickly, covering as much ground as possible in a single day.

Sanjay would observe those training under his command, and give instructions and encouragement to those who needed it. At the end of the day, he was expected to give honest assessments to his coordinating officer—Ayush—so that adjustments could be made now while there was still plenty of time.

But that was tomorrow morning. Tonight he would make a stop at the fruit stand, because he knew for sure Kusum would be there. She had told him herself.

With a wide grin, he hopped off the bus and headed to the market, happier than he'd ever been.

GILSTRAP HALL
HAWKINS UNIVERSITY
ST. LOUIS, MISSOURI

COREY WAS GETTING annoyed.

It had been several days since he contacted Hidde-Kel Holdings and requested an information pack about the company. He'd stressed the importance of getting it quickly, and had been told they would rush it right out, but, as his latest check of the mail just proved, it had yet to arrive.

It wouldn't be so crucial except for the fact he'd been hard-pressed to find other information about the company. Apparently it wasn't very big on publicity, as evidenced by its website, which was woefully devoid of useful information. He wasn't even sure where its headquarters were actually located. The address on the website corresponded to a tiny office in a multiple-tenant building in Portland, Oregon. He knew this because he'd looked it up on Google Maps, then switched to street view and saw the actual building. From that he was able to get the name of one of the other businesses that shared the same premises. He called and persuaded the woman who answered to give him a little information on her neighbor.

Turned out Hidde-Kel's address was more a mail drop than anything else. So was the company even *in* Portland?

As he walked back to his dorm room, he knew he had to come up with some other options. If he didn't, his paper wouldn't be much more than a page or two, guaranteeing him a failing grade.

There *was* one thing he could do. He'd been avoiding it because he'd hoped Hidde-Kel would be more cooperative, and because, technically, it would be breaking the law. But perhaps it was time to push things a bit.

His friend Blanton Kirn, also a student at Hawkins U, was working on a degree in computer engineering, a natural offshoot of his computer-hacking hobby. Corey thought that maybe Blanton could cut through the BS on the Hidde-Kel website and get to some real information.

Yeah, it was crossing the line a bit, but if Hidde-Kel wasn't going to help him, then he'd just have to help himself.

As he reentered his room, he pulled out his cell and gave his friend a call.

BUENOS AIRES, ARGENTINA

"SEE WHAT I mean?" Patricia said.

She'd convinced Rodrigo to come back with her to the not-quite-so-abandoned building. He'd been dubious from the start, but she had talked him into it, and now they were standing next to the collapsed portion of the wall, looking in at the blue metal box.

"You did this?" he asked.

"The wall? Well, yeah, but that's not important."

"Patricia, you damaged the building. Maybe you even damaged that." He pointed at the container.

"*That's* what's important. The wall doesn't matter."

"You don't know that."

"I *do* know. Look around! This place was already falling apart. I bet that wall was going to collapse soon anyway. All I want to know is what you think about the box. It's a shipping container, yes?"

Rodrigo looked at it and shrugged. "Could be, but I've never been this close to one before."

"Come on, come on," she said, stepping through the hole into the other room.

Her brother hesitated for a moment, then followed her. Now that he was within reach of the box, he seemed more interested. He ran his fingers up and down the metal surface as she led him toward the end. Before they got there, he stopped.

"Over here," Patricia said. "I want to show you something."

He pointed at the upper corner. "See that?"

She looked. There was a number painted near the top in faded white. She hadn't noticed it before.

"That's how they track this."

"So it *is* a shipping container."

"Yeah," he said. "It is."

"Well, then, maybe you can figure this out." She headed around the side.

When he joined her, she pointed at the odd locks on the doors. "They're not normal, are they?"

He bent forward for a closer look. "I've never seen anything like these before. Pretty elaborate. It's almost like you have to be inside to unlock it."

She looked at the container anew. "You don't think someone's in there, do you?"

"Did you hear any noise?"

She shook her head.

He raised his hand and rapped on the door. "Anyone home?"

"Don't!"

He smiled. "Relax. Nobody's in there. See? Let's take a look at the rest."

He headed around the far side, and she followed.

"That's unusual." He pointed at the top again, only this time not at a number.

"What?"

"There. Right at the top corner. Doesn't that look like a hinge?"

It was hard to tell for sure, but yes, it kind of did. "What could it be for?"

He shrugged. "Why don't I take a look?"

He jumped up and grabbed the top lip, then grunted loudly as he tried to pull himself up. When it seemed as if he wasn't going to make it, Patricia stepped over, put her hands under his butt, and pushed. That seemed to be the extra energy he needed. He flopped onto the top, and rolled onto his back.

"Well?" she asked, taking a few steps back so she could see him.

He flipped around. Since there wasn't enough room to stand,

he sat up. "It's a hinge all right. Runs all the way down the long edge." He looked away from her. "Well, that's kind of odd. There's another hinge on the other side. Same size. You know what? I think the roof's split in two, so it can open like shutters."

"Is that normal for a shipping container?"

"Not that I know."

"Maybe you should get down."

"Just a second."

He got on his knees and started moving toward the near end. At one point, he reached up, touching the ceiling so he'd know where it was and not bump his head. Only instead of continuing on, he stopped and looked up.

"What now?" she asked.

"The roof's made of metal."

"Well, yes. You can see that from outside. So what? Lots of places have metal roofs."

"Maybe." He continued to examine the roof, then crawled quickly toward the other side of the container. "It just seems…hold on."

Several seconds passed.

"Rodrigo?"

"I said, hold on."

Patricia backed up as far as she could to get a better view. Her brother had raised himself up so that his head was only a few inches below the ceiling. He was examining the point where the roof met the far wall.

"What are you looking at?"

He waved her question off without turning around. After a moment, he dropped to his hands and crawled several feet to his right. There, he looked at the roof and wall again. He repeated this two more times, ending up above the end where the side doors with the funny locks were. With his finger, he seemed to be tracing a line in the air that first moved across, then down the wall to the floor. He scrabbled to the near edge and lowered himself to the floor. As soon as he was down, he ran out of sight around the end.

Patricia stared after him. What was he doing? She was the one who brought him here. If he found something, he should tell her.

With an exasperated grunt, she headed after him, finding him around back kneeling next to the wall of the old building. He was gripping the sides of an old, narrow, wooden cabinet. If Patricia had to guess, she'd say it had probably been attached when the place was constructed. The screws holding it in place would surely put up little resistance. But as Rodrigo pulled, the cabinet didn't move.

"I thought so," he said.

"You thought what?"

"This is new."

"Are you kidding? Dad's younger than that."

"I think it's only supposed to look old, but I have a feeling it was put in here the same time the container was moved in. Think back to when we used to explore this place. Do you remember this being here? I don't."

She frowned, her mind searching through her memories, sure that the old cabinet must have been there, but her brother was right. She didn't remember it. In fact, she was positive now it hadn't been there.

"What's it doing here, then?" she asked.

"Hiding what's underneath."

Could he not just give her a full answer? "And what would that be?"

He shrugged. "Power, for sure. Probably some sort of controller unit."

"For what?"

"That," he said, looking at the container. He moved his gaze to the roof. "And that."

"Rodrigo, what are you talking about?"

He smiled at her. "There are motorized clamps along the high end of the roof." He pointed to where he'd been looking earlier. "And along the side walls I think there are rollers. You want my guess?"

She looked to the heavens. "*Por Dios.* Yes!"

He tapped the not-so-old cabinet beside him. "I think when this gets a signal, the clamps release, the roof rolls off, and the top of the container opens."

It took a second to process what he was saying. It was so far off from anything she expected. "Why?"

"I have no idea."

"Drugs?" she suggested.

Rodrigo suddenly grew wary. It was obvious he hadn't considered that possibility. "I'm not sure why they would set things up like this, but I guess, maybe."

She frowned. "We should tell Uncle Hector."

Uncle Hector was a member of the Buenos Aires police, and if this *was* some kind of illegal operation, he'd know what to do.

Rodrigo looked back at the container. "Yeah. I think you're right."

15

THE DIRECTOR OF Preparation—the DOP—was now in full charge of Project Eden. Until it came time for the Director of Recovery to take over, no one, not even the Principal Director, could overrule any order given by the DOP. This change of command had been worked out long ago, and had been written into the procedures of the Project. Each part was critical, and the appropriate Director for that segment of the plan would take charge for the duration of that particular phase.

The vote on moving forward had taken place two months earlier. Per protocol, all the Directors and the Principal Director had to vote in the affirmative if implementation was to occur.

Going in, the DOP had not been one hundred percent sure they had the votes. There were a couple of Directors he was just unable to get a read on. Turned out he needn't have worried. Everyone, without hesitation, voted yes, and from that moment until one month after Implementation Day, he was in charge.

The command center at Bluebird—known unofficially as the Cradle—was two levels below ground. Befitting its importance, the Cradle was large and impressive. It had five semicircular rows of desks, each home to over a dozen manned computer stations. They all faced the curved wall at the front of the room that was covered by over fifty monitors of varying sizes. The center monitor was, naturally, the largest, its high-definition screen providing a level of resolution few other monitors on the planet could match.

Any time the DOP was needed in the Cradle, he used a station in the center of the back row, raised slightly above the others. Ostensibly, this was so he could see everyone, but also, he knew, it reminded the others who was in charge.

He was sitting at the desk, his gaze on the main monitor, which currently was displaying a satellite shot of Australia. Overlaying this was a graphic containing over two hundred Xs representating locations where Implementation Delivery Modules had already been placed. If need be, he could push in on the image until he was looking at an overhead view of one of the IDMs.

Every region of the world had to be looked at on an individual basis. What would work one place might not work somewhere else. But they had known that from the beginning. That's why it had taken decades from when the plan was conceived to the point where they were only nine days away from actually making it happen. No, Project Eden was definitely no rush job. In the intervening years, extensive research had been done, hundreds of methods had been considered and tested, and best chosen for each need. All so that they could avoid any mistakes when the time to act came.

What they knew from the beginning was that covering every square inch of the planet was out of the question. Whatever virus they developed would have to be potent enough that they need only focus on dense population centers and a few outlining areas, and humanity itself could do the rest of the work, carrying the disease to other areas. If areas where the virus was unable to reach popped up, those could be targeted. KV-27a had turned out to be just that and more. There was no question in anyone's mind of its potential for success.

The same careful, detailed work had also gone into all other aspects of the Project—the selecting of candidates for survival, the long-range targeting and control of influential officials worldwide to ensure the Project would remain hidden and unhindered, the planning and preparation for after, and the development of the virus itself and its vaccine for those chosen.

With the start of the implementation phase, they had reached a point where everything was just logistics and coordination.

"What's the problem?" the DOP asked, his voice traveling straight from the microphone in front of him into the ear of the man at the Australia desk, four rows away.

"A ship with fifty IDM packages and one with thirty were delayed by a storm in the Indian Ocean. They're scheduled to arrive in the next two days. Our contractors in Sydney and Perth have added extra manpower to make sure they get to their destinations within twenty-four hours after offloading."

The time frame was still well within implementation parameters.

"All right," the DOP said. "Next."

The image switched to Southeast Asia, where a combination of several methods would be used throughout the area. Singapore, Malaysia, Indonesia, Thailand, and Vietnam would be dealt with using IDMs. Since Singapore itself was so small, four of the five containers assigned to it would remain right at the harbor, while the other would be on the back of a truck driven to Sembawang on the far side of the island.

Other areas, in places like Phnom Penh in Cambodia and Vientiane in Laos, would mostly be handled by teams of locals using handheld sprayers they'd been told were targeting the malaria-carrying mosquito population.

Which brought them to Burma.

Though the country had started to open back up to the world, its leaders were still highly suspicious. Chances were, at the first sign of a worldwide infection, they would seal the borders. A few carriers might sneak in, and some people might get sick, but the government would undoubtedly terminate them before more could be infected. Getting IDMs into the country wasn't going to be possible. They had tried to get permission for their anti-malaria spray, even offering to pay for everything themselves, but the Burmese generals who ran things wanted nothing to do with it.

So a third method would be employed. It was the same method that would be used in other troublesome areas like North Korea, Iran, several of the former Soviet Republics in the south, and much of the Middle East: modified passenger planes, painted to look like a local airliner, complete with correct transponder codes. Only instead of passengers, the planes would be carrying more than enough of the virus to drop a fine mist down over the targeted areas.

No nation would be immune.

"Any issues?" he asked.

"Nothing major, sir," the Southeast Asian supervisor said. "A few local labor problems, money mainly, but we're taking care of it."

"And Burma?"

"Planes are in position and ready to be loaded."

"Good." The actual loading of the virus would not occur until a few hours before the final Go signal was transmitted.

They worked their way through Southern Asia, the Middle East, Africa, and Europe without any major problems. In the North American report, the DOP was pleased to hear that one of his pet methods of distribution was prepped and ready to go. One of the Project's front companies had purchased a produce company that created, among other things, specialized produce misters for grocery stores. These misters included cartridges that enhanced the spray so that fruits and vegetables would stay fresh longer. Come Implementation Day, the cartridges—now all ready to go—would replace the standard cartridges the stores were currently using.

Central America went quickly with a no-problem report.

The next satellite image up was South America.

The DOP asked his standard question. "Anything?"

"Not…really, sir."

The DOP turned from the screen to the desk where the South American rep was sitting. "That sounded like something to me."

"Just a little issue we're dealing with."

"What?"

A pause. "We received a sensor fault on an IDM in Buenos Aires. It's probably nothing."

"What kind of fault?"

"The top hatch. One of the sensors was registering a downward stress. But on the next check, everything was fine."

"Is this the first time?"

"Yes, sir."

"Explanation?"

"Like I said, sir. I think it was just a fault."

"But…"

"But I'm sending someone to check."

"Good."

Another hesitation. "The closest person with clearance is in Caracas. I've told him to get down to Buenos Aires as soon as he can."

It probably *was* just an electronic glitch. There'd been a few others. Frankly, the DOP was surprised there weren't more. With a massive global operation, technical issues were bound to happen. "Keep me posted."

"Yes, sir. I will."

"Next."

The image was replaced by one of the Pacific Islands.

16

EIGHT PEOPLE. THAT was it.

It seemed so insignificant, microscopic even, especially when compared with the billions they were trying to save. But after going over everything again and again, it was decided that was all the resistance could spare for the mission to Bluebird. The argument was also made that with every additional team member, the risk of discovery would increase exponentially. If that happened, it was extremely possible the Project would order the immediate release of the virus into the world.

Though Ash had understood both positions, he didn't have to like them. As way of compensation, Matt let Ash choose all but three of the team. The first of the exceptions was—as Ash had already known—Pax. Ash would have chosen him anyway. The other two were members of one of the Arctic search teams—the same duo who had discovered the highly suspect wreckage of yellow team's boat.

That left four positions for Ash to fill. Tom Browne and Pat Solomon had shown their worth at the Bluff, though Tom really hadn't needed to prove anything after what he did for Ash earlier that year. On Tom's recommendation, Ash also included a man named Casey Nolan, known apparently to most people as Red.

"That's seven," Matt said when Ash gave him the names.

"You know who I want for number eight."

Matt smiled. "Yeah, I guess I do."

"And where will I—"

"Just outside San Diego. Pax will have the info."

It took three full days to get all their equipment together and compile as much intelligence as possible. It could have easily taken three more, but they all knew they couldn't afford any more time. Ash spent that final night in the room his kids were sharing. He lay on the floor listening to them sleep before finally nodding off himself.

At three a.m., his phone vibrated with the alarm he had reluctantly set. He slipped out from under his blanket, pushed himself up, and walked quietly toward the door.

"Be careful," Josie said.

She was lying on her bed but her eyes were open.

He went back to her. "I'm sorry. I didn't mean to wake you."

"You didn't wake me. I haven't slept yet."

"Oh, sweetie. You need to sleep."

She tried to smile, but failed. "I didn't…want to miss when you left."

He leaned down and kissed her on the forehead. "I love you."

"I love you, too, Dad."

"Keep an eye on your brother."

"I will."

He went over to Brandon's bed and kissed his sleeping son's temple. "I love you, buddy."

As he reached the door, Josie said again, "Be careful."

Not wanting to lie, he said, "I'll do my best."

The four other members of the team who were at the Ranch met Ash in the kitchen for breakfast. Matt and Rachel were there, too. There were no big speeches. In fact, few words were spoken at all.

When it looked like everyone was done, Ash said, "I guess we should be off."

One by one, they shook hands with Matt and Rachel. Ash went last.

"Josie and Brandon…" He couldn't finish.

"They'll be fine," Rachel said. "There's a whole group of people here who will take care of them."

He nodded. "Thanks."

He shook hands with Matt and headed for the door, but

stopped and looked back.

"We're planning on coming back."

"Good," Matt said. "We'll be waiting."

———————

"ALL RIGHT. ALL right," Madigan said between breaths. "Watch your left. You're vulnerable there."

"Like hell I am," Chloe shot back. She faked with her left, hit him with her right, then finally let her left fly.

He grunted as her fist hit the punching mitt he was wearing.

"Not bad," he said. "But I know you can do better."

He moved to his left, and she bounced around to the right.

They were outside the gym, on the large padded surface near the side entrance. Matt had set up the training facility years ago in the hills outside Escondido, California, about half an hour north of downtown San Diego. Ramona, Madigan's assistant, stood just off the mats, observing. Besides the three of them, there were only two others around, everyone else having shipped out on assignments.

Chloe had been waiting impatiently for hers, but it still hadn't come. She knew why—her leg. She'd nearly crushed the damn thing in the spring. Sure, she still limped a little when she got tired, but the leg *was* better. Anything Matt needed, she knew she could do. She'd made Madigan call and tell him that much, but the assignment still hadn't come.

"Getting tired?" Madigan asked.

"Maybe you are. Not me." Her brown skin glistened with sweat as she faked again. This time, instead of following up with a right, she kicked out with her foot, pulling back at the last second so that her outer arch merely slapped his ribs as opposed to breaking them.

"Hey, now," he said. "We're not working kicks today."

"Aren't you the one who's always telling me there are no rules?"

"Yeah, well—"

From out front came the sound of tires stopping in the gravel parking area.

"Hold," Madigan said.

Chloe took a step back, dropping her hands.

From their position, they could just see the hood of an unfamiliar dark sedan.

Madigan tossed the punching mitt to Ramona. "Take over. I'll be right back."

Ramona stepped on the mat and raised the mitt. "Let's go."

Chloe watched Madigan until he disappeared around the front of the gym, then released a rapid-fire combination that pushed Ramona back a few steps.

Ramona tossed the protective pad to the side. "No mitts on the outside as far as I'm aware. Spar?"

"Fine by me."

Ramona had always been more aggressive than Madigan. Chloe got her best workouts on the days she took over.

As they squared off, they could hear two car doors opening and closing again. Voices followed.

Ramona feinted left, then came in low and tried to land a punch to Chloe's ribs, but Chloe was ready. She twisted out of the way, swinging her leg around as she did, and knocked Ramona in the back.

"Lucky shot," Ramona said as she pushed herself off the mat. "My turn now."

Unfortunately for Ramona, Chloe was a good student, and remembered everything she was taught. Over the past several months, as they worked on strengthening her leg and improving her overall skills, she'd kept a keen eye on Ramona, learning the assistant's moves, perfecting them herself, and mentally marking the other woman's flaws.

So when Ramona came at her this time, Chloe knew where the hole would be, and perfectly timed a right uppercut that caught Ramona under the chin, knocking her backward in the air and then to the mat.

"Oh, shit," Chloe said, dropping down next to Ramona. "You all right?"

Ramona looked at her for a moment, unfocused, then said, "I think maybe next time we stick to the mitt."

From behind them, a voice said, "I guess that answers that question."

Chloe looked back and saw that Madigan had returned with

two others. When she saw who they were, she smiled broadly. "And what question would that be?"

Daniel Ash shrugged. "Just if you were in any condition to join us."

ASH HAD COME to trust Chloe like he trusted no one else. She had been at his side when he saved his kids, had almost permanently sacrificed her leg in the process. If he had to pick only one person to join him on this mission, she was it.

Chloe White was not her original name. That had been Lauren Scott. But after she was captured by the Project on a mission for Matt, the Project had done something to her that erased any memory of her past. In essence, Chloe White was born the day she was rescued.

It hadn't harmed her intelligence, though, nor robbed her of much of the education she'd picked up before the loss. The personal things were the areas most affected—the people who'd been in her life, her family and friends. They were like strangers to her. As much as she tried, she could remember none of them. Ash couldn't imagine how that must feel. Somehow, though, she had learned to cope.

Ash and Pax had left the other members of the team at the airport while they drove out to see her. They'd come around the corner of the building just in time to see Chloe knock the other woman to the mat.

"Ash and I need to have a conversation with Chloe," Pax said to Madigan. "Any quiet place we can talk?"

"You can use the gym. No one's in there."

"Thanks."

Since Chloe was the most familiar with the facility, she led the way.

As soon as they were alone, Ash gave her a hug. "Good to see you."

"You, too," she said.

Pax was next. "I could get used to a beautiful woman like you hugging me like this."

She playfully slapped his shoulder. "Well, don't. If anyone asks,

I'll be sure to say I've never let you within five feet of me."

Pax looked around, and motioned to some chairs in the free-weights area. "Why don't we have a seat?"

Once they were settled, Chloe eyed them both. "So, join you doing what?"

Before Ash could say anything, Pax held up a hand. "First, we need you to be straight up with us. How's the leg?"

She let out a quick laugh and nodded. "I get it. You need to be sure."

"That we do."

"I take it this is a mission."

"We'll get to that. Now, your leg?"

She got up and lifted her left leg so she was only standing on her right. She then began hopping up and down. "It's got some permanent pins, and there's a plate right here." She leaned down and touched a point on the side of her shin. "Sometimes when I get really tired, I limp, but my limp is faster than most people's walking pace. Along with everything else Madigan's been putting me through here, I go on a five-mile run every day, and on weekends Ramona and I go on a ten-mile hike." She sat back down and looked Pax in the eyes. "The leg is what it is, but it's never going to stop me."

"I'm sold," Ash said.

Pax shook his head. "All you had to do was say it's fine."

She glanced at Ash then Pax. "It's fine."

"You're in," Ash told her. "But only if you want to be."

"I want to be."

"Let me finish first."

"You don't have to."

"Yes. I do." Ash paused. "Chloe, this isn't going to be easy. Matt would probably put our chances of success at ten percent."

"Five," Pax corrected.

"The point being, I'm not sure how many of us are going to make it back, whether we succeed or not."

"How many of us are there?" she asked.

"With you, there'll be eight."

"Not a lot to start with."

"No."

She shrugged. "I'm still in. Better than hanging out here and waiting for the end of the world."

Pax stood up. "Great. Let's go get you outfitted in cold-weather gear and get under way."

"Wait," she said. "No one said anything about cold weather."

17

HECTOR RAMIREZ WAS supposedly out questioning suspects regarding a rash of burglaries at several boutique hotels in the Palermo area. What he was really doing was much more enjoyable.

There was no one who could get him as excited as Gabriella. At least once a week, he would sneak away for a few hours in the afternoon so they could have some time together.

Though Hector was married, he wasn't cheating on his wife. Gaby *was* his wife. Even after fifteen years together, she still was the most sensuous woman he'd ever met. While most of his colleagues wanted little to do with their spouses, Hector wanted everything to do with his. Happily for both of them, Gaby felt the same way about him.

They were on the living room couch, Gaby's body straddling his as she moved in a rhythm all her own. She gave him a devilish smile as she pushed her dark hair behind her ear.

Oh, God, how had he ever gotten so lucky?

As he reached up to caress her breast, his phone rang. Annoyed, he looked over at the coffee table where it lay.

Without slowing at all, Gaby said, "Go ahead."

"It can wait."

Up and down she went. "I want you to answer."

He sneered, knowing the possibility that it might be his boss—the danger of discovery—would turn her on even more.

Careful not to do anything that would throw off what she was doing, he reached over, nabbed the phone, and looked at the screen.

"Who is it?" she asked, her voice hushed.

"I don't know." There was no name, and the number was not one he recognized. "I'll let it go to voice mail."

"No, go ahead. See who it is."

She was crazy, this wife of his, and he loved that about her.

He accepted the call and put the phone to his ear. "Ramirez," he said.

"Uncle Hector? It's Patricia."

Immediately, he put his hand over the phone and whispered. "Stop. Stop."

His wife slowed, but didn't completely halt.

"Uncle Hector?" his sister's daughter said again.

"Patricia, how are you? Is everything okay?"

"Patricia?" Gaby whispered, confused. Then her eyes grew wide. "Our niece?"

Hector nodded. Gaby immediately rolled off her husband and sat down beside him.

"I'm…um…okay," Patricia said.

"You sound like something's wrong."

She hesitated for a moment. "Did you get my message yesterday?"

He had, but between the hotel robbery investigation and dinner out with Gaby and their friends, he'd forgotten. "I'm sorry. I was very busy and couldn't call you back."

"It's okay."

"So what's going on?"

"I, uh, found something, and showed it to Rodrigo. We both thought maybe we should show you, too."

"What is it?"

"I'm not sure. We thought it might have something to do with…drugs, maybe."

Hector sat up. "Drugs? What are you talking about?"

She briefly told him what she had found.

"Where is this?"

"In our old neighborhood. You know, the one we lived in when I was a kid."

If his niece was right, and the shipping container held drugs, then…good Lord, that could be one of the biggest seizes ever in the city. But if it *was* drugs, surely no one would have just left it there unwatched. According to Patricia, she'd been there twice already without anyone stopping her. That seemed inconsistent with what he knew about the business.

But he did have to admit that whatever it was, the situation was odd.

"Where can I meet you?"

"I'm using the payphone outside the store outside Cervantes Market. How about there? Remember? It's the one we used to get fruit at. It's close to what I want to show you."

"I know it," he said. "I'll be there in twenty minutes."

"Okay."

He hung up. Gaby said, "What's wrong?"

"Patricia and Rodrigo found something strange."

"Strange how?"

As he stood up and started pulling on his clothes, he repeated Patricia's story.

"Drugs," she said when he finished. "That's not your area. Maybe you should have someone else check it."

"I doubt it's drugs. In fact, it's probably nothing. Maybe the owner is just using the building for storage."

She didn't look convinced.

He leaned down and gave her a kiss. "I'll be all right."

———

"BACK THIS WAY," Patricia said.

They were at the old abandoned house. Hector didn't remember it from when he visited his sister's family in the past, but both Patricia and Rodrigo assured him it had been empty even back then.

His niece and nephew led him into the building, through an open spot near the top of a wall, then a secret hole at the back of a cabinet. They showed him the damaged wall, the container, the roof, and the peculiar box Rodrigo said he thought controlled everything.

It all confirmed what Hector had thought when Patricia told him about the place over the phone—it was odd. Beyond that, he had no answers.

"I've been thinking," Rodrigo said. He gestured at Hector and himself. "Between the two of us, I think we might be able to pry open the top a few inches and look inside."

Hector aimed the flashlight he'd brought along at the top of the container. The idea of climbing up there did not exactly appeal to him, but he was at least as curious as they were. "Are you sure?"

"When I was up there, there was one part that felt a little loose. So maybe we can."

Hector ran the beam along the side of the container, looking for an easy place to climb.

"I'll help you up," Rodrigo offered. "Then Patricia can help me like she did before."

"I want to go, too," she protested.

"You have to stay down here."

"Why?"

"Because I'm stronger than you."

She frowned. "Not by much."

"By enough."

Hector nodded. "Let's do it."

———————

PEREZ ARRIVED IN Buenos Aires just after lunch. Since he had no luggage and was using an Argentinean passport on this trip, he made his way quickly through Customs and was soon sitting in the back of the car driven by the local contact, a man by the name of Victor Flores.

Flores was a real estate agent used by the Project to procure properties in the Argentinean capital. The Project's cover was that they were representing a Korean company planning an expansion into the city. It was a variation on a ploy they were using in various countries throughout the world. Flores had received a substantial sum for his services, and was more than happy to drive Perez wherever he wanted to go.

In a way, it was a two-for-one deal. Perez's main reason for coming was to check out one of the IDM units and make sure there were no problems. While he was here, he had been instructed to eliminate Flores, too. It wasn't a necessary hit. In fact, if Perez hadn't needed to return, the Project would have left Flores alone. He would be dying in the coming weeks anyway, but since the Project's regional assassin was in town, Flores and his knowledge of the secured properties was a loose end that might as well be cleaned up.

But first, the IDM.

Flores, after several failed attempts at small talk, drove Perez in silence, first to a hotel where a small leather bag with a suppressor-equipped pistol was waiting in Perez's room, then to the neighborhood where the property was located.

"This is fine," Perez said.

"We still have several blocks to go."

"I said, this is fine."

Flores pulled the car to the curb.

As Perez opened the door and grabbed his bag, he said, "Wait here."

It was a beautiful, warm day. In the Southern Hemisphere, it was the end of spring, and in less than a week it would be summer. Perez had a brief thought about the millions of bodies in the city that would be rotting in the heat come January. He was not blind to the fact that he was working directly on making that happen, but it was for the greater good of humanity—the only way the human race would survive. At least he wouldn't have to experience the decay firsthand. He'd be on a completely different continent by Implementation Day, safely riding out the unfolding disaster in one of the Project's compounds.

He turned down the dead-end street where the building with the troublesome IDM was located. There were several cars parked along the block, but since there was no one on the street at the moment, he headed all the way back and entered the property.

The IDM had been sealed in the large, front room of the old building. There was, however, a disguised entrance that, with the right code entered into the hidden keypad, allowed Project members inside.

This particular entrance was all the way at the far end. The problem for Perez was that to get there, he had to go around the back of the building. As he walked along the rear area, he spotted fresh footprints in a patch of earth near the wall. He knelt down for a closer look. Two sets at least, and perhaps a third, pointing in the direction he was going.

Probably someone just taking a shortcut through the yard, or a couple teens hiding out from their parents.

He continued on, but as he reached a wall that had a group of bricks missing at the top, he noticed that the footprints simply stopped.

He opened the bag, pulled out the gun and two additional magazines. He stuck the gun in the holster under his arm and the spare mags in his pocket. He climbed the wall and dropped inside.

At first he thought maybe he'd been mistaken. The small room was empty. But then he noticed the door of an old cabinet in the corner hanging open. He pulled it out of the way and looked inside.

Well, look at this.

At the bottom was a hole that led into the sealed-off section of the house.

———————

BOTH HECTOR AND Rodrigo grunted as they tried to pull open one side of the container's roof doors.

"Wait, wait," Hector said, releasing his grip.

"We almost had it," Rodrigo told him.

Hector frowned. They had *not* almost had it. In fact, while Rodrigo had been right, and there was a spot that was loose, it wasn't loose enough.

"If we can't get it to open enough to peek through, then it's not going to work."

"Uncle Hector, just one more time. I'm sure we can—"

"No. I don't want to damage it. There's no proof that any law has been broken. Except for us being here."

"You've got to think there's something strange about this," Rodrigo said.

"Of course I do. I wouldn't be here if I didn't, but I think maybe I should call this in and get some help." He pointed at his nephew and down at his niece. "You two should go home."

"Home?" Patricia protested. "I'm the one who found it. I should be here when you open it!"

"I understand that," Hector said. "But if this *is* something bad, I don't want your names on any report. The last thing I want is some drug lord looking for you, understand?"

"I hadn't thought about that," Rodrigo said.

Patricia looked like she wanted to say something, but stayed quiet.

"I'm sorry," Hector said. "But you understand, don't you?"

Patricia, still silent, seemed to have stopped paying attention to him.

"I promise I'll tell you exactly what we find. Okay?"

A male voice from somewhere out of Hector's sight suddenly said, "I'm afraid you're not going to get that opportunity."

IT HADN'T BEEN something she'd heard. What had caught her attention was movement, a subtle shift in the layers of darkness at the far end of the container. At first she thought she was seeing things, but then the outline of a man emerged.

A man holding a gun pointed at her.

"I'm sorry," Uncle Hector said. "But you understand, don't you?"

She tried to open her mouth, to warn her uncle and brother, to scream, but all she could do was stare at the gun.

"I promise I'll tell you exactly what we find. Okay?"

The man with the gun grinned. "I'm afraid you're not going to get that opportunity."

His words broke her spell. "He's got a gun!" Even before she finished yelling, she started running toward the container end closest to her, hoping she could get behind it before the man shot her in the back.

She heard her uncle yell something, but her mind wasn't registering the words. Her focus was only on finding a place to hide.

Something thudded against the ground behind her. She couldn't help but look back.

Uncle Hector had jumped off the container and was standing between her and the man with the gun.

"Put it down!" he ordered.

Patricia reached the end and moved partially behind it. "Uncle Hector, please run."

"I'm a police officer," Hector said, still looking at the man. "You will toss the gun over here, then you will lie on the floor, your hands on your head."

For a second it looked like the other man was surprised by Uncle Hector's words, but then he said, "If anyone's breaking the law here, it's you. You don't own this property. My employers do. You have no right to be here."

"Your employers are the owners? Then what's inside this box?"

"Whatever's in there is not your business."

"If you move the roof away, and open the top, it looks suspiciously like you are going to release something into the air. Some kind of waste product, is that what it is? Something you're trying to hide?"

The man cocked his head. "Is that what you think? How interesting."

If it weren't for her fear of the gun, Patricia would have rushed out, grabbed the back of her uncle's shirt, and pulled him to safety. "Please, Uncle Hector. Please come."

A noise behind her startled her. It was her brother peeking at her from around the other corner. He motioned for her to come to him. She shook her head, and motioned with her eyes toward the other side where their uncle was.

"He wants us to go," he whispered, "while the other guy can't see us. He's trying to keep him busy."

Leave Uncle Hector behind? They couldn't do that.

"Who knows you're here?" the man with the gun asked.

"My colleagues," Uncle Hector said. "They're already on the way."

"Really? That's not what it sounded like to me. I got the distinct impression from what you told the other two that you hadn't called anyone yet."

"I called them on the way here. Told them where I was going. They should be here soon."

Patricia could hear the lie in her uncle's voice, and was sure the other man did, too.

"Tell your friends to come out. They're not going to get away."

Uncle Hector said nothing.

"Did you hear me?" the man said, raising his voice. "You're not going to get out. I've blocked the entrance through the cabinet. And I guarantee you that the bullets in my gun travel faster than any of you can run."

"Come on," Rodrigo said. "We have to go *now*."

"What about Uncle Hector?"

Rodrigo hesitated a moment, then said, "I have a plan, but you have to get out of here first."

"You heard him. He's blocked the cabinet."

"Then use the rat hole."

The rat hole? She had forgotten all about that. It wasn't really an exit, but it was a way to get out of sight. If she still fit.

Not knowing what else to do, she scrambled past her brother, and out through the collapsed wall.

"I said, get out here!" the man yelled again, his voice now partly blocked by the container.

"Okay," Rodrigo said. "We're…we're coming."

Patricia whipped back around. *What?* What was he doing? He wasn't really going to step out where the man could see him, was he?

She was about to go back to stop him, when she saw his shadow passing along the top of the container. Somehow he had climbed back up without her hearing him.

Now she understood what he was planning. He was going to get above the man and jump on him. That was actually a great idea. She should have thought of it herself.

Rodrigo noticed her through the opening in the wall, and waved for her to keep moving.

The rat hole. That's where he wanted her to go.

She nodded, and moved into the corridor. As she reached the room where the rat hole was, she heard something in the distance that sounded like a spit or a slap. It happened twice in a row, and after a moment, a third time. But she didn't have time to figure out what it was. She had to keep moving.

When she and Rodrigo were kids, they imagined the room had been used as an office by the factory's owner. It was the only room in the building with an actual fireplace. The rat hole was in the corner of the same wall the stone fireplace was located. It wasn't *really* a rat hole. It was a broken area near the bottom that, if she turned herself just right, she could squeeze through and slip inside the wall. She contorted her body into the position she'd used in the past, and hoped she was still skinny enough to fit.

She was. Just barely.

She shimmied to her left, toward the fireplace. There was a wide spot there, an open space behind the stones of the façade and mantel. As soon as she reached it, she crouched down and began to pray.

———

PEREZ EYED THE man who said he was a cop. *Were* there others coming? He doubted it, but he needed to know for sure, and the only way to do that was to force the man to tell the truth.

Perez heard a low creak come from the IDM container, but pretended he hadn't noticed. To try and surprise him from above was an obvious ploy. Inside he was smiling. Assistance, however unwitting, with his information problem was about to drop into his lap.

"Perhaps we should both walk away," the maybe-cop said.

"Perhaps we should," Perez agreed. "What do we call this? A misunderstanding?"

"I'd be willing to do that."

Perez smiled. "I bet you would."

In the silence that followed, Perez focused on the container. First there was a hint of a scrape, then a breath.

"So," the man asked. "Do we have a deal?"

No further sounds now, but Perez could sense the person looking at him. Though he couldn't know for sure, it was safer to assume it was the young man and not the girl.

"I think I've reconsidered," Perez replied.

The other man was doing everything he could not to look at the container. "A mistake is all this is. Walking away is not a bad thing."

Any second now. Any—

As soon as he sensed the man above him start to jump, Perez moved toward the IDM. The jumper—he was right, it was the man—arced over him, missing him by half a foot at most. He tried to grab Perez as he went by, but his outward trajectory was having none of it. When his feet hit the ground, he turned to take on Perez, but instead got a face full of pistol grip. Down he went, nose bloody, eyes rolling back.

"No!" the older man yelled, taking a step forward.

Before he could take another, Perez aimed his gun at the guy on the floor, really more of a teenager than an adult. The older man halted, getting the message.

"Now, who knows you're here?"

The guy stared at him for a moment, clearly running through options in his mind, but Perez knew he'd eventually realize he had only one.

"No one," the man said. "I haven't called anyone yet."

"So no colleagues on the way?"

Looking defeated, the man shook his head.

"What about family?"

"No. I've been at work all day. Haven't talked to anyone. Please, just let them go. They're just kids."

Perez remained silent, considering what the man had told him. After several seconds, he decided the guy was telling the truth.

"What I don't think you understand," he said, "is that the greater evil would be to let them go. What I can give them now, give *you* now, will save you a lot of pain later."

"What are you talking about? Please, harming us isn't necessary."

"Fine. If that's what you want. I *will* let them go."

Perez was waiting for it, that look of relief he knew would pass through the man's face. As soon as it did, Perez pulled his trigger twice, each bullet piercing the man's forehead. The guy dropped to the ground, dead before gravity even took hold.

In Perez's mind, what he'd done was humane. The man died thinking his two friends would be allowed to live. It was a small gesture, but a thoughtful one as far as Perez was concerned.

He turned his pistol to the kid on the floor, and put a single shot between his eyes.

With a sigh, he checked the older man for ID, wanting to know if he'd been lying about being a cop. Sadly, no. He'd told the truth. That meant it was all the more important to locate any car the man might have arrived in and have it moved.

That was second priority at the moment, though. The girl was number one.

Perez headed around the container and out of the room. Unfortunately, despite the condition of the building, the floor did not readily show prints. He glanced back at the room where the hole in the cabinet came out. Contrary to what he'd said, he hadn't blocked it.

Had she checked? Or was she somewhere else in the building?

His bet was that she was somewhere in the building, so he began a room-by-room search. What he found was…nothing.

For the first time, he felt angry. If she got away, she would surely bring others back. And if that happened, the IDM would be discovered, which might snowball to others being found, too.

How long before she might return? Minutes? Hours? A day?

No, not a day. At best, hours, but even that might be unrealistic.

There were contingency plans for situations such as this. The payload of this particular IDM would have to be destroyed immediately. Each of the devices was equipped with one of two different types of self-destruct mechanisms. This particular mechanism would superheat the interior to the point where the metal of the box itself would melt, and there would be nothing left for anyone to know what was inside. Perez preferred the boxes that simply exploded, but this would do.

He returned to the box, used the master combination to open one of the side doors, then engaged the self-destruct. To give himself enough time to get away, he set it on a ten-minute delay. If the girl and whoever she brought arrived before then, too bad. They'd be consumed by the blaze. If not, then there'd be nothing left to prove her story. Even the bodies of the two men would be gone.

Ten minutes. That would be more than enough.

PATRICIA HEARD THE board in the floor creak in the room just on the other side of the wall. She stopped breathing, afraid that even a slight sound might be enough to give her position away. If it had been Rodrigo, he would have called out her name, but whoever it was hadn't said a word.

Another creak, this one closer to the wall.

He's going to see the rat hole. He's going to see the rat hole and know I went through it.

She could hear him approach the hole. In her mind's eye, she saw him kneeling down, examining the opening, sticking his head in just enough so that he could look down the inside of the wall to her hiding spot behind the fireplace. She was so sure that was exactly what was going to happen, she at first refused to believe her ears when the sound of the floorboards grew fainter and fainter.

Not only did he *not* look through the hole, he wasn't even in the room anymore. The breath she'd been holding rushed out of her lungs.

He didn't know she was there. He didn't know. Her elation lasted mere seconds, though. *What about Rodrigo and Uncle Hector? If the man's walking around, had they gotten away? Or...*

She didn't want to think about it. She *couldn't* think about it. If she did, she'd start screaming and the man would know where she was.

She forced herself to calm down. She had to assume it was up to her to get away and find help. But how? She couldn't just crawl back through the rat hole and leave the way she'd entered the building. He'd said the opening through the cabinet was blocked off, so it would take time for her to clear it. He'd see her for sure. And if he had hurt either of the other two, they might need immediate help, so waiting until the man left wasn't an option. She couldn't hear him anymore, so it would be very unlikely she'd know when he was gone. In fact, she thought it was a very good possibility that he wouldn't leave at all but silently wait her out instead.

Patricia wasn't about to give up, though. Her brother and uncle were relying on her.

She looked around her cramped space, wishing there was some other way she could get—

Is that the sky?

Above her a slit of light glowed through an open seam in the ceiling. Could she get there? Was there a way to get through the old part of the roof if she did?

Once more she scanned her surroundings, but with different focus this time. The walls were out of the question. If she tried to climb them, there was no way she'd be able to do so without making a lot of noise. Plus, there was the very real possibility they might collapse under her weight.

There was another option—the chimney she'd been leaning against. It ran all the way up to the ceiling. In fact, the crack she'd seen might very well be where the roof met it. She twisted around and gave the stacked stones a closer inspection.

It wouldn't be easy, but if she was careful, she thought she could do it. Not could, she corrected herself. She *had* to do it. She *would* do it.

Examining each stone before she grabbed it, she began to climb. A little over halfway up, without thinking, she put a hand on the wall to steady herself. The wood groaned from the pressure, and she immediately froze in place. For half a minute, she did nothing but listen for the man, sure he would check the noise, but as far as she could tell, he hadn't returned. Maybe he just thought it was the normal settling sound of the structure. Or maybe he was gone.

She continued upward, moving past the height of the ceilings in the rooms, and into what had probably been the attic. Exposed beams, no floor, and not enough room for her to stand up if there had been. About twenty feet to her left, she could see where the attic had been sealed off, and beyond would be the recently installed removable roof.

The original roof was about four feet above her head. She could almost reach it with the tips of her fingers. She looked for a new spot on the chimney where she could grab and pull herself the rest of the way up, but there were no good options. She would have to use the beams, which meant noise.

She looked up again. The roof was definitely weak. She felt confident she could tear through it pretty quickly, but fast enough to make an opening, climb through it, then get off the roof and run for safety before the man came outside and found her?

Did she have any other choice than to try?

No. She didn't.

Once she started moving, she'd have to keep going, every second critical, so she needed to plan it all out. She checked the roof, looking for the best spot to break through. She settled on an area a few feet beyond the chimney, where it sagged as if the addition of a single leaf on top would cause it to completely collapse. Hopefully, it would take little effort to finish the job herself.

She took a deep breath, and another, imagining what she needed to do. She placed her hands on the beams to either side, slowly transferring her weight, and was pleased that they made little sound.

"Up. Through the roof. Down to the edge. And run," she whispered to herself as if giving an order.

Then, just as she was about to move, she heard a *whoosh*.

Out of reflex, she looked toward the part of the house the noise had come from, the part where the container was.

What is that?

Rather than fading away, the sound continued. Whatever it was, it was scaring the hell out of her.

Go! Go! A voice in her head screamed.

Not her voice. Rodrigo's or maybe Uncle Hector's. Maybe both.

She pulled herself up onto the beams, no longer concerned about the noise she might make. She needed to get out of there. That's all she knew. She needed to get out of there *now*.

She forced her fingers into one of the cracks near the bottom of the sag in the roof, and pulled with all her strength. The ceiling groaned and cracked and protested for as long as it could, then broke free.

While Patricia had tried to position herself as best as possible, part of the roof glanced off her arm. She fell backward toward the hole she'd had just climbed up through. The only thing that kept her from falling all the way to the ground was the beam she caught with her arm.

As she pulled herself back up, she could feel heat coming from somewhere in the house.

Fire!

With renewed horror, she scrambled to the break in the roof and climbed outside. She couldn't see the fire, but she could smell it now. There was an unfamiliar tang to it that was repulsive. She gagged and nearly threw up as she slid down the slope of the roof to the eaves. The second she got there, she took a quick look at the ground and jumped.

Safely away from the house now, she glanced back. Smoke had begun to billow out of cracks in the building, but that was nothing compared to the heat. It almost felt like she was walking on the sun.

Run, the voice ordered. *Run. Run!*
Patricia ran.

18

RICHARD HEATH HEARD shoes echoing off the concrete floor, heading in his direction. As much as he wished it was another member of the depot's security team, he knew it wasn't. No, it was one of them. Because, unless he was completely mistaken, he was the last one of NB328's detail left alive.

What he couldn't understand was how the attackers had snuck into the facility without sounding any alarms. It shouldn't have been possible, and yet it had happened.

Initially, he and his colleagues had thought it was simply some kind of raid to steal whatever could be grabbed. That was the type of incursion the security team had prepared for and been told by those above them in the Project to expect, but it quickly became clear that this wasn't a group of local thugs just looking for something they could sell. The people who snuck in were professionals who worked silently, and they had eliminated most of the security detail with single shots from sound-suppressed weapons.

Heath had no idea why he was still alive.

Luck? Not hardly.

If he'd been lucky, he'd already be dead. One against God-knew-how-many? He didn't have a chance. He checked his gun. Only five shots left. The way he figured it, that meant four for them, and the last for himself.

Dammit! Who the hell were these people?

The steps were much closer now. Surprisingly, he realized it was only a single pair. Did they not know he was here? Or did they think he was already dead? Whatever the case, the person walking in his direction didn't seem to be concerned that he might put a bullet through their head.

He leaned against the crate closest to the end of the aisle, and wrapped both his hands around the butt of his gun. *A little closer*, he thought as he listened. *Just a little closer, and at least I can take out one of you.*

The warehouse was as big as an American football field, and, full or not, the sounds inside were deceiving. Though the steps were still headed in his direction, he couldn't be sure if they were thirty feet away or seventy. He should be able to hit the target at both distances, but he wanted to ensure that he didn't miss, so the closer the other person was, the better.

With a suddenness that surprised him, the steps ceased.

Fifty feet for sure, maybe closer. He breathed deeply, trying to psych himself up. *Just do it. Just roll out and take the—*

"Hello. You hiding back there. I know you can hear me." The voice was female, coming from where the steps had stopped. "I'm sure you realize there's no way you're getting out of here, so I'm guessing you're probably trying to figure out how you can do the most damage while you have an opportunity. It's the way I'd be thinking, anyway. I should tell you, though, no matter what you try, you won't succeed."

The hell I won't!

Knowing it was now or never, the guard twisted out from the cover of the crate, and brought the barrel of his gun around to point at the spot where he knew the woman would be. His first shot left the chamber before he registered what he was seeing.

Rather, what he was *not* seeing. Where the woman should have been standing was…nothing.

He swung the gun left and right, looking for her, ready to pull the trigger at the slightest movement.

"Sorry to disappoint," she said, far closer than he expected.

Even before he could respond to her voice, something hit him in the chest, and his whole body seized in uncontrollable spasms. His gun flew from his hand as he fell writhing to the floor.

Finally, the source of the pain stopped.

A Taser, he realized, his mind able to focus again.

He lay panting on the floor, every muscle weak and tingling from the massive jolt of electricity. Though his mind was screaming at him to get up, he knew that was impossible.

He heard movement, then footsteps walking right up to him. *Clack, clack, clack.*

It was over. His end was coming. He trembled as the woman stopped beside him. She had short blonde hair, and what he would have called an Eastern European face—high cheekbones, slightly Asiatic eyes, and full lips. He had never seen her before.

"Go ahead. Do it," he said, his eyes glancing quickly at the gun in her hand.

She leaned down and touched something near his waist. When she stood again, she was holding his security badge.

"Good. You have full access." She smiled at him. "Relax. It's not time for you to die yet."

"SIR, WE'VE RECEIVED a message I wanted to make you aware of."

The DOP looked up from this computer. Major Ross had entered the conference room at the back of the Cradle, and was standing just inside the door. "What is it?"

"An emergency signal from NB328."

"What kind of emergency?"

"A break-in, sir."

The DOP frowned. "Verified?"

"No, sir. It was the automated signal. We haven't been able to reach the security team there yet."

"Where is NB328?" While the DOP was familiar with their storage depot locations, he didn't even try to remember what each had been designated.

"Costa Rica. Outside Carrizal."

Carrizal. A basic storage depot if he wasn't mistaken: food, clothing, fuel, some vehicles, and the standard weapons cache. Nothing particularly special about it.

"How long have they been out of contact?"

"We just received the message. I came straight here."

The DOP considered their options. If they weren't so close to

Implementation Day, he would have automatically said they should just wait for someone at NB328 to check in, but time was one thing they no longer had. "How quickly can you get someone down there to check?"

"There's a team in Monterrey, Mexico, but they'd have to fly commercial, so it would be at least four or five hours. There is another option."

"Yes?"

"Perez, in South America. He finished up with the job in Argentina last night, and is flying to Colombia as we speak. He should be landing in thirty minutes. He could refuel and be in Costa Rica in under two hours. The drawback, of course, is that he's alone."

"Send him, and get the Monterrey team moving, too. Perez can scope out the situation, and if it's more than he can handle on his own, the team will be there soon enough."

"Very good, sir." Ross turned to leave.

"Major?"

"Yes?"

"Keep me in the loop. I want to know everything that's going on."

"Yes, sir." Ross left.

The DOP returned his attention to his computer terminal, but instead of continuing what he was doing before, he brought up the specs on NB328. It was just as he recalled—a basic depot.

Potential raids on the warehouses had always been a possibility. The world was a violent place, and stores of goods were vulnerable. Because of this, the security had been beefed up at all the depots in anticipation of Implementation Day, so he was confident the team at NB328 could deal with whatever the problem was. If they ran into problems and losses were incurred, it would be unfortunate, but negligible when it came to its effect on the Project as a whole.

He switched back to his previous screen, certain that the matter would be satisfactorily resolved.

———————

AS WITH ALL the Project's warehouses, there was a vault on

the lowest level, protected not only by the secured entrance to the underground floors, but also by an impenetrable composite door on the vault itself. Impenetrable by force, at least, not if you had the key.

Karie and Gleason accompanied Olivia and the prisoner in the elevator to NB328's lowest level. When the door opened, Gleason pushed the man out, and Karie and Olivia followed.

There was no need for directions. While each of the facilities might vary in size, all were laid out basically the same. This way, if personnel had to be moved between locations, they could jump in immediately without the need of an orientation period.

Olivia led the way, passing contingency dormitories and the medical wing before turning down the short hallway to the vault. The first door they came to was similar to the others on this level, the only difference being that it needed to be opened via a security code.

"Enter the code," Olivia told the guard.

"No way."

She'd expected that response. She looked at Karie and held out her hand. "Radio."

The woman handed it to her.

Raising it to her lips, Olivia said, "We're outside the vault room entrance. Looks like we're going to need that information."

"Got it right here," a voice came back, crisp and clean. "You were correct, ma'am. Mr. Heath does have family on the survival roster."

The guard tensed.

"A sister and a teenage niece. They live in Arlington Heights, outside of Chicago. Both have already been administered the vaccine. You want their address?"

Olivia looked at the guard, an eyebrow raised in question. "Do I need it?"

"No," he said, then punched the code into the keypad.

The room inside was about the size of a small studio apartment. Along the opposite wall was the actual door to the vault. It had a blue-gray sheen and fit flush with the wall. There was a control panel mounted to the left.

"You know what I want," Olivia said to the guard. "And you

know what we'll do to your family if you don't cooperate."

"And if I do?" he asked. "You'll leave them alone?"

"As long as you do as I ask, yes."

He studied her face as if trying to determine if she was telling the truth. She was, but only because it would be a waste of time to bother with his family.

"Okay," he said. "I…I'll do it."

He started toward the control panel.

"Mr. Heath," Olivia said.

He looked back.

"I know there are two different codes you can use to get the door open. If you use the one that will activate the vault self-destruct, your family will die."

He shook his head. "I won't."

The control software was set up so that it needed not only the code, but also scans of the authorized person's eye and left hand. It could detect blood flow in the eye's capillaries, and the body heat in the hand.

Olivia watched him as he punched in the code, then scanned his eye and his hand. Once that was done, the code had to be input once more.

When he finished, there was a second of silence. Then she heard the locks pulling open.

As the door swung out, Olivia looked at the guard. "Thank you."

She nodded at Gleason, who raised his gun and shot the guard in the head.

———

THE PRIVATE JET carrying Perez from South America touched down in San Jose, Costa Rica, at 10:04 a.m. Thirty-seven minutes later, he pulled his car off the road, about half a mile from NB328, and covered the remaining distance on foot.

Judging by the exterior of the building, nothing looked amiss. That, of course, meant nothing. When he'd checked in with Bluebird upon arrival, they told him they still hadn't been able to reach anyone inside the facility.

Staying at least a hundred yards away, he made two complete

circuits of the building, but saw nothing unusual. Even the three satellite dishes on the roof that kept NB328 in contact with Bluebird looked untouched.

About the only thing he could say was that the place seemed to be too quiet. He knew that was his own bias, though, having spent much of the last several weeks in crowded, South American cities. Unless a depot was receiving a shipment, there was no reason for anyone to be outside.

The main door was in the middle of what was considered the front of the building. Perez watched it for several minutes, but decided not to approach it. If there were hostiles still around, they'd no doubt have someone posted just inside. The better bet was to use the emergency entrance. After all, it had been built for circumstances such as these.

He headed northeast to a point five hundred feet away from the building. The emergency entrances were all the same, designed to look like an abandoned concrete slab. He found it easily, but someone had released the locks that held it in place, and had slid it to the side, exposing the entrance to the tunnel.

He slipped his gun out from the holster, and pointed it at the opening. He couldn't see far. At this angle, the sunlight went down only ten feet. Beyond that was darkness.

He circled around the hole, checking the ground for footprints. He needed to determine if it had been opened from the inside by people trying to leave, or from the outside by someone trying to get in. If it had been the latter, that would definitely be troubling, because that meant the attackers knew ahead of time about the emergency entrance, and how to open it, which meant they knew about the Project, too.

Footprints. Leading *to* the slab.

So these weren't just some random thieves.

Perez looked at his watch. The team flying in from Mexico was not due to arrive for another hour and a half. Under normal circumstances, he would have waited, but nothing was normal anymore. He pulled out the small flashlight he carried in his pocket, and descended the steps.

"IT'S PEREZ, SIR," Ross said over the speakerphone.

The DOP snapped up the receiver. "Transfer him to me."

There was a click.

"Perez?"

"Yes, sir."

"Where are you?"

"I'm inside NB328."

"And?"

There was a pause. "Everyone's dead, sir."

The DOP didn't move for a full second. "Everyone?"

"Yes, sir. The entire security team."

"And the people who did this?"

"Gone, sir."

"What about bodies? Surely a couple of them must have been hit."

"If they were, they're not here now."

The DOP was stunned. A whole security team wiped out by a local gang? How in the hell did that happen?

"Figure out what they took," he said. "If any of it shows up somewhere, we can trace it back and deal with them."

Perez took a moment before he replied. "This wasn't a random robbery, sir."

"What do you mean?"

"None of the supplies are missing."

"That can't be right."

"I could be mistaken. I only did a quick look-through, but...well, sir, whoever it was entered through the emergency entrance using the code."

"The *what?*"

"It was open when I got here, so I checked the surveillance footage and the sensor logs, knowing there should be a record of the break-in. Whoever they were, apparently they were able to hack into the system before they came in, and turned off all the surveillance."

If the DOP wasn't stunned before, he was now. The emergency entrance? Knowing the code *and* hacking into the security system? What the hell was going on?

"And something *was* taken."

"What?"

"The vault was open. Two of the numbered boxes are missing."

The boxes were similar to deposit boxes in a bank. Each contained printed-out, detailed instructions to be used in specific situations. They were the hardcopy backups in case something happened to the computer system after Implementation Day. Another redundancy in the Project's desire to make sure nothing went off track when they set about rebuilding the world in the way they knew it should be. Every depot had a set of the boxes in its vault.

That someone had purposely broken into NB328 to get to them was unbelievable. The only people who *knew* about the boxes or the vaults were members of the Project, or at least that's what he had thought.

This was a serious breach. They had to find out who had done this and why.

"Which boxes were taken?" the DOP asked.

"J923 and T121."

The DOP brought up the vault database and typed both numbers in. J923 contained the list of all the other depots, and T121 a list of all the primary members of the Project. Both were disturbing, the second considerably more than the first.

"Go over every square inch of that facility," he ordered. "There has got to be some clue as to who these people are."

"Yes, sir."

"And make it quick. I don't want this becoming a problem."

For several seconds, the DOP stared out the windowed wall into the Cradle.

It's them, he thought. The ones who had been an annoyance to the Project for years.

Somehow they had found out about the vaults and the information they contained. He knew they'd been in one of the facilities before—NB7 in eastern Oregon. But every piece of security footage from that night had been reviewed, and neither Captain Ash nor the woman who'd been with him when he rescued his kids had gone anywhere near NB7's vault.

He picked up the phone again and called Ross. His first instructions were to assign extra protection to people on the list from box T121, and to put the depot security teams on high alert. Then he said, "Operation Pest Control is a go."

There was a pause, then, "Yes, sir. But…"

"But what, Major?"

"These added measures are going to stretch us pretty thin. If you want Operation Pest Control to happen right away also, we'll need to sacrifice in other areas."

The DOP closed his eyes and stifled a groan of frustration. "As soon as feasible, then," he ordered, and slammed the phone down.

———————

PEREZ HAD BEEN in error. Boxes J923 and T121 were not the only two that had been removed. In fact, the two boxes were of no importance at all to Olivia.

"These are the two we want to break into," Olivia had instructed, indicating boxes J923 and T121. They would be the smokescreen, specifically chosen to throw her former employers off and force them to allot manpower away from what she was focused on. She then pointed at a box near the bottom: G306. "This one we use the master key on."

Once they had the door to G306 open, Olivia removed the single sheet of paper from inside, slid the box back in place, and shut the door. She carefully folded the paper and put it in her pocket. No one would ever suspect the box had even been opened.

This was the only reason they had come to NB328.

19

"THERE'S NOTHING HERE," Blanton said.

Corey looked at his friend. "What do you mean, nothing?"

They were sitting in a booth at Old Tom's Pub just off campus, Blanton's laptop on the table. On the screen was the home page for Hidde-Kel Holdings.

"It's just a bunch of corporate BS that doesn't lead anywhere. It's not tied to their company computer system at all. It's just sitting on its own server all by itself."

"All by itself?"

Blanton nodded. "Nothing else on that server at all. I've triple-checked."

Corey wasn't the computer expert that Blanton was, but like most kids his age, he had a basic understanding of how it all worked. "You can't get into their internal systems from there?"

Blanton looked around. "Hey, hold it down. I'd rather not have a lot of people know about this, okay?"

"Sorry." It was early evening, and the place was starting to fill up. "So you can't get through?"

"Uh-uh. As far as I can tell, there's no tie between them."

"Dammit. I was really hoping you could get in that way."

"Well, I can't." Blanton paused. "Not *this* way."

Corey cocked his head. "There's another?"

A smirk grew on his friend's face. "This is like a challenge, you know?"

"Blanton, just tell me. Is there another way you can get me

more information about them?"

"Of course there is." Blanton began typing. "I was able to locate some of their business filings that had addresses on their main facilities. I should say, *facility*. Seems they only have one address."

"You mean the one in Portland? That's just a mail drop."

"I *don't* mean the one in Portland. I mean the one in Chicago."

"Chicago? What address in Chicago? I didn't find anything."

"That's because you're not me." Blanton hit one more key. A map of Chicago appeared on the screen with a red dot glowing northwest of downtown, right next to O'Hare Airport.

"That's it?"

Instead of answering, Blanton zoomed in. The dot turned out to be in an industrial area tucked in the southeast corner between I-90 and I-294. The building itself was probably about ten thousand square feet, and, at least when the satellite photo was taken, had a nearly empty parking lot.

"The whole building is theirs?"

"Yep."

"And you were able to get into their computer system?"

"Well, see, that's the challenge. I know they have something inside. I could figure out that much. Couldn't hack in, though. The only way to do that is if I got in close and tapped into their local signal."

"You mean actually go up there."

"Well, yeah."

Blanton sounded like it had been more of an intellectual exercise than anything else, but the idea appealed to Corey. Chicago was only about five hours away by car. They could be there around midnight.

"We'll take my car."

Blanton had raised his glass of beer to his mouth. "Uh, excuse me?"

"Better if I drive. I've only had a sip. That's your second."

"Drive where?"

"Chicago."

"I'm not going to Chicago."

"Come on, Blanton. Didn't you say this was a challenge? Don't you want to follow that through?"

"Dude, I have class tomorrow."

"Uh, no, you don't. Tomorrow's Sunday."

"Okay, not really a class, but a study group."

"Since when do you join study groups?"

"What?" Blanton said. "I can join a study group if I want."

Corey suddenly realized the truth. "What's her name?"

"Whose name?"

"The girl in your study group."

Blanton blushed but shook his head. "I don't know what you're talking about."

"Never mind. What time does it start?"

"Three."

"In the afternoon?"

"Well, yeah. It's not in the morning."

"We'll be back in plenty of time."

"I'm *not* going to Chicago."

"Who's going to Chicago?" Jeannie asked as she walked up.

Corey scooted over so she could join them. "Blanton and I."

"Oh, no. I'm not going."

Jeannie looked at her boyfriend. "When?"

"As soon as I can get no-boy here out the door."

"You're going to Chicago tonight? Why do you want to do that?"

Corey explained about the building Blanton had found.

"Maybe you should pick another company to do the paper on," Blanton suggested.

That was the simple solution, but Corey was way too curious about Hidde-Kel now to give up that easily. "Fine. I'll go by myself. You don't need to come."

"I'll go with you," Jeannie offered.

Corey smiled and squeezed her hand. He then looked at Blanton. "Not up for the challenge, huh?"

His friend groaned. "I don't want to miss my group tomorrow."

"I already said we'd be back in time."

"All right, all right. I'll go. But we're stopping at White Castle and you're buying."

WITH THE STOP for food and another two for bathroom breaks, they didn't reach Chicago until closer to one a.m. It took them another twenty minutes to get out to O'Hare Airport.

From there it was still a little tricky getting over to the area where the building was, but after a couple of wrong turns, Corey finally pulled his old Civic onto the right road. Driving slowly, both he and Jeannie read off building addresses.

"That's got to be it over there," she said, pointing ahead and to the left at a long, two-story brick structure.

The only sign on the building was an address number, the same that belonged to Hidde-Kel, according to what Blanton had found out. The parking lot beside it was sealed off by an eight-foot-high, chain-link fence with barbed wire strung across the top.

"Kind of fortress-like, don't you think?" she said.

Corey drove about half a block past, then pulled to the side of the road and looked back. There *was* something unusual about the place, but it hadn't been the barbed wire. He turned off the engine.

"You coming?" he asked as he opened his door.

"Hell, yeah," she said. "What about Blanton?"

He nodded in the back at his unmoving friend. "We'll let him sleep for now."

As they walked down the street, it felt like there wasn't anyone else around for miles. As they neared the building, they jogged across the street. Corey led Jeannie across a short expanse of brown grass to a row of leafless hedges in front of the windows.

There was no light on inside, which was odd, because in Corey's albeit-limited experience, most businesses left some kind of light on inside. Not Hidde-Kel, apparently.

He looked around and found a wide spot between two of the bushes. He thought if he was careful, he could squeeze between them. He gave it a try and made it cleanly. Jeannie wasn't quite as lucky.

"Ow!"

"You all right?" he asked.

She was clutching her neck just below her ear.

"Let me see."

She moved her hand. There was a one-inch scratch where a branch had whipped up and caught her.

He moved around and kissed her on the lips. "That'll make it feel better."

"You think so?" she asked, one eyebrow raised.

He kissed her again, longer this time. "Better?"

"Yeah. I'll live."

With a playful grin, he turned and leaned against the window, cupping his hands around his eyes. What he was looking at was obviously intended to be a lobby. But Hidde-Kel's lobby was devoid of any sign of use. There were no chairs, no magazines, no plants, no company name on the wall. Nothing. It almost looked as if the room had never been used.

Hearing footsteps on the street, Corey looked over. Blanton. He was walking down the road, munching on one of the White Castle burgers he hadn't finished earlier.

"Over here," Corey called out.

Blanton jerked to a stop, then headed over once he realized who it was. "Why the hell did you leave me there like that?"

"You were asleep."

"You could have woken me up. I was starting to think maybe this whole trip was some kind of practical joke."

"It just might be," Corey said. "This is Hidde-Kel. But it looks empty."

"Empty?"

Blanton pushed his way through the bushes, his backpack getting caught for a second before he finally reached them. He peeked through the window.

"That's weird."

"How old was the information you found?" Corey asked.

"Six months or so."

"They could have moved out," Jeannie said.

"I guess so, but what I found made it seem like they were going to be around for a while."

Corey frowned. "Did any of the info mention what the building was supposed to be for?"

"Corporate offices."

Jeannie glanced up and down the street. "Doesn't quite seem

like the setting for a corporate office, does it?"

Blanton pulled his backpack off his shoulders. "Maybe they just don't use the front." From inside the bag, he pulled out his laptop and flipped it open. Crouching down, he set it on his knees and began typing. After a few seconds, he looked back up. "The only Wi-Fi signals I'm getting are too weak to be coming from here."

This was totally not what Corey had expected. He'd set out to write a paper on a growing agriculture-related firm, and now he had what amounted to a mystery on his hands. There had to be some simple explanation, something that would probably make him feel like an idiot when he found out.

"I wonder if it's possible to get inside," he said.

Jeannie shrugged. "One way to find out."

She moved past the windows to the concrete pathway and up to the steel front door. She gave it a yank.

"It's locked."

Corey headed past her to the side of the building where he'd seen a gate, but it was secured by a thick chain and padlock. The property next door also had a chain-link fence around its lot, but it was shorter, with no barbed wire on top. Even better, the gate meant to close it off was open.

With the other two trailing behind him, Corey walked into the lot and moved along the fence that separated the two properties. About three-quarters of the way back, he stopped, figuring they were far enough away from the street not to draw any attention if someone just happened to be driving by.

He waited for his two friends to catch up, then said, "You guys stay here. I'm hopping over."

"You're going alone?" Jeannie asked.

"Better if only one of us gets caught trespassing than all three."

She stared at him. "Uh, excuse me. We're all trespassing right now."

He should have known better than to even suggest the solo trip. In the end, it was decided they'd all go.

One by one, they climbed over the fence and ran over to the Hidde-Kel building. There were no windows along the side, and only four doors. They tried each, and weren't surprised to find they were all locked.

Along the back of the building was a large loading dock. Here there was a single, very wide opening at least a story and a half high that was currently closed off by a rolling metal door. Beside it was another normal-sized door. As with the others, both were locked.

The far side of the building was identical to the first they'd checked—four doors, none open. Corey hadn't expected this to be easy, but he had been hoping.

"I guess that's that," Blanton said.

Corey ignored him and headed once more for the back of the building. He had seen one possibility. It was a bit more involved than what he would have liked, but he really wanted to see inside to make sure Hidde-Kel *was* gone.

The outer part of the loading dock had a six-foot wall on either side, but no roof. As the walls neared the actual building, they stairstepped upward in two-foot increments until they reached the roof.

"Give me a boost," he said to Blanton.

Both Blanton and Jeannie looked at him.

Jeannie was the first to realize what he meant to do. "I'm not sure that's a good idea."

"I just want to see if there's any way to look in."

She grimaced, but said nothing else.

Blanton created a cradle with his hands, and gave Corey the boost. Once on top, Corey stayed in a crouch to maintain his balance as he worked his way along the brick, then up and up and up until he reached the roof.

"What do you see?" Jeannie called out.

Corey scanned the roof. "Several air ducts, some machinery...maybe air conditioners or heaters?" He continued to look, then smiled. "Hey, I think there's an access door up here."

"Corey, be careful!"

"Don't worry."

It wasn't really an access door as much as it was an access hatch. When he pulled up on it, it moved a few inches, but then stopped. It felt more rusty than latched from the inside, so he tried again. It groaned as it opened an additional half-inch. His third try opened more, then on the fourth, there was a *pop*. The hatch flew open, and Corey rolled back onto his ass.

"Everything all right?" Jeannie called out, her voice distant.

"Fine!" he yelled back.

He knelt beside the opening. There was a ladder that went down four feet to a metal catwalk, but beyond that, all was dark.

He sat back. Up to this point, he'd technically been involved in only a little exterior trespassing. Okay, and some breaking in. What he hadn't done was actually enter anything. The moment he put any part of his body through that hole, that would all change.

While his head was saying, "Get the hell out of here," his gut was telling him, "Just check it out."

He decided to listen to his gut.

He lowered himself through the hole and climbed down the ladder. Testing the catwalk first, he moved onto it. Now that he was inside, he could see all the way to the nearest wall. There appeared to be another ladder there going down to ground level so that's where he headed. Less than a minute later, he was standing on the floor.

There was an eerie silence to the place, a sense of desertion reinforced by the stale air. If Corey had to guess, he'd have said no one had been there for at least several days. Devoid of people, yes, but not empty. Even with limited visibility, he could make out several large objects looming in the darkness.

Staying near the wall, he made his way toward the back. When he was about fifty feet from the end of the building, there were no more objects filling the space and the area beside him appeared to be empty. He reached the back wall, then felt his way along the inside of the metal roll door, to the small man-sized entrance at the other end. By touch, he unbolted two deadbolts, and pulled the door open.

Jeannie and Blanton turned in surprise from the other end of the dock near the wall he'd gone up.

"You made it," Jeannie said, relieved.

Corey gave her a smile, and looked at Blanton. "You wouldn't have a flashlight in that bag, would you?"

Blanton shook his head. "No, but my laptop screen works pretty well."

They used the illumination from Blanton's computer to locate several light switches near the door. One by one they began flipping them on, and soon there was enough light for them to see.

The problem was, Corey had no idea what they were looking at.

"What the hell?" Apparently, neither did Blanton.

As Corey had sensed, the area just inside the big metal door was an open space—for the most part, anyway. There were two metal shipping containers stacked on top of each other against one wall. Their doors were open and both were empty. If Corey had come that way, he would have run right into them.

In the rest of the open area, there were marks painted on the ground that roughly corresponded to the size of the containers, applied in a way that four could sit side by side with space in between.

Beyond the open area was where the weird really began.

Corey couldn't even guess what the nearest machine did. It was large and had a curling rail system that looked almost like a roller coaster, leading into the massive machine itself. There were several other machines past this that were unrecognizable. In fact, about the only things that were even halfway familiar were two rows of large, enclosed vats. They almost looked like something he'd seen on a brewery tour in St. Louis, but he was sure these weren't being used for beer.

"Have you noticed?" Blanton asked. "Everything looks so clean. No paper. No personal items. No dusty footprints. Nothing."

"They're gone," Jeannie said.

"Yeah," Corey agreed.

"What was this place?"

"I don't know."

Blanton pulled open a small side hatch on one of the vats and looked in. "Empty." He shut it again. "These Hidde-Kel people are supposed to be in agriculture, right?"

"Associated with agriculture, yeah."

"Maybe they're making some type of fertilizer?"

Jeannie grew instantly wary. "Or pesticide."

Blanton immediately began wiping his hands on his pants. "You don't think so, do you?"

"Relax," Corey said. "As far as I know, they're not into anything like that."

"Then what were they doing here?"

"Let's see if we can figure that out."

They spent twenty more minutes checking the rest of the manufacturing area and going through the rooms near the front. One thing was clear. This had never been a corporate office. There just wasn't enough office space, even for a small operation.

As they came back through, Corey opened one of the vats and looked in for himself.

What was he going to do about his paper now? As curious as he was about Hidde-Kel, writing what little he knew about them would not fulfill his assignment. He would have to do what Blanton had suggested at the pub—find another company to write about.

"I guess we should go home," he said.

Before closing the vat door, his fingers brushed the inside of the container. He was concerned for a second, worried that maybe Jeannie had been right about the pesticides, but there didn't feel like there was anything on the surface.

Unfortunately, there was.

20

THE LINK TO the online video remained active for exactly nine minutes and thirty-seven seconds before it was located and removed. In that time, of the 622 people who clicked on the link, only 51 clicked on it soon enough to watch the video in its entirety. For the others, the video stopped where their download had ceased, and when they tried to reload it, they were presented with a message about technical difficulties.

Of the 51 who did see it, only 24 actually watched the whole thing, and of these, all but three thought it was a viral marketing ploy for a new disaster movie. The three initially took it seriously, and were willing to believe at least part of it might be true. A killer virus, distributed by man. It sure sounded plausible to them. Unfortunately, when they realized the link had disappeared and they couldn't share it with like-minded friends, they began to lose interest.

Within five days, the three potential believers would barely remember the video at all.

"DAMMIT," TAMARA COSTELLO said. "Only nine minutes? They're getting even faster."

Bobby Lion frowned at the computer screen. "It lasted only three on Vimeo."

"Do they have somebody just waiting for us to upload? Is that it?"

"Well, yeah. I mean, it's probably automated to a point. Someone gets alerted when a suspicious video gets uploaded and they take a look, then do whatever they do to pull it down."

They'd tried everything—unassuming titles, benign descriptions and keywords. They even created a new account every time they posted. Without exception, their work got pulled down with no more than a handful of people seeing it. It was beyond frustrating.

Tamara and Bobby's job was simple: create and distribute video reports aimed at exposing Project Eden to the general public. Their talents were particularly suited for this. Both had been in the employ of PCN—Prime Cable News—before being recruited by the Hamiltons to help stop the Project.

Recruited was a relative term. What happened was Tamara and Bobby had run afoul of the Project while they were reporting for PCN from the front lines of the Sage Flu outbreak in April. Some of the Hamiltons' people had helped them escape before they became casualties, too.

They spent several months at the Ranch, learning about Project Eden. Bobby had believed right away, but it had taken Tamara some time to accept the horrifying reality. It was at that point they'd been asked to put their skills to use, and act as the public voice of the resistance.

They'd been set up in San Antonio, Texas, with false identities. Tamara was now Deirdre Murray, and ran a secondhand shop called Deirdre's Treasures. Bobby was Ralph Barber, a freelance handyman who never seemed to be freelancing anywhere. Instead, he and Tamara spent much of their time in the small studio built in the basement of Deirdre's Treasures, where he edited the pieces, and Tamara wrote the scripts and recorded the narrations, albeit with her voice altered to avoid identification.

They had tried to get their early video reports into the hands of the established media, hoping they would be aired on networks everywhere. They had met with zero success. They had tried blogs next, but quickly pulled the plug on that when one of the bloggers who posted their video turned up dead within twenty-four hours. They decided, in consultation with Matt and Rachel, that the only thing they could do was post the videos on public sites and hope for the best. Unfortunately, the best had yet to happen.

"How the hell are we supposed to get around this?" she said. It wasn't the first time she'd asked this. Not by a long shot.

"We have to hope that at some point, they're going to miss one long enough that people will copy it to their computers and repost so it goes viral. If it starts popping up all over the place, they won't be able to pull it all down."

She sighed. "Well, let's re-upload—"

Her cell phone rang. She answered it. "…this one now. And see if it sticks this time." The name on the phone's display read: UNKNOWN.

"Hello?"

"Tamara, it's Matt."

She switched to speakerphone. "Hey, Matt. You calling about the latest video? A whole nine minutes this time."

"Nine and a half," Bobby said.

"Sorry," Matt said. "I didn't know you were putting something up."

Tamara couldn't help but frown. They had sent Matt and Rachel an email like they always did before they posted. Matt had even responded with a simple "Thanks."

Bobby leaned toward the phone. "Fifty-one views before it got pulled down, though I don't know how many were able to watch it all. Did you get a chance to look at the script for the one we'd like to start this afternoon?"

"Whatever you were planning, you need to table it," Matt said.

Tamara and Bobby exchanged a concerned look.

"What's going on?" she asked.

"I need you to finish WC."

For several seconds, neither of them could speak. WC did not stand for water closet. It meant Worst Case, as in the video that would be placed if the worst-case scenario occurred. In other words, the video that would describe to humanity what was happening to them. They had started it months earlier, but had not finished it in hopes it would never be needed.

His voice dry and tentative, Bobby asked, "It's happened?"

"No. But if it does, it will be soon."

"How soon?" Tamara asked.

A pause. "Days. Maybe a week. Not much more than that."

"Are you sure?"

"About as sure as we can be. How soon can you have it ready?"

"We'll get right on it," she said, glancing at Bobby.

"A day or two, no more than that," Bobby added.

"When it's finished, I want you to close everything up and go to your backup safe house," Matt ordered. The safe house was a location not even Matt knew, just Tamara and Bobby. "If it looks like things are going to shit and you can't reach me, upload it. Don't wait for me to give you the go-ahead."

"Do you think…do you think we'll have to upload it?" Tamara said.

The silence stretched out for what seemed like minutes. "Yes."

The line went dead.

Tamara put her hand on Bobby's, wrapping it around the side and squeezing tight. He looked at her, the reality of what appeared to be coming reflected on his face.

Then he nodded. "We'd better get to work."

21

ASH HAD BEEN sure they would have crossed the Arctic Circle and been homing in on Bluebird's location by now, but the imaginary line was still several hundred miles to the north.

Their intent had been to fly from San Diego to Baker Lake in the middle of the Canadian territory of Nunavut, with a quick fueling stop in Winnipeg, just north of the US-Canada border in Manitoba. The weather, though, had a different idea.

Instead of lifting off from Winnipeg within an hour of landing, they ended up staying in the provincial capital for four nights, waiting out first a storm that passed through Manitoba, then one further north, cutting off their ability to get to Baker Lake.

Finally, the weather cleared enough for them to attempt the next leg of the journey. The flight was rough, but they were able to get into Baker Lake with only a few minor bumps and bruises. Waiting at the house that had been arranged for them to stay in were Gagnon and Wright, the two last members of their team.

Ash called everyone together for a meeting in the dining room, where he spread a map of northern Nunavut out on the table.

"The plan is for us to—"

"Excuse me, Captain," Pax said. "I don't mean to interrupt, but before we get started, I've been in contact with the Ranch and have some news I should share."

"Of course. Go ahead."

They all looked expectantly at the oldest member of the team.

"There's no easy way to put this," Pax began, "so I'll just say it straight. There's been a new outbreak."

Voices over voices:

"It's started?"

"Already?"

"Where?"

"When?"

"Should we go back?"

Pax gave everyone a few seconds, then held up a hand, silencing them. "The outbreak's in St. Louis. The good news is, it looks like it's both isolated and contained."

"So no cases anywhere else?" Chloe said.

"Not that anyone knows of. What Matt thinks happened is that there was accidental exposure, and that the so-called Implementation Day hasn't taken place yet."

"So we're still on mission here?" Browne asked.

"As far as I'm concerned." Pax looked at Ash. "Captain?"

"Absolutely. We keep going."

"If the snow ever lets up," someone threw in.

Ash pointed at a spot near the southern edge of the map. "This is where we are right now. Tomorrow, weather permitting, we fly to Grise Fiord." He touched the spot on the map where the small village was. "After that, Mr. Gagnon will fly us out to our first location in a specially modified plane he has there."

"What *is* the first location?" Chloe asked.

Ash looked down at the map. "Technically, we have three choices. Here, here, and here." He pointed first at Ellef Ringnes Island, then Yanok Island, then Amund Ringnes Island.

"That's a lot of ground to cover. We don't have a lot of time. Any way to rule out any of them?"

Ash studied the map for a second. "The wreckage of the boat was found right about here, correct?" He pointed at a spot south of Ellef Ringes, and looked at Gagnon.

The pilot nodded. "Yeah. Close enough."

"All right. If it was a setup and they were just trying to fool you, then I'd be inclined to rule out Ellef Ringnes. They wouldn't set up the crash that close to Bluebird."

"Unless they were trying to outthink us," Pax said.

"I'm not going down that road. Rachel was also sure it wasn't

Ellef Ringnes." Ash moved his finger along the map. "Which would mean it's either Amund Ringnes or Yanok Island. That cuts away a third of where we need to check. Happy to hear anyone else's thoughts."

"Sounds right to me," Pax said.

"Me, too," Chloe added.

The others chimed in their agreement.

"So which one do you want to check first?" Gagnon asked.

Ash frowned. "I don't know. If I guess wrong, we might not have time to adjust."

Pax put a hand on Ash's back. "No matter what we do, it's going to be a coin toss."

Pax was right, but it didn't make Ash's choice any easier.

"It's still a lot of ground to cover," Chloe said. "What if we split up? One group to Amund Ringnes, one to Yanok. Once one of us decides our location either is or is not Bluebird, we can regroup."

"We're already too small as it is," Pax pointed out.

"That may be," she said, "but do we have the time to check them one after the other?"

They went back and forth, neither fully able to convince the other they were right.

Finally, Ash said, "I'm reluctant to split up a group this size, but Chloe's idea has merit. I'd like to think about it for a bit so let's table it for now, and I'll make a decision when we get closer." He checked the time. "I want to head out as early as the weather will let us tomorrow. Let's eat up and get some sleep. We've got long days ahead."

22

SANJAY HAD BEEN working from daybreak until nearly ten p.m. every day for the last three days. According to the Pishon Chem managers, the schedule for everyone was likely to stay that way until they finished dispensing the anti-malaria spray. Thankfully, Pishon had thought ahead, and set up a dormitory complex on the grounds of the old factory they were renting so that the workers could stay there instead of going home each night.

The main reason things had become busy was due to the dozens and dozens of shipping containers that had begun arriving daily at the factory. Each was packed full with barrels of the chemical that was to be sprayed throughout the city. Sanjay and several dozen other temporary employees had been given the responsibility of unpacking the containers, and loading pre-determined numbers of barrels onto trucks that would take them south to Goa, north to Ahmedabad, and several locations right there in Mumbai.

The managers had assured everyone that working with the barrels was completely safe, but had also gone ahead and issued special gloves and paper surgical masks so that Sanjay and the others would feel even more at ease. While the gloves came in handy, most chose not to wear the masks, as they were more a hindrance in the humidity than a help.

Sanjay was supervising two teams of ten men each. Their job was to load the trucks with however many containers were assigned to each, so he was nowhere near the container drop-off zone when the accident occurred.

By all accounts, it was just a minor mishap, a truck hauling away an empty container scraping against another truck whose container was still full. Similar kinds of accidents happened in the city countless times a day. It was so minor, in fact, that Ayush, who was in charge of the delivery area, didn't even report the incident to the Pishon Chem managers. Not at first, anyway.

In a process that had become routine, the slightly dented but still-full container was removed from the truck and placed in the delivery area, waiting to be unloaded. When its turn finally came an hour and a half later, the door was unsealed, and a crew started moving the barrels out.

Because the contents of the barrels had been carefully designed to omit no odor, the men didn't discover the barrel with the broken seal until they neared it toward the back of the container. When they saw that some of its contents had been sloshed onto the walls and floor, they rushed out of the box, worried that they had been poisoned.

Ayush rushed over. "Why have you stopped? There are still barrels inside."

"One of them is open," someone said.

"The poison is everywhere," another added.

"What if we breathed it in? Are we going to die?"

The others began shouting variations on the same question.

"Wait, wait, wait," Ayush told them, patting his hands against the air to calm them down. "Show me."

"It's there," one of the men said, pointing at the open container. "Go see for yourself."

Annoyed, Ayush approached the container and looked in. It took him only a second to spot the mess.

The managers had briefed him and the other leaders about the spray. While it was apparently deadly to mosquitoes, it was harmless to human beings in all but extremely large doses. Did this qualify as that? He didn't think so, but it was probably better to check.

"Start on the next container," he ordered.

"But what about us? Should we see the doctor?"

"No. You are fine. The spray cannot hurt you. It is meant for mosquitoes, not humans."

"It still might be dangerous for us."

"It's not. But to be sure, you keep working and I will go check with the managers. They will tell us if everything is okay or not."

"You promise?"

"Of course, I promise."

The manager in the office at the time Ayush entered was a man named Dettling.

"Yes?" he asked as Ayush stood in the doorway waiting to be noticed.

"I'm sorry to disturb you, sir, but one of the barrels had opened."

Dettling looked surprised. "Are you sure?"

"Positive. The seal has broken on one, and much of what was inside has spilled into the container. The men who were doing the unloading are concerned and want to know if they should see a doctor. I told them everything would be fine, but I had them move on to a new container so I could ask you what we should do with the open barrel first."

"Did they breathe it in?"

The tone in Dettling's voice worried Ayush. "I think probably, yes. They were in the container for some time before they found the bad barrel. Is that a problem? I've been told the spray is harmless against us."

"No, no. It is harmless. It's just…supply is so tight…uh…losing even one barrel could be a…problem." He paused. "Go back out and tell them everything is fine. I'll be there in a few minutes."

―――――――――

AS SOON AS Ayush left the office, Dettling rushed over to the door and shut it. He didn't use the phone on his desk, but instead retrieved the sat-phone from his briefcase to make the call.

He was greeted with a recorded message, then a prompt. He said, "This is Dettling. Mumbai. I-7."

Dead air for a few seconds, then a click. "Go ahead," a live voice said.

Unconsciously, Dettling touched the spot on his upper arm where he'd received his KV-27a vaccination. "We have an accidental breach."

"Explain."

———————

SANJAY WAS BONE-tired when he dragged himself back to the dormitory at a quarter after ten that night. The only thing that kept him from heading straight up to bed was the growl in his stomach.

In the cafeteria, he piled the food onto his plate and carried it over to one of the common tables. Often, he had dinner with his cousin, but Ayush wasn't around.

Though the room was packed, few were talking. It seemed as if the only energy anyone could muster was used to move food from plate to mouth.

Once Sanjay was done, he made his way up to the dorm. He was assigned to a room that held ten people total. He shared it with others who had been given supervisory roles, including Ayush. Only Ayush wasn't there, either.

That was unusual, but not enough for Sanjay to think anything was wrong. Within five minutes, he was deeply asleep, unaware that Ayush and all the others who had been in contact with the contaminated container had been moved to the basement of a building three miles away, out of sight of anyone who might raise an alarm.

23

GILSTRAP HALL
HAWKINS UNIVERSITY
ST. LOUIS, MISSOURI

COREY FELT FINE when they arrived back in St. Louis just before dawn, but by the time he and Jeannie went out for breakfast at the Perch Café, he'd developed a case of the sniffles.

A cold, he thought, probably brought on by his lack of sleep and exposure to the freezing night air in Chicago. A couple cold tablets plus a few hours in bed and he should be fine.

At eleven a.m. he woke with a jolt, overcome by a coughing fit. He tried to get out of bed to get some water, but the room began spinning the moment he rose to his feet, causing him to drop back to the mattress. He closed his eyes, willing the dizziness to go away. It didn't work.

Maybe he'd been wrong. Maybe this wasn't a common cold after all. After three tries, he was able to grab his phone off the nightstand. He stared at it for a moment, not remembering who he'd wanted to call.

Jeannie. Right.

He spent longer than usual looking for her name at the top of his favorites list before calling.

"Hey," she said. "Thought you were sleeping."

"I...I..."

"Corey?"

"Not...I think...doctor..."

"Corey, are you all right?"

Her words faded away as the phone slipped from his ear, and he fell back on the bed.

———————

JEANNIE POUNDED ON the door. "Corey?"

She gave it five seconds, then tried again. When there was still no response from inside, she went in search of Corey's resident advisor, Barry Kellerman. Barry wasn't in his room, so she ran downstairs to the lounge.

The RA was on the couch with two other guys, watching SportsCenter on TV.

"Corey's sick," she said, running up to him. "He's not answering his door."

Barry pushed himself up. He was a good RA, and knew when to take things seriously and when not to. "Come on."

They ran up the stairs side by side, with Barry's buddies tagging along behind them. When they reached Corey's door, Barry knocked.

"I already did that," Jeannie said. "Just open it."

He hesitated a second before shoving the master key into the lock.

Corey was lying across the bed on top of the covers, his phone next to him.

Jeannie rushed over. "Corey? Hey, Corey. Can you hear me?"

She put her hand on his shoulder to wake him, but immediately pulled it back in surprise. He was burning up. She grabbed him again and shook him.

"Corey. Wake up. Corey!"

It was no use. He was completely out.

She looked back at Barry. "Call an ambulance!"

———————

IT TOOK TWELVE minutes for the EMTs to arrive. In that time, over half a dozen other residents of Gilstrap Hall poked their heads into Corey's room to see what was wrong.

At the hospital, he was put on fluids and anti-viral medication within two minutes of arrival. One of the upshots of the Sage Flu outbreak earlier that year was improved isolation protocol across the nation. Because of this, Corey was placed in a quarantined room. In addition, one of the nurses gathered all the names of people who might have come in contact with him.

Another improvement was the development of the Sage Test, a blood test that had an 85% accuracy at diagnosing Sage Flu. Several in the medical community thought this was overkill, their opinions gaining strength as months went by without any new Sage cases springing up, but after the outbreak, the public demanded its enforced use. That was the only reason the test was run on Corey.

Marcie Hayward was the doctor on duty. While Corey was in obvious distress, the doctor assumed it was just a particularly severe case of the flu. That in itself was disturbing, of course. The last thing they needed was a flu bug spreading through the school, but if there was one case now, there were bound to be others later. He told Nancy Batista, the senior RN on duty, that they should be sure they had enough supplies for a sudden influx of patients. He hoped it wouldn't be necessary, but knew the hospital couldn't afford to be caught off guard.

He then moved on to a broken arm suffered during an intramural game of flag football.

It was over an hour before Corey's preliminary lab results came in. Dr. Hayward was in the middle of a nasty case of road rash on the thigh of a girl who'd fallen from her bike when Nurse Batista rushed over.

"Sorry to disturb you, Doctor, but I need to see you for a moment."

Dr. Hayward smiled at his patient, and unintentionally lied. "I'll be right back."

Once they were outside the exam room, Nurse Batista showed the doctor the lab results. He read them twice, and looked at her in surprise.

"Are we sure?"

"I've drawn a new sample, so they can run it again."

That was also protocol if a positive result for Sage Flu was ever returned.

"Okay," he said. "But until we learn different, we need to assume this is correct. I want everyone who's been in contact with him isolated, including everyone on this floor. I'll inform the administration and the state health department."

"Yes, Doctor."

There was fear in her eyes as she ran off, the same fear that was probably in his. Both he and the nurse knew that the Sage Flu in its most virulent form meant one thing.

Death.

———————

MATT HAMILTON WAS in the Bunker cafeteria watching the video Tamara and Bobby had just emailed him. It wasn't the full WC report, just what they'd already completed over the previous months.

Tamara's voiceover—for the first time unfiltered so that it would be recognizable—had been done in an even, sure tone. There were no hysterics, just facts of the story. Even then, he couldn't help but frown. It played more like an over-the-top Hollywood thriller than something that could actually happen. But it was what it was. Besides, if they ever did need to play this video, it would mean the pandemic had started, and chances were people would be more keen on listening and believing.

Jordan was watching alongside him. With Pax gone, the younger man had assumed the role of Matt's top assistant. It was a job that would have normally fallen to Michael, but he was still watching over Janice, whose illness had turned into pneumonia after spending too much time on the freezing roof of the Bluff.

As Matt jotted down a few notes, he heard someone running through the hall toward the cafeteria.

"Matt!" Rachel's voice.

Forewarned by her tone, both he and Jordan jumped up and rushed into the hallway.

"What's going on?" Matt asked.

"Come! Come! I think it might have started."

With a feeling of dread, the three of them raced to the communications room. Nearly a dozen people were already there, including Billy. The TVs on the table were still tuned to the different networks, but only the volume on the PCN broadcast was turned up.

The image was a night shot of a multistory building. The

graphic at the bottom identified it as Hawkins Medical Center, Hawkins University, St. Louis, Missouri. The voice speaking belonged to Catherine Minor, one of the PCN anchors.

"…this time. We don't have the name of the patient yet, but we've been told he's a student at Hawkins University. The dormitory where he lived, and the emergency services area of the hospital have all been quarantined. Right now we need to go to a break. We'll have more when we return."

The image stayed on the screen for a second longer, then cut out and was replaced by a commercial for deodorant.

"What happened?" Matt asked.

"Apparently a student was brought into the hospital with flu symptoms," Billy told him. "When they ran the Sage Test, it came back positive."

"Just one case?"

"So far. According to the news idiots, they've isolated everyone he's come in contact with."

"Any reports from other locations?" If the Project had initiated Implementation Day, there should have been hundreds sick already, not just a single student in St. Louis.

"Nothing yet."

Matt nodded tensely.

An hour passed, then two. Through it all, the only words spoken were by those using the phone to see if there were outbreaks elsewhere.

As the end of the third hour approached, it was becoming clear that this was an isolated event. How? Sage Flu was not a naturally occurring disease. The student had been exposed to it somewhere. They needed to know where that was. It could provide crucial information.

He glanced over at Billy. "I want you in St. Louis as soon as possible. Jordan, you go with him. Find out how this happened."

———

"HOW DID THEY get in?" the DOP asked.

"Through the roof, sir," Ross said.

He stared at his aide for a moment. "The roof?"

"Yes, sir."

The DOP knew it wasn't worth getting upset over. Even this minor outbreak couldn't stop anything. It was annoying, though. It meant some people would be more cautious in the weeks to come, potentially skewing the survival rates in the wrong direction. Initially, anyway. At some point they would become exposed to the virus. This just meant that deaths might continue for months longer after the main event than he'd hoped. Statistically, the number would be infinitesimal, but it could still mean dealing with millions of sick people when they should already be moving on to the new reality.

"The factory needs to be destroyed," he said, forcing himself not to be distracted.

"Yes, sir."

"Immediately."

"Consider it done."

24

SANJAY KNOCKED ON the door of the managers' office. "Come in," a voice from inside said.

Reluctantly, he opened the door and walked in. In truth, he wasn't sure if he should be there at all. The last thing he wanted to do was anything that might upset his bosses. The money he'd already saved from the work they'd given him was more than he'd ever had at one time, and there was no sign this was going to end.

Though there were four desks in the room, the gray-haired senior manager was the only one there. The rumor was that he was German. Sanjay had never asked him, of course.

"Yes?" the man said.

"I am sorry to disturb you."

"What do you want?"

Sanjay hesitated for just a second, as he once more recalled the words he'd rehearsed. "I'm wondering if you might know where my cousin has gone."

"Your cousin?"

"Yes. His name is Ayush. He's a coordinating officer. He was here yesterday, but last night he did not return to the dorm."

"Ayush? How do you spell that?"

As Sanjay told him, the man typed his cousin's name into the computer. When he was through, he read the screen, and seemed to soften a bit. "Ah, yes. He's your cousin, is he?"

"Yes."

The man smiled. "Nothing to worry about. Ayush and one of

the work squads have been assigned to a task outside the city. They should be back in a few days."

"Thank you," Sanjay said, relieved. Then, feeling it necessary to explain himself, he added, "Usually we tell each other if we'll be gone, but he must have forgotten."

"You're probably right. It did come up quickly, so perhaps he looked for you but couldn't find you before he had to go."

"Thank you again."

SANJAY WOULD HAVE left it at that—in fact, had intended to leave it at that—if it were not for one thing. When he got back to the dorm that evening, someone else was using Ayush's bunk.

Why would someone else be given his bed if he was coming back in a few days? Sanjay asked around to find out who else had been assigned with his cousin, then discovered that their beds had also been filled.

So far, he had enjoyed working for Pishon Chem. Mainly it was the money, of course, but they had been fair in their other dealings, too. This seemed out of character, and he didn't like what it might mean about things to come.

A job is a job, a voice in his head reminded him. Ironically, it was Ayush's. And it was right. A job *was* a job, and questioning it after having spent so much time without a real one was not advised.

He headed out into the dark, warm night, thinking he just needed to take a walk and clear his mind. As he neared the building the managers used, he saw the youngest of the bunch, a man named Mr. Dettling, smoking a cigarette outside the main door.

Dettling had always been nice to Sanjay, and had been the person who delivered the news of his promotion. Maybe, if Sanjay worded things carefully, he could find out if there was anything going on he should be concerned about. He changed his course and headed toward the European.

"Good evening, sir."

Dettling jumped. "Sanjay. Jesus. I didn't...see you."

"I'm sorry. I didn't mean to startle you."

"What are you doing out here? Shouldn't you be asleep?"

"I was just out for a walk."

"Well, don't walk too long. Tomorrow's going to be really busy. We're just a couple days from starting."

"A couple days?" Sanjay said, surprised. "I did not know the official date had been set yet."

"Keep it to yourself for now. We'll make an official announcement in the morning." He tossed his cigarette on the ground and crushed it with his foot. "Well, I should get in. Have a—"

"One question, Mr. Dettling."

The man looked at Sanjay expectantly.

"I was told my cousin, Ayush, and several others would not be back for a few days. Will they be back in time? He is important to making sure things run smoothly."

For a second or two, there was uncertainty in the man's eyes, almost…fear. This was quickly pushed away by an accommodating smile. "They were needed elsewhere in the city. Your…your cousin will be replaced by someone else here who will do a fine job."

"Elsewhere *in* the city? But I was told—"

"I really need to go," Mr. Dettling said. "You should head back, too, and get as much sleep as you can." He turned toward the building.

In the city? The gray-haired manager had told Sanjay that Ayush and the others had been assigned somewhere *outside* the city. Was it possible Mr. Dettling just didn't know the details? Yes, but it seemed unlikely. In Sanjay's experience, the managers had always been in sync on information.

Could it be Mr. Dettling just forgot? Sanjay would have believed that more readily except for one thing—that look of uncertainty and fear before he answered. It almost seemed to Sanjay as if the man were making up a response that he thought would be satisfactory.

Sanjay didn't like this. Not at all.

Had Ayush gotten into trouble? Was he being punished or something? Or had he really been assigned to a new project? Whatever was going on, Sanjay wanted to know. Ayush was as much a brother as a cousin, and it was better to be sure that everything was all right than to wonder.

All this went through his mind in the seconds it took Mr. Dettling to walk over to the door, unlock it, and head inside.

Without even hesitating, Sanjay rushed forward and caught the door just before the lock clicked into place.

He waited, listening to Mr. Dettling's receding footsteps, then eased the door open a few inches. On the other side was a well-lit hallway that ran halfway through the building. There was no one in sight so he let himself in.

The ground floor was the working floor, where the managers' office was located along with several other rooms that were used for meetings and training sessions at the start of the job. Though Sanjay had never been above this floor, he knew upstairs was where the managers lived. Which meant he had to be extra careful to not be discovered.

An image of Kusum flashed through his mind. Working for Pishon Chem had brought him closer to a life with her. He knew how she felt about him now—the same as he felt about her. Because of his employment, her father was even coming around to the idea of them being together.

Just be careful, he told himself. *You can be in and out without anyone knowing.*

All he wanted was a look at the assignment sheet. On it would be the location where Ayush had been sent. If it wasn't too far away, he could go talk to his cousin himself, and make sure everything was okay.

The only copy he knew about was in the managers' office, so that's where he headed. The office was at the far end, along a small back hallway. Sanjay walked as quickly as he could, stopping occasionally to listen ahead, but always continuing toward his goal.

As he reached the short hallway, he peeked around the corner first, then immediately jammed himself against the wall. The door to the office was open, and there were voices coming from inside. He hesitated at first, then moved into the hallway, hugging the wall until he was only a foot away from the door.

He recognized one of the voices as Mr. Dettling's. The other belonged to a manager whom Sanjay had seldom talked to. They were speaking in German or whatever their native language was. Either way, he didn't know it, so he couldn't understand what they were saying. He was about to sneak away and return to the dorm when he heard Mr. Dettling say his name.

For half a second, he thought he'd been seen, but, no, Mr. Dettling was still in the room, not standing in the doorway. Sanjay paid closer attention.

His name again, then, "…Ayush…"

When the older man spoke, the only words Sanjay understood were "Ayush" and "Gamdevi."

Knowing he would be pressing his luck to wait any longer, he quickly made his way out of the building.

Gamdevi. Gamdevi…Road?

Gamdevi Road was where Ayush had taken Sanjay for his interview with Pishon Chem. He was told they were temporary offices, and figured they were no longer being used once the company moved to the compound.

Was that where Ayush had been sent?

There was only one way to find out.

———————

IT WAS NEARLY midnight when Sanjay reached Gamdevi Road. As was typical most anywhere in the city, there were still plenty of vehicles and pedestrians out and about.

He worked his way through the crowds to the building Pishon Chem had used. Their office had been in a storefront at the far end of the building on the street level. As he walked up to it, his heart sank. The windows had been partially covered with paper, but not enough to prevent him from seeing that the space beyond was completely empty.

His guess had been wrong. Whatever reason the man had mentioned Gamdevi, it apparently had nothing to do with either his cousin or the company's old office.

I'm making a big deal out of nothing. Ayush will probably laugh at me when I tell him about it.

Feeling like a fool, he wandered over to a food stall near the street and ordered some *pani puri*. Once it was ready, he sat down on an overturned bucket and popped one in his mouth. As he chewed, his eyes gazed down the street on nothing in particular. It would take him at least an hour to get back to the compound, which would probably mean he wouldn't be asleep until two a.m. He shook his head in self-annoyance. He would get three hours' rest at best before a day that was already going to be busier than usual. He would be a wreck by bedtime tomorrow night.

He shoved a second *pani puri* into his mouth and pushed himself to his feet, knowing to delay any longer would just make the next day worse. But instead of starting down the street, he remained where he was, frozen in place.

Getting out of a cab fifty feet away was Mr. Dettling. Sanjay watched as the man approached the building and walked up to an unmarked door between two of the shops. As soon as he was sure Mr. Dettling couldn't see him, Sanjay followed.

The manager pulled out a set of keys, unlocked the door, and went inside. Since it had worked one time already this evening, Sanjay raced forward to grab the door before it completely closed. Unfortunately, this time the distance was too great and the door clicked shut.

Sanjay sprinted around the building, looking for an alternate entrance. Everything was locked. Frustrated, he scanned the building again, looking for any possibility, and spotted one. At the back of the building, one floor above ground level, was a wide terrace. If he could get up there, it might lead to another way in.

Using a large bush and the rough surface of the building itself, he climbed the wall, and was soon high enough to pull himself onto the terrace.

The space was not part of an apartment like the balconies on the floors above, but rather an extension of a restaurant that had apparently just closed for the night. While there were no customers around, there were still a few employees inside cleaning up.

Sanjay waited until they had stepped into another room—the kitchen perhaps—then entered through the back door and cut across the dining area. There was another door at the far end that led to the interior of the building, a lobby with access to a staircase and elevator.

Sanjay chose the staircase and raced down to the ground floor. He took a moment to get his bearings, and tried to find the entrance he'd seen Mr. Dettling go through. He finally discovered it through a narrow hallway that seemed to be used by the people who took care of the building. It snaked around the elevator shaft, and around to the front of the building where the door was.

But all it really told him was that Mr. Dettling could have used it to get to the lobby and then taken the elevator to any floor. Sanjay headed back toward the lobby, thinking he might be able to figure out which floor the man had been on when he came back down, only he didn't make it all the way. There was a door he had missed when he came through the first time. It was on the same side as the elevator shaft. Sanjay turned the knob and the door opened.

Just inside, stairs led down to a basement level. If there hadn't been a light on at the bottom, he would have closed the door and moved on, but there was, so he knew he had to check.

Quietly, he descended the concrete steps into a long corridor that ran off to the left and right. He listened, not knowing which way to go.

Voices. Faint, and…from the right.

He went toward them, making his way past several doors until he reached the one where he could hear two distinct voices behind. Like at the managers' office, they were speaking a language he didn't understand. The door had two different locks. He carefully tried the knob, but it didn't budge.

Sanjay was trying to figure out how he was going to get on the other side when one of the voices—Mr. Dettling's, he realized—suddenly increased in volume.

Sanjay knew he'd never make it to the stairs in time. There was, however, a doorless entryway only ten feet back that opened onto a dark room.

He ducked inside, and had just moved into the shadows when the locks on the other door turned, and Mr. Dettling and a second person entered the main hallway. As they passed his hiding place, he tensed, sure he would be discovered, but the two walked by without stopping. When they reached the staircase, Mr. Dettling continued to talk for several minutes, then the other person said something. A woman's voice.

Sanjay peeked out, and saw that the woman had her back to him. Mr. Dettling was completely out of sight on the staircase. If Sanjay wanted to see what was on the other side of the locked doors, this was his only chance.

He moved into the hallway and crept quickly to the door with the locks. Behind him it sounded like the conversation was ending.

He put his hand on the knob, hoping they hadn't locked it again when they exited. It turned. He pushed it open, slipped inside, and closed it again.

He was in a short hallway. There were three doors that led off it. Out of the farthest one, he could hear a low, rhythmic beeping noise. Not just one pattern, he realized, but several, at slightly different speeds.

In the hallway behind him, he could hear footsteps approaching the door. Having little choice, he stepped over to the nearest room and opened the door. It was dark inside so he went in, but left the door open just a crack so he could keep an eye on the woman when she walked by.

He heard the outer door swing open and shut. Locks were turned, then the woman's footsteps passed his doorway and continued down the hall. He watched her through the crack. Not surprisingly, she entered the room the noise had been coming from. What *did* surprise him was that she was wearing a nurse's outfit.

As soon as she disappeared, he reentered the hallway and followed her. When he reached the doorway the noise was coming from, he paused at the jamb and leaned forward just enough to get a look inside.

It took him a moment to process what he was seeing. There seemed to be a plastic wall about a third of the way into the room, cutting the space into two. On the larger, enclosed side were five beds—*hospital* beds—each occupied.

No longer thinking about being seen or not, he stepped inside so he could get a better look. Yes, definitely hospital beds, and the beeping was coming from equipment set up next to each of the patients.

Though they all had tubes taped across their faces and looked in pretty bad shape, Sanjay recognized them. He'd seen four of them on and off around the Pishon Chem compound. The fifth he'd seen almost every day of his life.

Ayush.

"What are you doing here? Who are you?"

The sound of the voice knocked him out of his trance, and for the first time he looked at the front half of the room. There was more medical equipment here, most set up on tables that lined the plastic wall. There were also several chairs, two of which had been occupied until a moment before by female nurses. Both women were now on their feet.

"What's wrong with them?" he demanded. "What have you done to them?"

"You can't be here," the closest nurse said. "These people are very sick. You need to leave."

He looked at her, still trying to comprehend the situation. "Sick? How? From what?"

The other nurse grabbed something off a back table, and seemed to be fiddling with it.

"You need to get out *now!*" the first said.

Sanjay pointed at the plastic wall. "That's my cousin! What's wrong with him?"

His words seemed to startle the women. They looked at each other, and back at him.

"Where did you come from?" the second nurse asked.

"What do you mean, where did I come from?"

"How did you know to come here?" the first asked.

"I saw Mr. Dettling. He was down here a few minutes ago."

"You know Mr.—" The first nurse paused. "You work on the Project?"

"Of course." He pointed at his cousin again. "Ayush and I both do, and so do the others you have there. What happened to them?"

The second nurse had moved closer now. Whatever she'd grabbed earlier was out of sight behind her. "They're very sick," she said. "You shouldn't have come here. You've probably made your-self sick, too."

"How can my cousin be sick? He was fine yesterday. No prob-lems at all."

"I'm sorry," the first nurse said. "Sometimes it just happens quickly."

As he looked at her to ask, "What happens quickly?" the other nurse stepped toward him, her hand moving out from around her back.

He turned just as she was bringing her hand forward. In it was a syringe. He twisted to the side and thrust out his hand to push her away. She fell back into the table, her ribs smashing against the edge, and the wind rushed out of her lungs. With a groan, she fell to the ground and gasped for air.

The other nurse stared at Sanjay for a moment, then tried to run past him for the door, but he blocked her way. As she retreated, he reached down and picked up the syringe that had fallen from her friend's hand.

"What's in this?" he asked.

The nurse shook her head.

"Tell me! What did she try to give me?"

The nurse refused to answer.

He stepped quickly forward, grabbed her arm, and moved the needle toward it.

"No!" the woman shouted.

"What is it?"

"Something that would put you to sleep. But that much..."

"This much what?"

"Would...kill you."

His eyes widened. He looked at the woman writhing on the floor. She had tried to kill him. *Why?*

He turned back to the other one. "What's going on here? What are you trying to hide?"

It looked like she wasn't going to answer again, so he moved the needle toward her arm once more.

"Tell me!"

"It's not going to help you if I do. You're going to die anyway."

"Why do you say that? Why would I die?"

She glanced over her shoulder at the five prone figures in the other part of the room, then locked eyes with Sanjay. "They have Sage Flu."

At first he didn't understand what she meant, but then it hit him. *Sage Flu.* Earlier in the year there'd been an outbreak in America. But it had stopped, hadn't it? No more illnesses reported? He was sure he'd heard that on the news.

"How can it be here?" he asked, the needle still hovering near her skin.

She hesitated, her gaze nervously flicking down to the syringe.

He touched the tip to her arm, breaking the surface. "Tell me!"

"The spray."

He shook his head for a second, not following. "The mosquito spray?"

She nodded. "It's not what you think."

"What is it?"

She looked over her shoulder at Ayush, then back at Sanjay, her meaning clear.

"No," he said. "No. That can't be true."

"Believe what you want. By this time next week, you'll be dead."

"No. No!"

"If you let me go, I'll…I'll give you the vaccine."

He squeezed her arm. "Have you given it to my cousin?"

"It's too late for him."

"You're lying. It's not too late. You can save him."

"Once the virus took hold, nothing could save him. You haven't been exposed yet. You could still live."

He barely heard the last part, his mind reeling from the idea that his cousin was as good as dead.

"I can save you," she said. "But only if you let me *go*!"

"I'll…I'll go to the police. I'll tell them what's going on."

"Try it, and you'll be in a jail cell when the sickness finds you. No one will listen to you."

She was right. He was a poor man from a line of poor men. His word against that of a group of Europeans "helping to rid India of malaria"? He *would* be thrown in jail.

He almost let her go right then, but he realized there was something he could do. Something he *had* to do.

"How do I know you're not lying about the vaccine?"

"There's no way you can know."

He thought for a moment. "You'll take it first."

"Okay, but I'm already vaccinated."

"I don't care. I just want to see if it kills you."

She nodded. "I understand."

"Where is it?"

25

I.D. MINUS 51 HOURS

IT WAS AMAZING what the right set of credentials could do. Authentic or not, if they looked good, they were good, and the Centers for Disease Control credentials Billy was carrying looked great.

After donning a protective suit, he was allowed entry into the now isolated Emergency Care area of Hawkins Hospital. There, he first interviewed Dr. Hayward and Nurse Batista, the people who had been caring for Corey Wilson, patient zero of the current outbreak. There was nothing new the two professionals could give him that he hadn't learned after a quick perusal of the patient's file, but if he'd really been from the CDC, they would have been the first people he talked to, so he had to keep up appearances.

Next, he was taken into the patient's room, but it was clear he would get nothing out of the boy. From the condition he was in, Billy was sure Corey wouldn't last more than a few hours, a day at most. This, of course, he kept to himself.

"Who found him?" he asked Nurse Batista.

"His girlfriend."

"And where is she?"

"They've sectioned off a part of the hospital that's connected to our area, and put all the people who needed to be quarantined there."

"Can you show me?"

They found Jeannie Saunders in a room with several others, staring sullenly at a TV mounted on the wall. As with the other televisions Billy had seen, this one was tuned to the news.

"Jeannie?" the nurse said.

The girl took a second before she looked over, her expression unchanged.

"This is Dr. Grimes from the CDC. He'd like to ask you a few questions."

Jeannie stood slowly and shuffled toward him, her arms wrapped around her chest. As she neared, he could see her eyes were red from crying.

"Is there someplace I could speak to her alone?" he asked the nurse.

"Not a lot of private space left, Doctor," she told him. "There's a linen closet at the end of the hall that's fairly roomy. It's possible no one's claimed it yet."

"Thanks."

She pointed him in the right direction then headed back to Emergency Care.

The linen closet was unoccupied. In the back corner was a folding chair stuffed between shelving units. He pulled it out and opened it for the girl. Once she was sitting, he leaned against the wall so that he wouldn't tower over her.

"I know this has been a very difficult time for you, and that some of the questions I'm going to ask you've already answered. I want you to understand that this *is* important, and that whatever you can tell me is going to be a big help."

"Sure, no problem." She sounded even more defeated than she looked.

"Corey's your boyfriend?"

She nodded.

"Do you know how he might have gotten sick?"

A headshake, but with a slight hesitation.

"Before you found him, when was the last time you saw him?"

"Uh…the night before. At Old Tom's."

"Old Tom's?"

"It's a pub. We had a drink and then…he went home."

"Alone?"

"Of course."

Billy leaned back. "You're lying," he said. There was no time to waste trying to slowly extract what he needed from her.

She looked up, surprised. "What?"

"You're lying, Jeannie."

"I'm not."

"Let me lay it out for you. Your boyfriend is dying. You could very easily be next. Potentially thousands of others could be in danger, too. If you know something and aren't telling me, their deaths will be due to your inaction. Do you understand what I'm saying? If you think telling me is going to get you into trouble, you're wrong. I'm just looking for the source so I can stop this as quickly as possible."

Her eyes shifted to the floor as she clenched her hands to stifle her shaking fingers. "We…we weren't supposed to be there."

"Where?"

"IT'S SOME KIND of factory, I think," Billy told Matt over the phone as he made his way to Lambert-St. Louis International Airport. "From her description, it sounds similar to the virus factory in the video. She said it looked like the place had been cleared out, though. Corey—patient zero—apparently looked inside one of the vats. She said they appeared empty, but…"

"…but you can't see a bug," Matt finished for him.

"Right."

TWO HOURS LATER, Billy was in the Chicago area, hunting down the address the girl had given him. When he finally turned down the right street, he wasn't surprised to see a dozen emergency vehicles parked next to the building he was looking for.

Fire had completely gutted the structure, and while the machinery inside would, no doubt, still be partially intact, there was no way he could get to it with all these people around. Not that he really needed to anymore. The blaze was more than enough confirmation of the girl's story.

At some point within the last several weeks, this building had been churning out the virus and shipping it off to God-only-knew-where. He was sure of it.

There was a silver lining, though.

"Why were you there?" he'd asked the girl before he left St. Louis.

"Do you really need to know that?"

"It might help."

She took a breath, then said, "It was Corey's idea."

"Same question. Why?"

"He's writing this paper…was, I guess…oh, Jesus."

"Stay focused. What paper?"

"He was supposed to write a company profile, only he wasn't having any luck finding information about the company he chose. Then his friend found an address in Chicago, so…so we decided to go up and check it out."

"The address you visited."

"Yes," she said.

"Do you know the name of the company?"

She thought for a moment, then shook her head. "I don't remember. Hid-something, I think."

She coughed. If she realized what that meant, she didn't show it.

"The other friend you went with, would he know the name?"

"He should."

Before leaving the hospital, Billy located the kid named Blanton Kirn.

"Sure, I remember. Hidde-Kel Holdings. With a hyphen after the first 'e.'"

Hidde-Kel.

It was a start.

26

I.D. MINUS 39 HOURS

Ash AND HIS team arrived in Grise Fiord after eight p.m. It had been a mind-numbing, exhausting two days. They had tried to leave Baker Lake the day before, but had barely gotten into the air when it became obvious the weather wasn't going to cooperate. The storm had finally broken around 6 a.m. that day, but by the time the runway was cleared and they could get on their way, it was the middle of the afternoon.

Grise Fiord was as far as the jet would take them. Unless needed elsewhere, the pilot and plane would remain there for exactly one week. If Ash or another member of the team failed to show up prior to that, the plane would return to the Ranch. From Grise Fiord, Gagnon would fly them in a smaller, more agile craft equipped with a combination water pontoon/snow skid.

The first thing Ash did was check the weather report. It didn't look good. One, maybe two days of relative calm, then another storm, a big one that might last several days—several days they couldn't afford to sit idle.

Once they arrived at the CF Guest Quarters, he told the team what he'd decided. "We'll have to split up. Four in one, three in the other, with Gagnon in the plane."

Chloe nodded in agreement, but Pax didn't look as comfortable with the idea.

"The weather isn't giving us a choice," Ash said to him.

"I know. It's the decision I'd make, too, but I still don't like it."

Ash nodded. He felt the same way. "I want you to head up the second group. Browne, Solomon, and Wright will go with you. Chloe and Red will be with me. Which island do you want?"

"You're the boss. Which one do you want?" Pax asked.

Before Ash could respond, Chloe said, "We'll take Yanok."

They all looked at her.

"If you know something, you should tell us," Ash said.

She shook her head. "Just a feeling."

Ash stared at her a moment longer. He knew firsthand that her instincts were far better than average, but kept the thought to himself. "Okay. Gagnon, you'll fly the first group out to Amund Ringnes in—" He looked at his watch. "—six hours. As soon as you get back, you'll take us to Yanok. Anyone have any questions?"

There were none.

"Then that's it, I guess. Tomorrow we start what we came here to do. No pressure, but the whole human race is hanging in the balance."

"There is that, isn't there?" Pax said.

———————

SECURITY HAD ALWAYS been a priority for the Project. The last thing they wanted was for Bluebird to be discovered. They had come close already with the men who'd made it all the way onto the island, but it seemed as if Major Ross's diversionary tactics had been successful in cutting off any trail that might have led back to their headquarters.

From even before they had taken full control of the facility on Yanok, they had stationed a two-man observation team in Grise Fiord. The men—Rogers and Perry—posed as climatologists for a European consulting group, and had slowly worked their way into the tolerance of the locals, if not their trust.

Because of this, whenever something happened in Grise Fiord, they heard about it almost right away, like everyone else in town. This was particularly true of new arrivals.

When the news got around that evening about a jet touching down with a group of scientists, Rogers had been having a beer with a few of the local residents. Upon hearing the story, he casually finished off his Molson's and excused himself for the night.

He did not, however, return home. Instead, he took the cold

bumpy drive out to the airstrip.

Just like he'd been told, there was a private jet sitting off to the side. They didn't get a lot of traffic out here, especially not jets. Usually those who arrived in one were oil and energy people looking for a new resource to exploit.

Unable to recall ever seeing this particular plane before, he wrote down the tail number so someone back at Bluebird could run it through the system. Next, he went to see if the plane might be open. He wasn't worried about being seen. Chances were he was the only one outside for a thousand miles in any direction. The aircraft, however, was locked up.

He drove back into town and woke up Perry. Together they headed over to the building the supposed scientists were using for the night.

All the lights inside were off, so it was a pretty good bet that everyone was asleep. Over a period of time, he and Perry had been able to make keys to all the buildings in town as a precaution. Not that they needed them often. There was no crime up here, so most places were seldom ever locked.

That message had obviously not been passed on to the new arrivals yet since the door to the CF Guest Quarters was secured. Rogers thought for a moment, bringing up a layout of the building in his mind. If he remembered correctly, there was a long, narrow mudroom on the other side of the main entrance, then another door that opened into the central room where everyone would be sleeping.

Easy enough.

He found the appropriate key from his master ring, slipped it into the lock, and turned it. The door opened with barely a protest. He motioned Perry in first then followed.

The front room was pretty much empty. Unfortunate. He'd been hoping their luggage would be there. Having no other choice, he moved quietly to the other door, listened for a second, then turned the knob and pulled the door open.

———————

CHLOE'S EYES OPENED.

She'd heard something, but didn't know if it was real or in her dreams.

She tried to recall the noise. Something bumping something else, maybe? A click?

Even as this thought was going through her mind, the wind suddenly howled across the roof.

Maybe that's what it was?

Click.

No, not the wind. Not even from outside. The noise had come from somewhere in the room.

She raised herself on her elbow and looked around. All the other cots were full, so whatever was making the sound was either the building itself, or…

A shadow moved over near where they'd left their backpacks.

Son of a bitch! Someone was trying to steal their things.

Silently, she slipped from the cot, and moved along the back end of the beds in a crouch, using them as cover to get closer to the packs. She stopped behind the last cot.

Not one shadow. Two.

They seemed to be carefully looking through the bags. Why? If they were thieves, they would just grab and go. It was almost like they were looking for something in particular.

She glanced around for anything she could use as a weapon, but apart from a pair of boots, there was nothing handy.

To hell with it. She didn't need a weapon.

THE PACKS WERE stuffed with all the items one would expect for cold weather survival—clothes, goggles, extreme-rated sleeping bags, and similar items. But so far, Rogers and Perry had found nothing identifying the people sleeping on the cots.

Rogers leaned toward his companion. "There are a couple bags by the door," he whispered in Perry's ear. "I'm going to check 'em out. You stay on these."

CHLOE SMILED. WHOEVER the intruders were, they'd just made a critical error.

There was no question which one she should go after first.

The guy sneaking across the room was headed straight for the bags containing weapons and other specialized gear.

Being sure to stay out of either man's line of sight, she quietly closed in on her target.

THERE WERE THREE large, duffel-type bags shoved against the wall. Rogers started with the one farthest from the door, and carefully unzipped it. When he had it open enough to look inside, he pulled out his flashlight and aimed the beam into the bag.

Guns. At least half a dozen. And not the kind that might be needed in the unlikely event they ran into a wild animal. These were handguns.

Why would a group of scientists need *pistols*? Only one answer came to mind: because they weren't scientists.

He turned to get his partner's attention.

WHEN THE MAN finished looking in the bag, Chloe was two feet behind him, her arm drawn back.

He paused for a second, undoubtedly working through what he'd just found. Then, as she knew he would, he turned.

The base of her palm rammed into the side of his jaw before he even registered her presence. The blow sent him reeling backward. His feet caught on one of the bags, and he fell across them, his head slapping loudly against the wall.

Chloe whirled around and sprinted across the room toward the other man. He was staring at her, surprised. His hand suddenly shot to the pocket of his jacket, where it began fumbling with the opening, going for a weapon, no doubt. But by that point, he was too late.

Chloe all but leaped the final few feet, hitting him in the chest and sending both of them to the floor. She tried to pin him down, but he had a size advantage on her, and easily shoved her off to the side.

"I could use a little help!" she yelled.

The intruder pushed himself back up, but was on his feet for only a second before Chloe grabbed his ankles and yanked his legs out from under him.

"What's going on?" a sleepy voice called out.

The man jerked Chloe toward him by her hair, and threw his arm around her neck, choking her from behind. She slammed her elbow repeatedly into his ribs, but he held on tight. Gray started to invade the edge of her vision as the blood flow to her brain decreased. Desperate, she brought her leg up into the air, bending it at the knee, and slammed her foot down into his groin.

Air rushed out of his lungs as his grip around her throat loosened.

Chloe twisted free, hopped to her feet, and looked back toward the other guy. He was still on the floor in the same place she'd left him.

Suddenly, the lights came on.

ASH WAS FIRST to jump up. He ran across the room to the light switch and flipped it on.

Chloe was standing in the middle of the room, her fists hovering ready at her waist. She was looking back and forth between two figures on the ground. The one nearest her was rocking in obvious pain. The other one lay unmoving only a few feet away from where Ash stood.

The rest of Ash's team were throwing off their blankets and hopping out of their cots, ready if another fight broke out.

Ash jogged over to Chloe. "Are you all right?"

"Yeah. Why wouldn't I be?"

There was a patch of red on her neck, but otherwise she looked fine.

"What happened?"

"These two assholes were taking a look through our stuff."

"Who are they?"

She frowned at Ash. "I didn't stop to ask."

The one who'd been rocking had recovered enough to put his hands on the ground and try to stand.

"Uh-uh," Chloe said, shoving him back down with her foot.

Ash pointed at the unconscious one. "Pax, check him." He then knelt next to the nearer guy. "What the hell are you doing here?"

"Nothing, okay?" the guy said defiantly.

"*Not* okay. Why were you going through our stuff?"

The man remained silent for a few seconds, then shrugged. "Looking for something we could sell. That's all. You got us, okay?"

"Sell? Here in Grise Fiord? I'm guessing there's not much of a black market."

"You'd be surprised."

"You got that right."

Chloe moved up next to Ash, and put her foot on the man's neck. "Who the hell are you?"

"Stop!" the man croaked.

"I think you should probably answer her question," Ash said.

"Just a couple of guys, all right? Trying to entertain ourselves."

Chloe pushed down on his throat.

"Come on…stop…it." His voice was even more strained.

Pax walked up behind them. "Ash, a moment if you don't mind." Once they were several feet away, he whispered, "The other guy's dead. I'd say he cracked his head against the wall."

"Dammit," Ash said. That was a mess they didn't need.

"I wouldn't worry too much. I don't think these guys were just burglars."

"Why not?"

Pax held up his hand. In it was a small notebook. He opened it to a page near the back, and showed it to Ash. There was a date, a number, and the words: 7 MEN 1 WOMEN, PLUS 2 MAN FLIGHT CREW. Pax pointed at the second item. "That's the tail number of our jet."

"You're sure?"

"I've flown in the thing nearly a hundred times. Yeah, I'm sure. Now take a look at this." He flipped back to earlier pages in the book. It was a log with more dates, both arrival and departing; plane numbers; and passenger descriptions. "He's been tracking visitors. I'll bet this is everyone who's set foot in this town since he's been here." He paused, and locked eyes with Ash. "I think they're with the Project."

Ash looked at the book, and pointed at several dots that were printed at the end of each entry. "What are these?"

"I'm not sure. But if I had to guess, I'd say those were times they reported in."

Ash flipped to the last entry. Theirs. At the end was a blue dot.

With a nod, he walked back over to their captive. He motioned for Chloe to remove her foot, then crouched down beside the intruder, making sure the man could see the notebook in his hand.

"I have a very simple question for you. Where is Bluebird?"

"Bluebird? What's that?" The response was automatic, too quick.

Ash opened the notebook to the page containing the team's information. He tapped the blue dot. "What did you tell them?"

The guy snorted and shook his head, but kept his lips sealed this time.

Ash stood up and looked over at Browne and Solomon. "Search him."

They pulled the intruder to his feet and checked him over, but the only items they found were a pistol, a flashlight, and a key ring with four keys on it.

"Where is Bluebird?" Ash asked the man again.

For a second it looked like the intruder was going to deny any knowledge of the Project's base again, but then he smirked and said, "You really expect me to tell you?"

"It would be better for you if you did."

The man laughed. "You're all going to die, you know that? All of you. There's nothing you can do!"

Without warning, he lashed out to the side, knocking Solomon backward, then ran for the door. Ash and Browne sprinted after him. The intruder reached the mudroom five seconds before the others. He raced to the main door and threw it open.

Neither Ash nor Browne were dressed for the outside, and would risk serious exposure if they stepped into the Arctic night for more than a few seconds.

With no choice, Ash returned to the other room, where he threw on heavier pants and a jacket, and yanked on his boots without tying them.

"Take this," Pax said. He tossed one of the pistols through the air.

Ash grabbed it in mid-stride and headed for the main door.

Browne was standing just inside, holding the door partially open.

"Which way did he go?"

"Left," Browne said.

Ash ran out the door.

The cold was like a wall, slapping him hard and nearly stealing his ability to breathe. He forced himself forward, ignoring the shock, and focused only on finding the man. If the intruder really was part of the Project, they had to stop him before he could report back to his bosses. If that happened, their mission would be compromised, and their minimal chance of success would drop to zero.

CF Guest Quarters was located at the northern end of Grise Fiord, not far from the landing strip. The bulk of the town—not much to begin with—was to the left on the other side of a short bridge.

Ash ran as fast as his loose boots let him, his gaze on the road ahead, looking for the man in the darkness. Wind was whipping around him, sending up swirls of ice and snow, and playing tricks with the shadows.

He had just crossed the bridge when he heard someone running up behind him. He twisted around, thinking maybe he'd somehow passed the man, but the person was too small.

Chloe, he realized. In her hand was a gun.

With a nod of acknowledgment, he started off again, his run turning more into a jog as the cold zapped the energy out of him. Even then, within half a minute, he was in the main part of town.

Here and there, lights shone outside some of the buildings. Each structure was raised above the ground, making them all look like they'd fit better in a mobile home park farther south than this northern bit of barren island. Even the church looked like a shoebox on a wooden stand.

The road ahead was split, one part continuing straight and paralleling the coast, while the other curled to the left, back to a few other buildings on the eastern side of town. He glanced at Chloe and pointed for her to take the coast road. He then followed the curve.

Where is this guy, dammit?

It wasn't that big of a place. Ash doubted there were even one hundred buildings in the whole area. He was also confident the man couldn't have gone into any of the buildings unseen.

Stopping in front of the church, he looked around.

Nothing. Just night and snow and frigid cold. He was the only one—

Wait. Something had moved behind a large storage tank to his right.

He ran toward it, stumbling once but managing to remain on his feet. As he neared the tank, he saw another behind it, and there, outlined against the side of the second tank, was the intruder.

Breathing hard, the best Ash could muster was a quick walk, but it was faster than the other man, who could do no better than to shuffle around the tank. Soon, Ash could hear the man breathing.

"Stop!" he yelled when only fifteen feet separated them.

The intruder looked back, but kept moving.

Ash raised the gun. "I *will* shoot you."

The threat did nothing to stop the other man.

On willpower alone, Ash increased his speed until he caught up to the man. He reached out and grabbed the back of the guy's jacket. The intruder tried to pull away, but Ash held tight.

In a desperate move, the guy spun around and threw himself at Ash. Ash's feet slipped on the icy snow, and they both slammed to the ground. The man grabbed the barrel of the gun and twisted the weapon, popping it free. Ash tried to snatch it back, but the man pushed away, creating a few feet of distance between them.

Ash scrambled to his right, wanting to get behind the cover of the tank, but knowing he wouldn't make it in time. When the gun went off, he tensed, waiting for the bullet to hit.

It never did.

He looked back.

The man was sprawled on the ground, a hole in his head.

Chloe was about thirty feet away, her pistol in her hand. "You all right?"

"Why wouldn't I be?" Ash huffed, climbing to his feet. "Thanks."

She shrugged. "That's like a dozen you owe me now."

"How do you figure that?"

"I'm rounding up."

THEY HID THE two bodies under the CF Guest Quarters. Come summer, if it warmed up enough, the smell of the thawing corpses would signal their location. Hopefully, there would still be someone alive in Grise Fiord to notice.

27

"YOU'LL WANT TO see this," Jordan said.

Billy came around the table, and leaned over Jordan's shoulder so he could look at the computer screen. The two had been holed away in one of the small meeting rooms in the Bunker since Billy's return to the Ranch from Chicago. Though it was well after midnight, going to bed had not even crossed Billy's mind.

"What am I looking at?" he asked. On the screen was what appeared to be a night-vision video of a street.

"Just watch."

Jordan tapped one of the arrows, speeding up the image for several seconds, then hit the space bar. The video ramped down to normal speed.

On the right side of the frame was the edge of an industrial-type building, and on the left, the road the business was located on. Most of the shot, though, was focused on a chain-link gate fastened to the building. It was an obvious security shot meant to monitor who went in and out. At the moment, the gate was closed and no one was around.

"Where is this?"

"Give it a second, okay?"

Billy watched the screen, unsure of what he was supposed to focus on. He was about to say as much when two headlights appeared in the upper left corner, coming out of a driveway a block down on the other side of the street. When the lights turned onto the road in the direction of the camera, Billy could see that it wasn't a car, but a semitruck. It continued toward the camera for several seconds, then passed out of sight.

Jordan stopped the playback, and looked triumphantly at Billy.

"So what? A truck on a street."

Jordan dipped his head in disappointment. He pointed at the screen. "Look again. That's not just any street. *You've* been there. That's the one where the Hidde-Kel building is. And this truck…" He backed the video up and paused on the frame right before the semi moved out of view. "Just came out of Hidde-Kel's lot."

Billy studied the picture. "You're sure?"

"Positive. It took a little finagling, but I was able to hack into the security system of a company just down the road. They keep two months' worth of footage on their backup drives. Just had to hunt around until I found this."

Billy moved his finger toward the screen, hovering it just over the load on the back of the truck. "And is that…?"

"Yes. It is."

A shipping container. An identical match, as a matter of fact, to the shipping containers in the footage their inside person had sent them.

MATT AND RACHEL arrived within seconds of each other, both responding to urgent phone calls from Billy.

"I need to go back out," Billy told them.

"Why?" Matt said, surprised.

Billy nodded to Jordan. "Show them."

Jordan turned his laptop so the others could see the screen, and hit the space bar. While the video of the truck played, he and Billy took turns filling in the details.

"But that's not even the best part," Billy said as the video finished.

It sounded pretty damn good to Matt. Knowing the public face of the Project had been an elusive goal to this point, but now, with the discovery of Hidde-Kel, they had a name. It meant they might be able to stop just reacting and go on the offensive. They might not be able to kill the Project's plan completely, but they might be able to create some big problems.

"So what's the best part?"

Billy smiled. "Jordan was the one who figured it out."

Jordan shrugged. "All I did was enhance the video enough to get an ID number off the truck."

"And?" Billy urged.

"Well, from that I found the company who owned it. These days, nearly every truck on the road has a transponder so that its owners can track them. I, um, was able to get the truck's transponder ID and tap into it."

Matt was not surprised. Jordan was a tech expert who routinely hacked into satellites and computer systems for the cause. "I take it you found something."

Jordan minimized the video and brought up a static image of a map. Superimposed on it were several bright yellow lines, each overlaying existing roads and creating loops that seemed to always start in Chicago before going somewhere else in a two-state radius.

"The lines represent routes the truck traveled in a two-week period surrounding the time the video was shot." He clicked a button and all but one of the loops disappeared. "And this is the trip he started that night."

The line went southeast into Indiana, then almost due east across the state and into Ohio, where it terminated in Cleveland. From there it looped back, following basically the same route home.

Jordan clicked on Cleveland, and the map zoomed in. He didn't stop until the image area was filled with a roughly four-square-block section of the map. The yellow line stopped right in the middle.

"This is where they dropped off the container," Billy explained.

"Where you guys *think* they dropped it off," Rachel corrected him.

"No. Jordan, show them."

Jordan brought up a satellite image.

"The angle's a little skewed," he said. "The closest satellite I could get access to wasn't directly overhead, but you can still see it."

The focus area of the shot appeared to be part of an industrial zone. In the center was a large open lot behind a warehouse-type building. Even from the slightly angled view, it was apparent the lot was not seeing much use. There were several abandoned cars along one fence, and a couple of semitruck trailers in the middle. Sitting right next to the trailers was what looked like a brown shipping container.

"It's the same container?" Matt asked.

"I think so. Yes. Look at it. It's a match to the one that was on the back of the truck that we now know stopped at this very location. I found a few images of the area from a month ago, and the only thing different is that there's no container."

"Matt," Billy said. "That lot is only a few blocks from the airport, and a mile or so west of a huge residential area."

"So if it is a delivery system, it's perfectly placed," Matt said, more to himself than anyone else.

"Exactly." Billy paused. "This is a perfect opportunity to find out how these things work. I want to go check it out."

"I'm not sure that's such a great idea," Rachel said.

"Look, if I can figure it out, we might be able to dismantle others. Jordan's already started the process of trying to locate more. Don't you see? This will save lives."

"Do it," Matt said. "Take whoever you need with you."

"Shouldn't we talk this over?" Rachel asked.

"We don't have time. If there's a way to stop these things, we need to know that now."

Rachel frowned but made no further arguments. Matt knew what she was thinking, though. Even if Billy figured out how to dismantle the death box, it would probably be too little too late.

28

I.D. MINUS 29 HOURS

THE DOP RECEIVED his regular morning briefing from Foster, the night watch officer, at six a.m. on the dot in his quarters.

"There have been no additional problems with the situation in Buenos Aires. We've hired some local freelancers to keep an eye on Patricia Mendes in case she tries to stir up anything."

The DOP waved a dismissive hand in the air. "We're too close for anything she might say to matter at this point. You can let her be."

"Very well, sir." Foster provided updates for several other minor incidents, including the small outbreak in Mumbai, India. "It appears to be contained with no further infections."

The DOP sensed hesitation. "What is it?"

"It seems, sir, that the two nurses watching the patients have…left."

"What do you mean, left?"

"When the next shift came on, they weren't there. It's believed they fled."

"Are they Project members?"

"Yes, sir. Um, some of their cache of vaccine is missing."

The DOP stared at him. "They stole vaccine."

"Yes, sir."

Unbelievable, the DOP thought. "Put their names on a list to be dealt with after everything is over. This kind of lack of loyalty cannot be tolerated."

"Yes, sir."

"Has there been any information leak on the outbreak?"

"None."

"Good." An outbreak associated with the people working on the "malaria problem" could have caused some serious questions to be raised, and jeopardized their operations not only in Mumbai but other places where they were using the method.

"What's next?"

"Have not heard back yet from the team at Grise Fiord," Foster said.

The men at Grise Fiord had reported the arrival of a science group the previous evening, and were going to check them out, but it wasn't unusual for them to take up to twenty-four hours to learn anything useful.

"All right," the DOP said, glad that these types of issues were not something he'd have to think about for much longer.

"Our lookout in Savissivik reports that the Danish cultural committee is leaving as scheduled this morning for the south," Foster said.

Savissivik on the northwestern coast of Greenland and Grise Fiord in Canada were the two closest manned locations to Yanok Island, so it had always been a priority to keep an eye on them.

"Anything else?"

"Yes. There's a storm heading our way."

"When?"

Foster smiled. "Just in time for Implementation Day."

The DOP chuckled. He liked the idea of that.

The briefing finished, Foster headed off to bed while the DOP got dressed. He then went to the cafeteria for a leisurely breakfast before joining Major Ross in the Cradle.

They were approaching twenty-four hours from activation, the moment he'd been working toward for so many years. The anticipation was intoxicating. He wanted to make sure he savored every last second of it.

29

BILLY ARRIVED IN Cleveland just after seven a.m. via a chartered jet. He'd brought only one other person with him, a woman named Karen Pruitt. She had a degree in electrical engineering, and was one of the people who kept the Ranch's equipment running.

After obtaining a rental car, it took them only a few minutes to get to the container's location, just as the early winter sun was coming up. Live and in person, the lot looked even more abandoned than it had from above. There was a rusty chain-link fence, topped by three strands of barbed wire, surrounding the entire lot, and another, slightly newer fence partially cutting the lot in half. The row of neglected vehicles was a mix of cars and a couple of old tow trucks. None looked like it'd been on the road for years.

Billy pulled the rental into one of the spaces at the west end of the lot, and got out. Though he could hear a low rumble coming from the freeway several blocks away, the area itself was quiet. At this early hour of the morning, he and Karen were probably the only ones around.

After exiting the car, Karen went to the trunk and removed the case containing the specialized tools and equipment they thought they might need. That was one of benefits of chartering a plane from a company the Ranch had worked with before—they didn't have to worry about a security check. She joined Billy at the misaligned gate in the fence, only about twenty feet from where they'd parked.

Though the gate looked like it had been there for decades, the chain and lock holding the two halves together were new. Karen selected a couple tools from the case, set to work on the lock, and opened it in seconds.

From the sidewalk, the brown shipping container was out of view, blocked by one of the aging trailers, but as soon as they walked on the lot, they could see it. Billy's first impression was that it was a normal container, just like the countless others he'd seen over the years in ports or on the backs of trucks and trains. Then he noticed the top edge. At the point where the side panel met the roof, there seemed to be a hinge. *That* was definitely not normal.

He pointed it out to Karen. "Goes all the way along the edge."

She frowned, and disappeared on the other side. "Same over here, too," she called out, then came back around to where he was. "I think the roof splits in the middle."

Billy located the number at the top back corner of the box, and checked it against the one Jordan had seen on the container in the security footage. "Numbers match," he said. "It's definitely the same one."

When they stepped around the far end, they found another surprise. While the doors for loading and unloading the container were right where they should be, the locking mechanism keeping them closed was decidedly not standard, and seemed to be attached to something within the box itself.

Karen set the case on the ground and moved in for a closer look. "I've never seen anything like this."

"Can you open it?"

"Maybe if I had time and the right software. But I don't think I'd even want to try."

"Why not?"

"If I got it wrong even once, what do you think the chances are something inside would be triggered? I mean, *if* this is one of the Project's devices."

"Then how are we going to see what's inside?"

"Give me a few minutes."

While she conducted a closer examination of the box, Billy pulled their communication gear from his jacket pocket, and put his wireless earpiece on. Matt's one caveat for letting Billy come to

Cleveland was that once he and Karen were on site, they had to be in constant communication with the Ranch.

"This is Billy. Anyone there?"

"This is Echo Four. I got you, Billy," a voice said on the other end. He recognized it as belonging to Leon Owens, one of the communications operators.

"We're on site, doing a visual check of the container."

"All right. I'll let Matt know."

"Billy!" Karen called out. "Bring me the scanner, would you?"

Billy knelt down next to the tool case, and removed the scanner from inside. The device looked like a tablet computer, but was really a down and dirty imager that could see through solid objects for about half a foot. He brought it around and gave it to Karen, who held it against the side of the container and activated it. The image that appeared on the screen was grainy and devoid of color. As she moved it along the surface, shades of gray seemed to recede then start again.

"What is it?" he asked.

"I'm not sure, but whatever it is, it's packed right up to the inside of the wall."

When she was just a few feet from the end of the box, the screen became more black than gray.

"It's empty right here," she said. "I think we could probably cut through the wall and get in that way. Can you bring the case over?"

Billy retrieved the tools, and Karen pulled out a compact metal cutting torch that had been included in their kit.

"Billy? It's Matt."

Billy touched his earpiece. "I'm here."

"So what have you found?"

"It's definitely the same container. Not sure beyond that yet. One thing we do know is that it's been modified." He explained about the roof and the odd locking setup, then told him about the scans. "Karen's cutting a hole in the side. Once she's done, we should be able to see what's going on inside."

"All right." Matt paused. "Billy, I have some bad news."

Billy stepped away from the container so he could hear better. "What?"

"The student in St. Louis, the one who got sick?"

"Yeah?"

"He died an hour ago."

That wasn't unexpected, but Billy had hoped his prognosis had been wrong. "I'm sorry to hear that. What about the others?"

"That's actually the bad news."

"Oh, no. How many?"

"No other deaths yet, but the number of infected just reached one hundred percent."

Billy's lips parted in resignation. "All of them?"

"Yes."

"Dear God."

"Find us an answer there, Billy. We're counting on you."

A few minutes later, Karen turned off the torch and removed a two-and-a-half-foot-square section of the container's wall. As they'd seen on the scan, there was nothing in the immediate space beyond. Karen moved right up to the opening and slowly stuck her head inside.

"Careful," Billy said.

"There's a wire mesh netting about a foot away from me. Goes clear across. Looks like it's supposed to keep everything on the other side from moving into this part."

"What's it holding back?"

"Metal drums and hoses running between them, and…." She paused. "You know what I think?"

He was standing beside her now. "What?"

"This is *definitely* a delivery device. There are hoses hooked into rails along the top. Looks to me like what's in the barrels is supposed to be turned into an aerosol and shot through the roof. If the wind catches it, God knows how far it will spread." She twisted around and looked toward the short end of the box. "Huh."

"What is it?"

"Can you hand me a flashlight?"

She held out a hand without removing her head from the hole. Billy grabbed a flashlight from the case and gave it to her. She shined the beam around for a few seconds before extracting herself from inside.

"There's a control system mounted on the wall. I think I can hook into it with my laptop and download whatever information it might contain."

"Are you sure?"

"It's pretty straightforward. I don't think they ever expected anyone to get in like we did."

Though Billy wasn't as confident as she was, he nodded his agreement and reported to Matt, who agreed it was worth a try.

Karen retrieved a cable from the case, snipped off one end, and attached a different type of connector to it. She hooked the other end into her laptop, and motioned for Billy to stand right next to her.

"Hold the computer as close to the opening as you can, so I have as much play with the cable as possible."

"Sure."

Though a small woman, she was just barely able to get both her arms and head inside. She grunted a few times, her body stretching and twisting, then she let out a brief "Ha" of triumph, and pulled herself back out.

"Let's see what we've got," she said, turning the computer so she could type on the keyboard. It took several seconds, but finally she smiled. "I'm in."

Billy touched his earpiece. "We're linked into the container's computer."

"Excellent," Matt said, sounding relieved. "And?"

"Hold on. Karen's sorting through things right now."

"It's pretty bare bones," she said. "Looks like there's some kind of communication module. Most likely the way the Project remotely contacts the container. If we look hard enough, we'd probably find an antenna built into the roof." She paused. "Huh. What's this?"

Billy leaned over so he could see the screen, but it was full of unreadable code, at least to him.

She shook her head. "I think it's just a…wait a minute…" She stared at the screen, her eyes widening in concern.

"What is it?" Billy asked.

"I…I thought it was just a normal clock. You know, to sync computers. But…" She looked at him. "It's a countdown."

The reality of what she said hit him immediately. "How much

time?"

"No…no, this can't be right."

"Karen! How. Much. Time?"

She studied the readout and clicked a few keys. "Oh, shit. Run!"

—————————

BILLY HAD LEFT his mic on so Matt could hear everything.

"No…no, this can't be right," Karen said.

"Karen! How. Much. Time?"

A brief pause, then, "Oh, shit. Run!"

Before another word could be spoken, a loud rumble burst over the line, then the signal cut out.

"Billy?" Matt said. "Billy, can you hear me? What's going on there?"

"We've lost the signal," Leon said as he typed in commands on his computer, trying to reconnect the signal. "I can't get through. I don't know what's wrong."

Matt threw the headphones off. "Keep trying!" he ordered as he moved to the empty station on Leon's right.

The others in the communications room started crowding around Leon and Matt. Fearing the worst, Matt searched online for feeds from Cleveland-area radio stations. He found a news station, and pumped it through the external speakers.

For several tense minutes, there was nothing. Matt wanted to think it had just been an equipment failure, but couldn't. Then, as if to confirm his intuition, the announcer said, "We are just receiving reports of a large explosion south of the airport. As of yet, there is no information on the cause. We have a reporter on his way to the scene, and should have more in a few minutes."

Though there was no reason to listen any longer, Matt let the radio play. It was soon determined that the explosion did not involve any aircraft and seemed completely unconnected to the airport. According to the on-scene reporter, a two-block area of industrial-type buildings had taken the brunt of the damage. Unnamed fire department contacts said it had been a particularly intense blast, but so far no bodies had been discovered.

The people at the Ranch knew it wouldn't stay that way.

30

Ash WOULD NEVER again complain about the cold. Forget fire. The frigid Arctic was the true Hell.

"There it is," Gagnon said.

Ash peered out the windshield and could just make out the lump of Yanok Island on the horizon through the near perpetual darkness of late afternoon. They were flying low in hopes of keeping their arrival a surprise, the ocean a mere thirty feet below the bottom of the plane.

Before leaving Grise Fiord, Ash and Gagnon had gone over the map and decided their best approach would be from the southwest, the opposite end of the island from where the research station was located. Gagnon felt confident he could get the plane into the small inlet that was located at that point, and bring the team all the way up to the land. Ash was all for that. Anything that ensured solid ground under his feet was a good idea.

The closer they got to the island, the lower Gagnon took the plane, until it finally felt like they were just inches above the surface. As the pilot had warned them, the ice that had been missing from this part of the ocean only a week earlier had started to make its return, and the sea around Yanok was crusting over. The problem was, in some places it was barely an inch thick, while in others it was already over a foot.

"Hold on," Gagnon said. "This might be rough."

There was a handle next to Ash just below the window. He wrapped his fingers around it and squeezed tightly. He didn't look in back to see how Chloe and Red were doing, but he doubted they were any more comfortable with this than he was.

With the island still half a mile away, Gagnon lowered the plane onto the ice. As smooth as it looked from even a height of ten feet above, it wasn't. The craft jumped and lurched as it whipped across the frozen ocean. At one point, it leaped into the air for several feet before slamming back onto the surface. Still, the plane raced ahead.

"Shouldn't we be slowing?" Ash asked, his voice raised above the roar coming from outside.

"Working on it,"   Gagnon said.

With a bang, the right side of the plane raised into the air, the skid on that side having hit an uneven spot on the ice.

"Whoa! Whoa! Whoa!" Red called out from the back.

For a second it seemed like the plane was going to right itself, but then a gust of frigid wind caught the underside. The opposite wingtip dug into the ice, pivoting the plane briefly into the air before the craft smashed down on its back.

It skidded forward, twisting around and around.

Ash and the others hung upside down, caught in their seats by their straps and unable to do anything as the plane slid across the ice. He had no idea which direction they were heading. He only hoped it wasn't toward an area of open sea.

The wind and the engine and screeching of metal on ice blended together in a cacophony of chaos.

Someone yelled from the back, but whatever they were trying to say, Ash couldn't make it out. He tried to look back, but quickly gave up. The plane was jumping around too much, and all he ended up doing was knocking his head against the seat.

"Just hang on!" he yelled, knowing that wasn't much help.

A loud bang, then a groan from the right side of the plane. Their speed rapidly decreased and the spin nearly stopped. Ash turned his head enough so he could peer out the window. The wing on his side had apparently hit something and was now at a different angle to the plane than it had been earlier. If the crash itself had not already made the aircraft worthless, the damage done to the wing did. Ash knew it would never fly again.

Their speed continued dropping, until finally their forward

motion stopped altogether. The plane turned slowly for several seconds more, eating through the last bit of momentum.

The only noise now was the wind.

Ash caught his breath, and looked over at Gagnon. The pilot hung in his seat, unconscious.

"Anyone hurt?" Ash called to the back.

There was a pause, then Red said, "Just a cut on the side of my head. I think I'm okay."

"Chloe?"

"What?" she said.

"Are you all right?"

"I'm hanging upside down in a plane in the middle of the Arctic Ocean. No, I'm not all right. I want to get out!"

He had forgotten about her bouts of claustrophobia. "Out is a great idea. Careful when you unhook yourselves. First one out, make sure to check the ice first. I don't want anyone falling through."

There were grunts and groans from the back as the other two released themselves from their seats.

Ash used one hand to pull himself as tight to his seat as possible, then unhooked the belt with the other. Freed, he twisted as he fell so that he landed on his back. He flipped around and crawled over to Gagnon.

He felt for a pulse. The man was alive, but Ash didn't like the way he was breathing. He checked the pilot for any obvious wounds, and found a nasty gash on the man's leg and at least two broken ribs. Ash couldn't be certain, but he was willing to bet one of them had punctured a lung.

He tried to wake up Gagnon, but the most he got was a groan.

Cold air suddenly rushed into the cabin as someone opened the door. Ash could hear the person hop out onto the metal underside of the wing.

"Looks pretty thick here," Chloe called out.

Ash twisted around. "Can you see the island? How far are we?"

"Hold on. Let me check." Several seconds passed, then, "Can't make a damn thing out in the dark. Red, can you find me the night vision binoculars?"

"Sure."

Red rummaged around one of the packs that had fallen onto the roof, and handed the glasses out the door.

"Thanks," Chloe said.

"Red," Ash said. "Come up here. I could use your help."

Together they eased Gagnon out of his seat and laid him down on an open area of the ceiling.

"First-aid kit," Ash said.

Red quickly retrieved it.

Ash cleaned up Red's face first and slapped a butterfly bandage across the cut. Then they turned their attention to Gagnon. As they were patching up the pilot, Chloe returned to the doorway.

"Found it," she said. "The plane's facing away from it."

"How far?" Ash asked.

"At least half a mile."

A half-mile on its own didn't sound like much, but across the ice of the Arctic Ocean, in the wind and cold and dark? It sounded like forever.

"Okay, you and Red get the gear out. We'll also need to make a stretcher."

He finished up with Gagnon while the other two unloaded the plane. For the stretcher, they worked off a loose piece of sheeting from the wing, and attached ropes to it so they could pull it along the ground. To keep Gagnon from freezing against the metal, they lined it with the carpet from the cabin, and one of the spare jackets.

They headed out.

———

IT TOOK THEM over an hour to reach the cove that had been their initial destination. Ash knew he should feel relieved to have the solid ground of the inlet's beach underfoot instead of the ocean ice, but they still had to get up the incline that surrounded the small bay, so their work was far from done.

"I think our best bet is right over there," he said, pointing at a rise along the eastern end of the beach. The slope was slightly less vertical than elsewhere.

Getting Gagnon up the natural ramp was the hardest part.

They ended up having to carry him and bring the sled separately.

Once they were finally on top, Ash pulled out the satellite phone and first tried to reach Pax, then the Ranch. As with the few times he'd tried during their journey across the ice, he couldn't get through.

"Hey, did you see this?" Red called out.

He was back near the slope they'd just taken.

Ash put the phone back in his pack. "What is it?"

"Looks like boot prints. Couldn't have been made too long ago. They aren't filled with snow yet."

Though they'd hit some storms further south in Canada, the weather reports Gagnon had pulled together indicated that Yanok Island, a thousand miles to the north, had not experienced the same. The forecast did predict that was soon to change.

"Which way were they headed?"

"Can't tell." Red stopped and leaned down. "What's this?"

Ash and Chloe moved next to him for a closer look.

There was a five-inch-wide band of puncture marks in the ice that came out from under a pile of snow next to the boot prints and headed north.

"That pile doesn't look natural to me," Chloe said.

"I was thinking the same thing," Ash agreed.

Using the entrenching tool that had been strapped to his pack, Ash broke off some of the looser pieces of the pile and shoved them to the side. The other two joined in. After a few minutes, they stopped.

"What the hell is this doing here?" Chloe asked.

Under the pile of snow was a highly modified motorcycle with metal-studded tires.

"Yellow team's," Ash said as way of explanation.

Before leaving the Ranch, he had been fully briefed on all aspects of the missing team's mission, including what gear they'd brought.

He knelt down and took a closer look at the ground around where the bike had been buried. It was possible that yellow team ditched its cycle and covered it up, but he was sure that wasn't the case. Yellow team had consisted of only two men. By his count, there were at least five distinct sets of boot prints surrounding the pile.

No, yellow team hadn't done this. Someone else had. Someone who didn't want the motorcycle to be seen again.

———————

THEY FOLLOWED THE tire tracks to a rocky overhang that had been walled off with tarps and snow. What they discovered inside left Ash with zero doubt that Bluebird was located on Yanok Island.

It was the yellow team's camp, and it had been deserted in a hurry.

They put Gagnon into a sleeping bag on one of the cots first, then did a thorough search. Food and weapons and sleeping bags and spare clothes were all still there.

"No radio," Red said.

Ash scanned the room again. Red was right.

"If I was trying to get out of here fast," Chloe said, "that's the only thing I would grab."

"The question is, why leave in a hurry?" Ash said.

No response was necessary. They were all thinking the same thing.

"See if there's any kind of journal or notes anywhere," Ash said.

He stepped back outside and took another look around. Unlike near the buried motorcycle, there weren't a lot of boot prints. More likely than not, Bluebird hadn't even looked for the camp. And why would they? They had everything they wanted—the boat, radio, and codes they'd obviously learned from the yellow team that had allowed them to send the false messages to the Ranch.

Back inside, he found Red and Chloe looking at a map of the island spread across one of the open sleeping bags. Though identical to the one they'd brought with them, it had seen considerably more use.

Ash knelt down beside them.

"This mark right here," Red said, pointing at a blue circle on the map. "That's where we are. Which puts us about three miles from them." He moved his finger to the north end of the island,

and tapped on the words BRULE INSTITUTE OUTPOST.

A gust of wind whipped past the opening, blowing in some snow. Chloe walked quickly over and pulled down on the tarp rigged to fully enclose the shelter. Using two rocks on the ground, she anchored the bottom so the covering wouldn't flap around.

"Not exactly a pleasure walk," Ash said to Red.

"Hence the motorcycle."

"We don't have that option." Ash stood up. He could see the weariness in the others' faces, and knew his looked the same. His initial plan had been to get as close to the outpost as possible after Gagnon dropped them off. The crash and subsequent hike threw a wrench in that. "A few hours' sleep. No more. Then Chloe, you and I pay our Project Eden friends a visit."

31

THE MOOD AT the Ranch was somber. Billy might have been a disagreeable sort at times, but his heart had always been in the right place, and he'd been part of the team trying to stop the Project since early on. In his role as doctor, he had treated nearly everyone there, so in one way or another, he had touched all of their lives.

That, of course, was not to diminish the loss of Karen Pruitt. She had also been a valuable team member, and there were those at the Ranch who had been very close to her.

But for Matt, losing Billy was like losing a brother. It was simply…inconceivable.

If not for the fact the day they had been both fighting against was looming, he would have been sitting alone in his room, numb to everything around him. He couldn't afford that now. None of them could.

At the moment, there were teams all around the world trying to find ways of stopping, or, at the very least, limiting the damage from the plague the Project was about to unleash. Which was why Matt was in the communications room, monitoring events. But even knowing that automated shipping containers were one way the virus would be spread, his people were having very little luck finding them. Jordan had been able to track down a handful, but it was just a drop in the ocean. The containment, if that was even possible, would only be a moral victory at most.

"What's the latest on Ash's team?" Matt asked.

The man assigned to monitor the Arctic mission was Oscar Guerrero. "The last report was that Pax's group had already been taken to Amund Ringnes Island, and that Ash and his group were about to leave for Yanok. We should be getting another report at any time."

"Let me know as soon as that happens."

"Yes, sir."

Matt doubted Ash would even find Bluebird, let alone get inside and do something to stop Implementation Day, but he hoped, oh God, he hoped. It was, after all, the only way the coming hell could be avoided.

"Matt?"

He turned and found Jordan standing a few feet away, a closed laptop in his hand by his hip. If anyone had taken Billy's death harder than Matt, it was Jordan. He clearly felt responsible since he was the one who had found the container. Matt had told him he had nothing to do with Billy's and Karen's deaths, that finding the container had been vitally important. It didn't seem to help.

But now, Jordan looked different, almost excited.

"What's up?"

Jordan took a hesitant step forward. "I think I might have figured it out."

"Figured what out?"

"How they're distributing everything."

"We already know it's the containers, at least in part."

"No, no. I mean *who.*"

"Who?"

"The front."

Matt stared at him.

"Here. Let me show you."

Jordan set his laptop on Matt's desk. As soon as it was open, a web browser page appeared for Hidde-Kel, the company whose factory the container that killed Billy had come from.

"We already know Hidde-Kel's the front," Matt said.

"Not the front. *A* front. I know how we can identify the others."

He brought up a new page. It was a map of an area surrounded by four rivers.

"Recognize it?" Jordan asked.

"No."

"There are hundreds of variations, so that's understandable. This is Eden."

"Eden?"

"Yes. These four rivers are the Pishon, Gihon, Tigris, and Euphrates."

"Okay. So?"

"The Tigris and Euphrates had different names when the story was written. The Euphrates was called the Phrath, and the Tigris the Hiddekel. Hidde. Kel."

Matt felt the skin on his face tighten. Project Eden had taken its name from the Christian version of the origins of man, when people were few and resources plentiful. Had they used the reference beyond that?

"I found several other companies around the world utilizing the name Hiddekel or Hidde-Kel, and one even using Hid-de-kel. Not all of them are involved, but some definitely are. And that's not all. I broadened the search and found suspect companies using Gihon, Phrath, and Pishon as part of their name."

He brought up another web page. The header read PISHON CHEM.

"This company has supposedly developed a spray that it says will eradicate mosquitoes carrying malaria. It's hired thousands of locals and is going to do a trial in dozens of major cities throughout Southeast Asia, South Asia, and Africa." Jordan looked over at Matt. "It's scheduled for Friday."

It was as if every centimeter of Matt's skin had gone numb. Not only had Jordan potentially discovered how to ID those distributing the virus, he had also turned up a date.

Friday was the day after tomorrow.

Then Matt realized something else—it was also the day before Christmas Eve. In the predominantly Christian countries, the streets would be full of shoppers, easy targets for the virus.

"We've only got two days?" Matt said. It wasn't nearly enough.

"No," Jordan said. "Not two days. Friday starts in some of these countries in less than six hours."

32

LOCAL TIME 12:24 P.M.

SANJAY DIDN'T RETURN to the dormitory after he found Ayush. Instead, he fled to the slum where he grew up and hid in the small, single room that belonged to Ayush. He stayed there all the next day, then through another night, scared out of his mind.

Sage Flu. Ayush. The spray. Kusum.

Sleep came in fits and starts—an hour here, another there—only occurring when his exhaustion momentarily won out over his fear. But it never lasted long.

The last thing he'd eaten was the *pani puri* he had in front of the building on Gamdevi Road. That was over thirty-sixty hours earlier, and though he still wasn't hungry, he knew he should eat something. He began rummaging through Ayush's things, and had just discovered a warm bottle of cola when a rumble of voices and shouts began moving in his direction.

He moved to the doorway and sneaked a look outside. The narrow passageway that ran in front of Ayush's home was lined on either side by the huts that had been built with whatever material could be found—metal, wood, rubber, plastic, paper. It snaked off both ways so that Sanjay could see only thirty or forty feet in either direction.

The noise seemed to be coming from the right. He leaned farther out until he was able to see a sliver of the alley another seventy feet down. Everything looked normal—a few people passing by, and the back of a woman who seemed to be talking to someone. Then suddenly the woman jerked around and pressed against one of the homes as three men walked by. The two in front were big and angry-looking. But it was the one behind them, the European man, who made Sanjay race out of Ayush's room and down the passageway in the other direction. It was the mean, older man from the Pishon Chem compound. The senior manager.

They had to be looking for him. They must have figured out he was the one who'd discovered his cousin. Of course, he'd made it easy, not showing up at work. That was all the admission of guilt they needed.

Staying under the shelter of the slum, Sanjay cut back and forth through several alleys, trying to get as far away from the men as possible. When he finally reached an opening to the street, he paused, checking the road to make sure no one was out there waiting for him.

It appeared to be clear, so he sprinted across, and into another warren of huts on the other side.

When he emerged again twenty minutes later, he knew his only choice was to get out of the city. Subconsciously he touched the top of the pouch that he'd stuffed in his pocket. Inside were the syringes the woman had filled from the same vial of vaccine he'd made her take a shot from. He hadn't been sure at first whether to believe her story, that the contents of the barrels he and the others were going to spray around the city was not intended to kill mosquitoes but the residents themselves. It seemed too crazy to even consider. But there, on the other side of the plastic wall, had been his cousin and the men who had been working with him, all suffering from a severe flu. And now, the people from Pishon had come after *him*.

Get out of the city. It was the only thing he could do to survive. But there was something else he needed to do first.

When he reached the market, he feared Kusum wouldn't be there. Then, as soon as he saw her, he feared he wouldn't be able to talk her into coming with him. The plan he'd thought up while he was running seemed weak now, but he had nothing better.

"Sanjay," she said as he approached. "What are you doing here? Shouldn't you be at work?"

"Not today," he said. "They have given me the day off, for working so hard."

Kusum's mother was sitting nearby. "Really? Since when do companies give time off for working hard? Isn't that what you are supposed to do?"

He forced a smile. "Apparently they do it differently in Europe."

"A waste of a good day, I think."

It was too good of a lead to pass on. "For them," he said, "but not for me."

"Oh? And why is that?"

"Because I can take you and Kusum to lunch as a thank you for your kindness."

"And who would watch the shop?" Kusum's mother asked.

"Is no one else coming today?" He already knew the answer. On Thursdays it was just the two of them.

"Do you see anyone else?"

Sanjay bowed his head. "I'm sorry. I had only been hoping. You cannot go, so I understand." He glanced at Kusum, then back at the mother. "Unless…it would be okay…"

The mother raised an eyebrow. "For you to take Kusum alone?"

"It would only be for lunch."

"And how long would you be gone?"

"An hour. Two at the most."

"Two? And I am to be here alone the whole time?"

"Mother," Kusum said. "Don't worry. I will stay with you."

Her mother huffed under her breath. "You would only mope around here all day if I don't let you go."

"So she can?" Sanjay asked.

The mother gave him a sideways glance. "As if this was not your plan all along. Yes, she can go."

"Thank you," Kusum said, smiling.

"Don't tell your father. He won't be happy."

"Of course."

Sanjay wanted to rush Kusum out, but he let her take her time making sure there was nothing else her mother needed her to do. Finally, they were walking through the market toward the street.

"And where will we go to eat?" she asked.

"Someplace special."

"Really?"

He nodded, worried if he said anything more, he would give himself away.

When they reached the street, it took him only a few minutes to find someone who would rent a motorbike to him.

Surprised, Kusum said, "Are we going far?"

"A little far, but don't worry. You'll like it."

She seemed a little hesitant, but climbed onto the back of the bike and put her hands on his waist.

An hour later, as they were riding—now heading east out of the city—she demanded to know where he was taking her. It was another hour, though, before he pulled onto a side road and they got off.

"Take me back! Take me back right now!" she demanded.

"I can't."

"Why not? Are you kidnapping me? My parents do not have any money."

"I'm not kidnapping you. I'm saving you."

"What do you mean? Saving me?"

Without warning, he stabbed the needle into her arm and depressed the plunger. She tried to pull away, but he injected all the vaccine before she did.

"What is this?" she asked, staggering back from him. "Are you drugging me? What is *wrong* with you, Sanjay?"

"I'm not drugging you. I told you, I'm saving your life."

He put the other needle into his own arm.

"What is that stuff?"

"A vaccine."

"A vaccine? For what?"

When he told her, she didn't believe him.

Not at first.

33

Palmer GROANED. THE phone was ringing again. How was he supposed to ever get out of there if he had to keep answering it?

As usual, he was the last one in the office. He'd been hoping that in another five minutes, he'd be out the door and on his way to his friend Curtis's house for the waiting beer and steak he'd been promised. But the damn phone! Every time it rang, it pushed his departure back further and further. Unfortunately, as the owner, he couldn't quite bring himself to let calls go to voice mail if he was actually there. You never knew when the opportunity for new work might come in.

On the third ring, he grabbed the receiver. "Palmer Transport & Shipping. This is John Palmer."

"Mr. Palmer, thank God you're still there. This is Jordan Evans with the World Health Organization."

Palmer paused, caught off guard. "I'm sorry. Where?"

"WHO. The World Health Organization."

Palmer leaned back. Maybe this *was* more work.

"And what can Palmer Transport do for the World Health Organization?"

"We understand that you may have been hired to do some work for a company called Hidde-Kel Holdings. Is that correct?"

Frowning, Palmer said, "I don't make it a habit to talk about clients."

"But Hidde-Kel *is* a client, right?"

"I've done some work for them. Why is that important?"

"Did it involve the transportation of any shipping containers?"

"That's a large part of the work we do here, so it wouldn't be unusual."

"And where did you take them?"

"Listen, Mr. Evans. I don't care who you are with. If you don't tell me why you're asking these things, I'll hang up right now."

Silence at first, then, "There was apparently a mix-up when Hidde-Kel's containers were loaded. We believe the contents have been contaminated with material that was meant to be shipped to the Centers for Disease Control in the States."

Centers for Disease Control?

"What kind of…material are we talking about?"

"Contagious material."

"*What?*"

"Mr. Palmer, some, if not all, of the containers you handled for Hidde-Kel could be extremely harmful to whoever opens them up."

"This is a joke, right? Who is this, really?"

"I'm sorry, Mr. Palmer. I wish it were a joke."

Palmer was stunned.

"There's another problem," Evans said. "According to our experts here, there's a good chance that by tomorrow, the contamination will leak out of the containers and affect anyone nearby." He paused. "Are you there?"

"I'm here," Palmer said.

"Listen very carefully. We need you to collect all of the containers that came through your facility and—"

"I'm not going to let my men near those things!"

"I understand your feelings, but I can assure you that at this point, your men won't be harmed. You have a chance to do something about this. If you don't, and it starts to affect others tomorrow, *you* will be responsible."

"Don't you try to put this on me."

"I'm not," Evans said. "You're just in the unfortunate position of being caught in the middle. The people who will blame you will be the media when they realize who put the containers in their neighborhoods. How long do you think your business could last after that happened?"

As much as Palmer hated to admit it, the man was right. It wouldn't matter that he'd just been doing the job he was hired to do. Once he was associated with any problems—or, God forbid, deaths—he'd be ruined.

"What…what do I do with them once I have them?"

"You need to dump them in the sea so that they are completely submerged."

"I'm sorry. Dump them in the sea?"

"It's a drastic measure, but the only one that will ensure no one is harmed. We have dispatched a crisis team to your location, but they won't arrive until tomorrow. They'll deal with things at that point. But *all* the containers need to be disposed tonight."

"Tonight? Do you realize what time it is? It's getting on nine p.m."

"This is a health emergency, Mr. Palmer. The time of day is not important."

Palmer thought for a moment. He could probably round up enough drivers to get the containers in the Perth area, but elsewhere? "Some of the containers are quite far away. I don't see how I could possibly get them all tonight."

"It doesn't matter where they are. It *needs* to happen. Can you do it?"

Palmer stared blankly at the wall across from his desk. "I'll…try."

"Good. Let me give the number you can call if you have any further questions."

————

THERE WERE NEARLY two dozen people in the Bunker making calls around the world, doing whatever they could to put a dent in the Project's plans.

As soon as Jordan hung up, Matt asked, "Did he buy it?"

"I think so."

"Will he be able to do it, though?"

"He wasn't sure, but he was going to try."

"Okay," Matt said, wishing the answer had been more definitive. "Don't let me stop you."

Jordan nodded, looked down at his list, and dialed the next number.

———————

PALMER LOOKED OUT his window at the night sky.

Contaminated. Extremely harmful to whoever opens them.

How the hell had that happened?

He turned back around and reached for his phone, intending to call his assistant Cora at home and have her get as many drivers as quickly as possible, but he paused, his fingers touching the handset.

Why hadn't Mr. Vanduffel called him about this? Did the people at Hidde-Kel Holdings not even know? That seemed unlikely.

He hesitated a few seconds longer then called Cora anyway, so that the drivers would be ready to go. As soon as he finished with her, he dialed a much longer number.

"Hidde-Kel Holdings," a male voice said.

"Mr. Vanduffel, please."

"May I tell him who's calling?"

"John Palmer. Palmer Transport & Shipping in Perth."

"One moment, Mr. Palmer."

It was over a minute before the line clicked.

"Mr. Palmer? I didn't expect to hear from you. Is there a problem?"

"A big problem. Why didn't you tell me your containers are contaminated?"

Silence. "Did something happen?"

"I got a phone call is what happened, from someone at the World Health Organization. He tells me your containers are contaminated and I need to dump them in the sea before tomorrow."

More silence. "Who exactly called you?"

"A man named Jordan Evans."

"Did he give you a number?"

"Have you not heard from them?"

"No. We haven't."

"So you know nothing about this?"

"Not a thing."

Palmer frowned. "I thought they'd have called you first."

"Of course they would have. Which leads me to believe this Mr. Evans isn't who he claims to be."

"So you think he was lying about them behind contaminated?"

"Mr. Palmer, I can assure you, the only things in those containers are what *we* put there. Whatever this man told you is a lie. Now, could you give me the phone number? I'd like to check it out."

After hanging up, Palmer didn't know what to think. If Mr. Evans had truly been from the WHO, surely he would have called Hidde-Kel by now, but could Palmer take the chance of ignoring the warning?

There was one thing he could do that might answer the question. Check out one of the containers himself. If he took appropriate precautions, he should be able to protect himself from anything inside. The closest one was only ten minutes away, right in Perth.

Making up his mind, he called Cora again. "I'll be back in thirty minutes. Just tell everyone to hold tight until I return."

"Can I at least tell them what you want them to do?"

"I'll explain everything when I get back."

He never got that chance. The explosion that killed him when he opened the container meant that no one at Palmer Transport & Shipping knew anything about Mr. Evans's warning.

34

"ROWAN, REPORT," SECURITY officer Phillips said into the radio.

Nothing.

"Rowan, this is base. Are you receiving me?"

No response.

Rowan was a minute overdue checking in. Ten minutes ago, in his last report, he had made no indication of problems, radio or otherwise, but with the severe conditions on Yanok Island, that could change in seconds.

"Rowan, this is base. Report."

Still receiving no response, Phillips contacted the watch officer. This being the day it was, the DOP's personal aide, Major Ross, was serving in the role.

Ross's voice came over the receiver. "This is the watch officer."

"I have a non-response from perimeter security."

"Who's out there?"

"Benjamin Rowan, sir."

"How long is he overdue?"

Phillips glanced at the clock on his screen. "Two minutes."

The patrol officers were drilled on keeping religiously to their check-in schedules, so even a delay of half a minute was unusual.

"Had he reported any previous problems?"

"No, sir."

"Send out a search team."

"Yes, sir. Right away."

35

ASH CHECKED THE map, then nodded ahead. "We should be able to see the outpost from that ridge."

Chloe gave him a nod, but said nothing, conserving her strength.

Around them, the wind was gusting, pushing at their backs as if urging them onward.

When they finally neared the top of the ridge, they dropped to their stomachs and inched the rest of the way up. The outpost was right where he'd expected it, about a quarter-mile away. It was a large structure, clad in snow, with light streaming out through several windows. There was no one visible through them, but it was early so that wasn't surprising.

"They're not going to be expecting anyone at this time of morning," Chloe said. "Might be a good time to try and get in close."

Ash pulled out their binoculars, flipped them to night vision, and surveyed the landscape ahead. Between the ridge and the outpost, there was no place to hide except against the building itself. As he searched for some way they might be able to sneak in, he couldn't help but wonder how many people they'd have to get through to stop the Project's plan before it could begin.

Stop it, he told himself. *One task at a time. Just get to the building, and then you can figure out what's next.*

"Take a look," he said.

As he handed the binoculars to Chloe, something crunched on

the ice behind them.

He whirled around just in time to see the dark shape of a man rushing at him. He tried to roll out of the way, but the person piled into his shoulder, knocking him flat on his stomach.

He shoved back against the man's chest, hoping to push him off so he could get away, but the guy was not only big, he was strong. The attacker pulled Ash to his feet, lifted him in the air, and slammed him back into the hard ice. For several seconds, Ash lay there, unable to move.

As soon as he could, he turned his head to look for Chloe, hoping she'd gotten away. But she was pinned to the ground, by a clone of the guy who'd jumped Ash.

Footsteps again, crunching toward him. Then a new figure stood above him. A hand went up to the face and removed the protective mask. A flashlight flicked on, and suddenly he could see who it was.

"Ash. What a nice surprise," Olivia Silva said.

———

THE LAST AND only time Ash had seen Olivia in person was through a transparent wall that looked into the cell she lived in beneath the Bluff. Now their positions were reversed and he was the captive.

"I understand my information helped, and you were able to save your kids," she said.

He and Chloe were on their feet now, three armed men standing behind them to make sure they didn't try to run.

"It did. Thank you," he said, meaning it.

"And my message? Were you able to deliver it?"

Her only request had been that he give a message to the man who'd taken Ash's children, the same man who had left Olivia to be captured by Matt's people.

"I did."

"Good. I knew I could count on you."

No one said anything for a moment. Then Ash asked, "So are you going to shoot us here? Or take us inside so your friends can watch?"

"Friends?" she asked, as if she didn't understand. Then her

eyes widened and she smiled. "Oh, I see. Who do you think freed me from my prison?"

"We know who freed you," Chloe said. "Assholes from Project Eden."

"I agree with your assessment of them," Olivia said, "but they weren't the ones who freed me. It was my friends. Others who had become…disenchanted by the Project."

Ash looked at her warily. "Then what are you doing here?"

Her gaze turned momentarily in the direction of the outpost hidden behind the ridge. "I have no love for anyone in that building," she whispered. She looked back at Ash and said in a stronger voice, "I have a feeling you and I have a similar goal."

"I doubt it."

"Oh, come, now. Don't you want to get inside?"

Ash said nothing.

"I thought as much." She stood up again. "The only way you'll get in there is with my help."

"And why would you help us?"

She said nothing for several seconds, then, "Because the last thing I want is for the people who left me to die to be in control of the world they're trying to create. I'm here to kill them. I assume that's why you're here, too."

There was an edge to her words, a hatred that made him know she was telling the truth. "We're here to stop them," he said.

She grinned, her eyes twinkling. "Given the circumstances, isn't that pretty much the same thing?"

Ash remained silent.

"So are you coming with us?" she asked.

He glanced at Chloe. He could see she was reluctant, but had also come to the same conclusion he had.

"We'll come with you."

36

THE DOP WAS furious. "I should have been told about this immediately!"

"Yes, sir," Ross said. "I'm sorry. I thought you might want a bit more rest before the day began."

Not just any day, *the* day. Implementation Day. There, in the bowels of Bluebird, it was eight fifteen a.m. on December 22nd, but in a little less than three hours, at eleven a.m. Central Standard Time, it would be six in the morning in New Zealand on the 23rd— given the island country's proximity to the International Dateline, it was designated as the initial release location of KV-27a. At that moment, the DOP would enter the Go code into the system and messages would be sent across the globe—activating timers on the IDMs and other automated delivery devices so that they would begin releasing their contents at the busiest time of the day, and notifying those teams who were relying on manpower to spread the virus, such as the spraying operations in Africa and Southern and Southeast Asia, and plane operations scattered all across the world.

Ross had been right to let him sleep. It was a momentous day, one at which the entire directorate of Project Eden would be present to witness from the start. What he didn't like, however, was beginning this day of all days with news like this.

The suit he was going to wear had been laid out the night before. He grabbed his shirt, yanked it on, and started buttoning it up. "How? How could this happen?"

"We're…not sure yet."

From his bed, the DOP picked up the paper detailing the conversation between the Australian transport company owner and the Project member who had been his contact. "This phone number——anything on that?"

"It's a dummy. It reroutes half a dozen times then splits in several directions. Basically untraceable."

The DOP snagged his pants off the hanger. "It's them. I know it is," he said, sure the people who had been a thorn in the Project's side had just taken things to an unacceptable level.

"I agree."

"Major Ross, since everything is in place now, surely we can spare some manpower to deal with them."

Ross nodded. "Actually, sir, I've already pulled together an assault team, and they're en route to the Montana location right now."

The DOP strung his tie around his collar, tied the knot, and pulled on his jacket. He looked over his shoulder at Ross, locking eyes with his aide. "I want them dead. All of them. And not by the virus."

"Yes, sir. I understand. I'll make sure that happens."

"You had better. Is there anything else?"

Ross seemed to hesitate, but then shook his head. "No, sir. That's it."

37

BLUEBIRD TIME 8:39 A.M.

TWICE THEY HAD to lie low to avoid patrols, so it took over an hour and a half to reach the camp Olivia and her people had set up three-quarters of a mile to the southeast of Bluebird. Ash could feel every passing second, and knew they needed to keep moving, but Olivia had been in no hurry to start out again. If he had known how to get into the building himself, he and Chloe would have been long gone.

Finally, Olivia deemed it was time. The hike took them to the coast, then along the hilly edge. She still didn't seem to be in any hurry. He tried to get her to pick up the pace, but she only said, "Don't worry. We'll be there right on time."

Finally, Olivia stopped them and sent two of her men ahead.

"Usually they don't guard the entrance we're going to use. It's almost impossible to get into, but I guess that's to be expected today."

"What do you mean today?"

She looked at him, amusement in her eyes. "Why do you think?"

"This is it?" he asked. "Implementation Day?"

"Oh, very good."

"How much time do we have?"

An exaggerated look of pain clouded her eyes. "Don't you trust me? I told you, we'll be there on time."

Chloe leaned toward Ash and whispered just loudly enough for him to hear, "I *don't* trust her."

"Can you at least tell us what the plan is?" he asked.

Before he knew if she would answer or not, her men returned. She conferred with them for several seconds, nodded, and said to the rest, "Looks like we're all set. This way."

The new path led along the face of a cliff, sloping downward until it dead-ended at a pile of snow-covered rocks that went all the way to the ice of the ocean.

When Olivia started climbing down, Ash called out, "How are we supposed to get to the outpost from there?"

"I guess you'll have to see, won't you?" she yelled back.

She continued down, her people following without question.

"I don't like this," Chloe said.

Ash shook his head. "Neither do I. But what choice do we have?"

They caught up to Olivia on a narrow strip of land that ran above the beach about twenty feet. The path wasn't a natural occurrence, but had been carved out of the cliff face. The darkness made it difficult to see ahead, but it appeared that the trail simply ended after fifty feet.

"We should probably hurry," Olivia called out as she neared the end of the path. "Less than twenty-five minutes left."

"Are you joking?" Ash asked.

"Why would I joke?"

With a step to her left, she disappeared.

The path, it turned out, led to the opening of a cave in the cliff that had been almost invisible in the darkness. As Ash and Chloe stepped inside, several of the others turned on flashlights, giving them a better look at their surroundings. Not a cave, Ash realized, but a manmade tunnel. And on the ground just inside were two bodies. The guards, Ash guessed.

Olivia took the lead again, and didn't stop until they reached a secure-looking metal door mounted in the tunnel wall. The door had no handle, and whatever hinges it swung on were either recessed in the metal frame or were on the inside. For all intents, it was impassible.

Olivia stepped over to the wall several feet from the door. Putting her hands on part of the rocky surface, she began moving them counterclockwise. To Ash's surprise, the rock underneath turned with her, then hinged open. In the space where it had been was a twelve-inch-square monitor with a single button at the bottom.

"The box," Olivia said.

One of her men came forward, carrying a long case almost the size of a box for roses.

"Warm it up," she told him.

He undid the clasps and opened it. Whatever Ash thought would be inside, a severed forearm with a hand still attached wasn't it.

"What the hell is that for?" Chloe said.

Without answering, the man removed a device from the bag he'd been carrying on his back and flipped a switch on the side. It started to hum, faintly at first, but grew louder as the seconds passed. Once one of the ends started glowing red, he hit another button, doubling the strength of the noise, and aimed the glowing end at the hand.

He let this go on for half a minute, then touched the palm with a small plastic strip. Seemingly unsatisfied, he aimed the device at the hand again for another thirty seconds. This time, after he put the strip against it, he said, "Ready."

Olivia turned back to the screen, but instead of pressing the button at the bottom, she tapped the monitor in the upper right corner twice, and once in the middle. As soon as she lifted her finger the last time, the screen came to life.

She tapped twice more, and each time the screen changed as soon as she was done. She then motioned for the man holding the arm to join her. She moved the fingers of the detached hand just enough so that there was separation between each, and pressed the palm and fingers against the screen.

Nothing happened for a moment, then there was a loud *clunk*, and the door began to swing open.

Olivia smiled at Ash. "After you."

38

MATT STARED AT the world map on his computer screen. Marked on it were the locations where companies with variations on the names Hiddekel, Pishon, Gihon, and Phrath had been conducting suspicious operations that had so far gone undiscovered. While there were many marks, they represented only a fraction of the number that he knew must have been out there. Worse yet, Matt's people were having spotty luck getting through to people who might be able to do something about those they did know. And even when they did reach someone, convincing them that something terrible was about to happen was more miss than hit.

"Mr. Hamilton?"

Matt looked up. Everyone seemed to be busy at the different stations. "Who called me?"

"I did, sir." A hand went up across the room.

Matt stood up. "What is it?"

"Security breach, sir. PB position two."

PB was the codename assigned to the dirt road leading to the Ranch. Position two would mean whoever it was would already be halfway to the Lodge from the highway.

"Do you have visual?"

"They'll be coming up on a video point in about fifteen seconds."

"Route it to one of the TVs."

"Yes, sir."

There was a delay of five seconds, then the monitor on the

end of the table filled with an image of the empty dirt road.

"Sir, second contact."

"Also on PB?"

"No, sir, from the southwest, but coming fast and low. I think it's a helicopter."

On the screen, three large SUVs suddenly appeared. Though it was impossible to tell for sure, each looked like it was filled with men wearing helmets and holding weapons.

Matt shoved himself out of his chair. "Get everyone who's outside into the Bunker *now* and lock us up tight! I don't want whoever is coming this way to get even a hint of where any of the entrances are."

The alarm began blaring throughout the Bunker to let everyone know they were about to seal things up.

"Prep full cover," Matt said.

Silence descended on the room.

"Are…are you sure, sir?" one of the men asked.

"I said prep, I didn't say set it off. But if I do, I don't want any hesitation."

"Yes, sir."

Full cover would mean igniting both the Lodge and the dormitory so that they would burn down on top of two of the entrances to the Bunker. The third entrance, accessed via a long tunnel, would be left open unless it was found. If that happened, it could be collapsed once the intruders were inside.

"Let me know as soon as everyone is in," he said.

"Sir, another contact. Looks like a second helicopter. Coming from the northeast."

Rachel rushed into the room. "What's going on?"

"Someone's coming at us."

"Who?"

He looked at her. "I'll give you one guess."

"We don't know that for sure."

"If we could find them, they certainly could find us."

"Sir, fourth contact." It was yet another helicopter.

"Is everyone back inside yet?"

"Jon Hayes is still out there. He went to the barn to check on the horses."

"Get him on the radio."

Several seconds passed. "I've patched him through to the speaker, sir."

"Jon, this is Matt. Where are you?"

"Running up from the barn."

"How long will it take you to get here?"

"Three minutes."

Matt glanced at the center screen. The security image from the road had been replaced by a map of the Ranch, with moving dots representing the contacts heading their way. Three minutes would be too late.

"You're not going to make it," he said. "You'll have to—"

"Matt, I'm not alone. Brandon Ash came with me."

Ash's son? "Who authorized that?"

"No one. He was going a little stir-crazy, so I thought maybe if he helped me with the horses, he'd feel better. I...I didn't think anyone was going to show up like this."

No one had thought that, but still, taking the kid out? What was Matt going to tell Ash?

"You need to hide. *Now.* When it's clear, get to one of the emergency supply dumps in the woods, fill up a pack, and hike out. They may keep coming back, so it's your only chance. After you're away, operate under emergency contact conditions. Do not, I repeat, do not try to come back here."

"What about you?"

Matt hesitated. He could no longer ignore what was heading their way. "We're going full cover right now." He nodded at the man monitoring the security system, confirming the order.

"I understand. Good luck."

"Jon. Don't let anything happen to the kid."

"I won't."

———————

"THEY'RE NOT GOING to let us back in?" Brandon asked, trying not to sound as scared as he felt.

"There's no time," Hayes said. "You hear the helicopters?"

Brandon nodded. Distant *thump-thump-thumps* were coming from several directions.

"We'd never make it back before they got here. It's okay, though. Don't worry. We just need to hide out until they're gone." Hayes looked around quickly. "This way." He started for the woods south of the path.

"What about the horses?" Brandon asked.

"They'd see us if we were on them."

"No, no. I mean, won't the others see the barn? Couldn't the horses be in danger?"

"I'm sure no one will bother them."

He took another step toward the trees, but Brandon held his ground. "We *can't* leave them there! Mr. Hamilton said they were going to full cover. I know what that is. I've been trying to learn everything so I could help if I was needed. If they get rid of all the ways in and out of the Bunker, who's going to feed the horses? Don't you see? We have to at least let them go so they can take care of themselves."

Hayes stared at him, and sighed. It was only a minute back to the barn. Chances were, the people in the helicopters would head straight for the Lodge, buying Hayes and the kid a little more time.

Hayes couldn't help also feeling a little ashamed with himself. Brandon was right. Leaving the horses pent-up would be inhumane. The two of them could probably let the animals out and slip into the woods to the east without anyone ever suspecting they were there.

He stepped quickly back on the path.

"If I yell 'hide,' you run as fast as you can for the closest trees, you understand?"

"So we'll let the horses out?"

Hayes nodded.

———————

AS SOON AS the alarm went off, Josie went looking for her brother.

Surprisingly, he wasn't in any of the places he usually hung out. Thinking that maybe he'd gone to the communications room to see what was going on, she headed there. A quick scan of those present revealed that Brandon wasn't one of them.

She walked quickly up to Rachel. "Miss Hamilton? I can't find my brother."

Rachel looked surprised to see her, then her face turned serious. "I don't want you to worry. He'll be okay."

The words had the exact opposite effect. "What do you mean?"

"He's outside," Rachel said. She put a hand on Josie's arm. "But Jon Hayes is with him and will take care of him."

Josie pulled back. "Somebody needs to go get them."

"We can't, Josie. We're being attacked."

Josie's eyes went wide. "A...attacked? But you just said Brandon's still out there."

"He's going to hide in the woods. They won't know he's there."

"You've got to let him back in! You've got to!"

She ran out of the room, not waiting to hear any more. She headed straight for the exit that would take her up to the basement of the Lodge. But when she got there, a massive door that had never been closed blocked the way to the exit.

She headed for one of the other two ways out of the building, but it, too, was sealed tight. And, she soon found out, so was the last.

She stared at the door, not knowing what to do. Her father had wanted her to watch over Brandon, but now she couldn't even get to him.

WITHOUT ANOTHER WORD, Brandon and Hayes sprinted down the path, and rushed into the barn just as one of the helicopters came into sight.

"Don't move," Hayes ordered Brandon. The man peeked outside through a crack between two of the boards. "Dammit."

"What's wrong?"

"I think they might have seen us. They're coming this way. I'm an idiot. We should have stayed in the trees until they passed by."

Outside, Brandon could hear the beat of the helicopter rotors drawing nearer.

Hayes suddenly grabbed Brandon by the arm. "Come on."

They raced back to the horse stalls, stopping next to one housing a brown mare. Hayes opened the gate. "Get in there and stand right up against Maggie."

"Why?"

"Those people out there might have a thermal scanner. If they do, they'll be able to see your heat signature and know you're not a horse, but if you're next to her, it's possible they won't see the difference. Now go!"

Feeling more than just a little nervous, Brandon entered the stall. Feeding the horses was one thing, but standing next to Maggie was something else entirely. As Brandon pressed against her, he was sure she would pull away, or maybe even bite and kick at him. But while she did turn her head and look at him for a second, she remained where she was.

Two stalls away, just above the sound of the helicopter, one of the horses huffed several times. Mr. Hayes said some soothing words, and the animal seemed to calm down.

The barn began to shudder from the wind generated by the aircraft as it slowed to a hover near the front and began circling the building. As it worked its way past the stall Brandon was in, he closed his eyes tight and repeated to himself, "Don't see me. Don't see me. Don't see me."

After what felt like forever, the helicopter rose higher into the air, and headed west toward the Lodge.

Five minutes later, the horses wandered out into the meadow, and Brandon and Mr. Hayes were safely under the cover of the trees.

39

I.D. MINUS 10 MINUTES

BLUEBIRD TIME 10:50 A.M.

THE DIRECTORS WERE gathered in the conference area at the back of the Cradle. The DOP thought it was an excellent location. While those on the other side of the glass wall wouldn't be able to hear the final vote, they would be able to see the Directors, and could tell their children someday that they'd witnessed the start of the new world.

The only non-Director in the room was Rosemary Eames. She was the Principal Director's personal aide, and, as such, was tasked with making sure the recording devices were working correctly and the meeting went smoothly.

For a brief moment, the DOP imagined future generations listening in awe to the playback of this momentous occasion. Hell, he would probably listen to it himself in the coming years, a reminder of how hard they had worked, how hard *he* had worked, to reach the future they knew was humanity's only chance at true survival.

"The time is now ten fifty a.m., Central Standard Time," Rosemary said for the record. "All the Directors are present." She nodded at the Principal Director, who stood up.

"Today marks a beginning, not an end," he said, his aged voice gravelly. "Though we have put considerable effort into bringing this moment about, the task ahead will be even more difficult as we shape the new human civilization. So as this day proceeds, let us reflect on where we are and where we are going, and let us not forget our brothers and sisters who will be sacrificed for the betterment of mankind." He turned to the DOP. "The floor is yours."

The DOP rose to his feet. "Thank you, sir." He looked around at the others. As was decided when Project Eden was established, a final vote by all the Directors had to be taken prior to the Go signal being transmitted. A single No vote would delay implementation until the issues were resolved. "Directors of Project Eden, we have but a single item before us this morning. Implementation Day. Yes or no. Does anyone wish to say anything before the vote is taken?"

A few of the Directors shook their heads, while the others stared back stoically.

"Very good. Then we will proceed."

He sat, and motioned for Rosemary to begin.

"Director of Survival," she said.

"Yes."

"Director of Recovery."

"Yes."

"Director of Facilities."

"Yes."

She continued down the list.

"Yes."

"Yes."

"Yes."

"Yes."

"Principal Director," she said.

A pause, and then, "Yes."

She looked at the DOP. Since this was his operation, he was honored with the final vote. "Director of Preparation."

"Yes," he said.

Rosemary looked at the tablet of paper in front of her. "On the matter of moving forward with Implementation Day, nine votes yes and zero votes no."

Excitement and anticipation burned in the DOP's chest, but he was careful to keep his demeanor neutral. This was a solemn event, after all. Seven billion people were about to die.

But for a better world, he thought. *A much better world.*

"The vote is to move forward," he said. "May the new world we create be a lasting tribute to the old."

As if on cue, the other Directors began standing. One by one, they made their way to the DOP and shook his hand. As each Director finished, he headed out into the Cradle to be in place when the DOP entered the code that would make what they'd just voted for a reality.

Finally, it was just the DOP, the Principal Director, and Rosemary.

"Are you holding up all right?" the Principal asked as he shook the DOP's hand.

The question was unexpected. "I'm fine, sir."

The Principal looked at him for a moment, then said, "Good. Let's start our new beginning."

As they walked out, it finally hit the DOP what the Principal had probably meant. In minutes, it would be by the DOP's hand alone that the order to exterminate ninety-nine percent of the human race went out—a genocide unlike any genocide the world had ever seen. He would be the one directly responsible.

But he'd long ago come to terms with that. It was the greater good that was important.

For the first time since he'd woken up that morning, he allowed a smile to grace his lips.

———————

WHILE THE VOTE was going on in the room at the back of the Cradle, security officer Phillips frowned at his monitor. One of the indicators on the screen had just switched from Red to Green, letting him know someone had entered Bluebird through the emergency tunnel. He clicked on it to bring up the details.

AUTHORIZED ENTRY: ROWAN, BENJAMIN—SECURITY DETAIL RANK 2

Phillips signaled Ross that he wanted to speak with him.

"Yes?" Ross said over the intercom, his voice impatient.

"Rowan's turned up, sir."

"Rowan? Where?"

"He just entered through the tunnel."

"He's been gone for hours. Where the hell has he been?"

"I haven't been able to talk to him yet, sir."

Ross paused before responding. "Send someone to check on him, and recall the search team."

"Yes, sir."

40

OLIVIA HELD UP a hand, stopping everyone.

In the distance, they could hear footsteps. She looked around quickly, and pointed at a door fifteen feet back the way they'd come. Without wasting a second, they filed into the room and closed the door behind them.

They heard the footsteps enter the hallway where they'd been, and walk past their current position. There was only a single set.

Olivia pointed at two of her men, then opened the door wide enough so they could slip out.

When they returned forty-five seconds later, they were carrying a man with a sidearm strapped to his belt. Though there were no obvious wounds, it was apparent the man was dead.

Once the body was on the floor, Olivia said, "Everyone ready? We're not going to have time to stop again."

Nods all around.

"They'll all be in the Cradle."

"The Cradle?" Ash asked.

"It's what they call the command center. There's bound to be some security there, but not much. The rest will be upstairs covering the ground entrances. Once we have the Cradle secured, I'll lock them down so they can't get to us."

"We're going to have to deal with them at some point."

She smiled. "Trust me."

Ash frowned, uncomfortable, but said nothing.

"Any other questions?" she asked.

He shook his head.

"So we can go?" she asked.

"Please."

As they reentered the hall, Ash couldn't help but think there was something she wasn't telling him.

41

BLUEBIRD TIME 10:58 A.M.

As THE DOP entered the Cradle from the conference room, everyone sitting at the monitoring stations stood. There was no applause. Silence seemed to be the appropriate response to the moment.

Solemnly, he made his way to the empty station that sat by itself, front and center in front of the monitor wall. Once he reached the desk, he turned and faced the personnel of Bluebird. Along with the Directors who were standing in front, and those at the stations, there were two dozen others squeezed in along the walls, nearly everyone at the outpost who wasn't needed on security detail elsewhere. All eyes were on him.

He felt a surge of pride. These were some of the most dedicated members of Project Eden, most had been a part of the organization for at least a decade, and many of them for more. What he was about to do was as much for them as it was for everyone else.

Though it wasn't part of the plan for the day, he felt he needed to say something, something everyone would remember. He'd been wrestling with what that should be for days. Finally he decided to just go with the first words that came to mind.

"Our actions here today are meant to accomplish only one thing—the ability for humankind to reach its full potential. With your dedication, heart, and service, we will achieve this."

All right. Perhaps it wasn't *One small step for man*, but no one in the room seemed to care.

Exit 9

He looked at the digital clock on the wall. They were eighty-three seconds away, less than a minute and a half until the time finally arrived.

42

THEY PAUSED AT the junction, each of them listening closely for anyone who might be in the intersecting hallway.

For several seconds there was nothing, then a distant voice drifted toward them.

"...here today...meant...one...for...to reach...potential..."

Ash glanced at his watch. It was almost eleven a.m. If Olivia was right, they were seconds from being out of time.

"We need to go now," he whispered.

43

BLUEBIRD TIME 10:59 A.M.

As THE DOP sat down at the computer, a hush fell over the room.

Ross had already brought up the activation screen, so all the DOP had to do was input his personal password and the correct code. He typed the alphanumeric combination he'd memorized long ago into the password box.

The code itself he didn't know, not yet, anyway. It was currently in the Principal Director's possession. Per protocol, the Principal would not hand it over until thirty seconds prior to the time assigned for Implementation Day to begin. Which meant, as the DOP noted, he would have it in twenty-five seconds.

He clasped his hands and set them in front of him. He heard the door at the back of the room open.

"Well, I'm glad we made it in time."

44

THE DOOR WAS open about an inch. Through the gap, Ash spied several people, all looking away from the door at an angle. The voice they heard earlier had stopped and been replaced by an eerie silence.

Olivia quickly divided her people into two groups, and made it clear where she wanted them to go. She looked at Ash and Chloe, and indicated they were to follow her.

She put one hand on the doorknob, and began counting down with the other.

Three.

Two.

One.

She pushed the door open. The two small groups went in first, then she stepped through with Ash and Chloe behind her.

"Well," she said loudly enough for everyone to hear. "I'm glad we made it in time."

The entire room seemed to turn as one to look at them. Immediately, the five security men scattered throughout the space went for their handguns. They could have saved the effort. Before any of them had their weapon above their waist, Olivia's people opened fire. The security guards dropped to the floor, dead.

Screams of terror and surprise filled the room, as those nearest the new arrivals moved away as quickly as they could. Several people went for the doors, trying to get out, but when gunfire rang out again, slamming into the wall near the exit, they pulled back.

Olivia rushed toward the front of the room, where an unremarkable middle-aged man sitting in front of a computer on a solitary table had just been handed an envelope by an older, but similarly unremarkable man.

"I'll take that," she said, snatching it out of his hand.

45

THE DOP FROZE. Standing at the back of the room was Olivia Silva.

She had once been one of the brightest stars of Project Eden. In fact, KV-27a would not have been possible but for her early work. Up until that previous spring when they learned otherwise, they had thought she was killed in the raid on the lab where she had been doing her research.

For the initial seconds, he thought she'd come back to join them, but that idea immediately vanished when the people who'd come in with her opened fire on the security detail. Joining them was *not* on her agenda, he realized.

The Principal seemed to have come to the same conclusion. He rushed forward, his hand moving under his jacket. Just as he pulled out an envelope, there was another round of gunfire, this time aimed at the doors to keep anyone from leaving.

"Here," the Principal said as he handed the DOP the envelope. "Input the code!"

The DOP turned the envelope over, and stuck his finger under the end of the flap. But before he could rip it open, Olivia was standing in front of him.

"I'll take that," she said, grabbing it.

She had come to stop them. He couldn't believe it. The Project was something she'd believed in just as much as he had, but now she was going to keep it from happening.

"Why?" he asked.

"You *know* what we're trying to do," the Principal said. "If you stop us, you'll damn our whole species."

"Oh, will I?" she asked. She pulled out a pistol from her pocket, and pointed it at the old man's forehead.

"You wouldn't dare," he said.

"Oh, please. I would."

She pulled the trigger.

A collective gasp filled the room as the Principal Director dropped dead to the floor.

Olivia pushed the DOP out of the way, and sat in front of the computer. Without closing the activation window, she opened the program that ran Bluebird's security system. Navigating it like an expert, she began sealing off different sections of the facility until the only exit from the Cradle would be out the emergency tunnel.

"There," she said, standing. "I think we can relax a little now. Everyone move to an outer wall and have a seat."

Slowly at first, but with growing speed that was encouraged by Olivia's team, the Project Eden members did as ordered. All, that was, except for the Directors. Olivia made clear with her gun that they had to remain where they were. A few glanced at the floor where their former leader lay, while the others kept their eyes on her.

"How long did you know I was being held captive?" she asked them.

"We didn't know," one of them blurted out. "We were told you were dead."

She looked at him with faux compassion. "Perhaps that's what *you* thought, but what about the rest of you?"

Most nodded their heads, indicating they'd heard the same thing, but the DOP and the Director of Survival did not.

She looked at the DOP. "You knew, of course."

"Not until recently," he admitted.

"Let me guess. Last spring, when my friend over there delivered my message to Dr. Karp." She nodded toward a man standing in the aisle.

The DOP looked at him, and squinted his eyes. Yes. It had to be.

Captain Daniel Ash. The very man whose immune system

made it possible for the Project to come up with a vaccine for the virus. It was almost fitting he was here, though the look in the captain's eyes was anything but friendly.

"So, over half a year," Olivia continued.

Again, the DOP made no reply.

"Did you try to get me out at any point during that time?" She shook her head. "Don't answer. You'll only embarrass yourself."

She returned to the computer and accessed a new area of the security program. When the DOP saw what it was, his eyes widened. On the screen were the controls for Bluebird's self-destruct mechanism, intended to be used if there was no other way to protect the Project. But there was no way she could set it, was there? She would need the correct security sequence, and it was kept safely locked away in—

The vault in Costa Rica.

In the security boxes at every depot, there was always one that contained the self-destruct code for Bluebird in case it had to be remotely activated. The other boxes that had been opened had been a ruse to cover up what she really wanted.

Activating the sequence would still need one of the Directors to sign on, but he'd already done that for her.

Dear God.

46

ASH HAD NEVER felt so relieved as he did when Olivia stopped the man from activating the release of the virus. He didn't even flinch when she killed the older man. But when she started working on the computer again, he moved forward so he could see what she was doing.

She'd accessed a self-destruct system. *Good.* This place needed to go.

He watched as she set the timer to fifteen minutes, then hit Start.

Without getting up, she turned to the men she'd kept at the front of the room. "You'll stay here. The world won't be needing your services after all."

One of the men said, "You can't let us die in here."

Ash started to scoff at the irony, but was cut off by the sound of Olivia's gun. The bullet ripped into the man's leg, sending him crumpling to the ground.

She looked at the others. "If any of the rest of you want to try to leave, I'm happy to make sure that doesn't happen."

There didn't seem to be any takers.

"Good." She glanced at Ash. "You and your friend should move out into the hallway with my men. We're not going to have a lot of time to get out of here. I'll join you as soon as I've had a final, private conversation with my old colleagues."

There was a tingle at the back of Ash's neck, that sense there was something he was still missing.

But the threat *was* over. Olivia had stopped it, and in less than fourteen minutes the entire place was going to be destroyed. If he wanted to get back to Josie and Brandon, Olivia was right. They needed to leave.

He nodded, and started for the door. Ahead, Chloe and the members of Olivia's team were already filing out.

A few of the Project Eden people tried to go, too, but they were shoved back. Those that Ash passed pleaded with him with their eyes, as if he might take them along, but he had no compassion for any of them. They had chosen their path when they joined the Project. They could all go to hell as far as he was concerned.

47

Olivia TORE OPEN the envelope the late Principal Director had given to the Director of Preparation. This was it. The activation code.

The DOP had been so very close to being the one who carried it out. She couldn't have that.

She removed the piece of paper, and read what was written on it—the code that simply had to be input on the screen, followed by the Enter key. One word followed by one number: EXIT 9.

Was there a hidden meaning to them? she wondered. Did it matter? The only important thing was that they were the two most powerful words in the world.

Five simple characters that could wipe out mankind.

If anyone was going to bring on that kind of chaos, it would be her.

She placed her fingers on the keyboard.

E-X-I-T-9

48

As ASH REACHED the door, he heard paper ripping behind him. It was a familiar, distinct sound. Not a sheet being torn in half, but something slower with stops and starts along the way. As he turned to see if he was right, he heard the tapping of keys.

The Go code for the virus! Olivia had opened it and was entering it in the system.

His weapon was in his hand before he even realized he'd reached for it.

Olivia struck another key.

"Stop!" he yelled, moving forward.

She looked over at him and smiled. This was what she'd intended to do from the beginning, he realized. This was what she'd been hiding. She wanted to both destroy the Project *and* bring its nightmare to reality.

"Olivia, don't do it!"

She raised her right index finger, letting it hover over the edge of the keyboard.

Over the Enter key.

49

THE ONLY THING Sanjay has tried that keeps Kusum from running away is to promise that if nothing happens in the next few days, he would take her back and turn himself over to the police. He knows she can tell he's not lying, and eventually she gives in.

He drives them deep into the countryside, where neither of them has ever been before.

He assumes Ayush has died. His cousin looked nearly dead the last time he saw him, so Kusum is the only thing he has left.

As long as he can save *her* life, she can hate him forever.

———————

JESSICA WHITNEY SITS numbly at her brother's desk. She still cannot comprehend that he is dead.

Killed by an explosion? It just doesn't make sense.

The only reason she has come to Palmer Transport & Shipping is to find a list of his contacts and clients, so that she and a few of her cousins can start letting people know in the morning that he's gone.

Her eyes wander over his desk, stopping momentarily on a pad of paper near his phone. On it, in typical John fashion, there are the doodles and scribbles he often made when he was on the phone. It's a new sheet so there aren't quite as many marks as usual. Some are impossible to read, while others—"H-K," "WHO," and "container"—are clearer.

What any of it means, she has no idea.

Unexpectedly, her sadness overwhelms her. She rips the sheet from the pad, and crumples it into a tight ball. When she finally gets up, she drops the paper into the trash and never thinks of it again.

———————

PATRICIA MENDES IS also in mourning. In her case, it's for a brother and an uncle. Their deaths are surprisingly similar to the man in Perth's, and two other people in Cleveland, though she will never know this.

The police have already decided that Rodrigo must have discovered a drug lab and had let Uncle Hector know. It's as good a story as any, and both her brother and uncle come out heroes who were trying to do the right thing.

The true story of what happened, she keeps to herself, along with the guilt she will carry until she takes her last, gasping breath.

———————

JEANNIE SAUNDERS IS coughing again.

Thankfully the attack only lasts for a few seconds. Her chest muscles are so sore, and her throat so raw, she is sure that soon she'll pass out from the pain. It would be a blessing, actually. A way not to think about anything.

Corey is dead. No one has told her this, but she knows. She can see it in their eyes, even behind the protective suits they wear when they come into her room.

What happened to Blanton, she has no idea. She should ask, but she doesn't have the strength.

What she really wants is to go home and lie on her bed.

She closes her eyes, that thought on her mind, and dreams that's exactly where she is.

———————

IN A VACATION home on North Carolina's Outer Banks, Tamara Costello and Bobby Lion spend their time either watching TV or walking along the nearly deserted shore. It is cold and the ocean looks angry, but the only thing on either of their minds is the phone Tamara carries in her pocket. Will it ring? And when it does, will Matt tell them it's time? That the video they hope they never have to show anyone needs to be released?

There is no way to know the answer. All they can do now is wait.

———————

RICH "PAX" PAXTON once more tries to reach Gagnon on his satellite phone. For hours his calls have gone unanswered, and he is concerned. He has tried Captain Ash, too, but received the same results.

He and his team know the research facility on Amund Ringnes Island is exactly what it claims to be and not home to Project Eden. This means either their assumption about Bluebird's location is wrong, or it's on the same island Ash and Chloe and Red are on.

That's why the unanswered calls trouble him so much. If Bluebird is on Yanok, he worries that something has happened to the others. He wants to go there right now and make sure they're all right, but even if Gagnon answers, Pax and his people won't be going anywhere soon.

A storm is moving in, and it's a big one.

———————

IN A SECRET basement known as the Bunker, below the burning hulk of a building that was once called the Lodge, a teenage girl named Josie Ash sits alone in her room, her back against the wall.

Though there are others in the Bunker with her, she has never felt so isolated. Her thoughts run to her father, off on some unknown mission, and to her brother, trapped outside the Bunker where the killers are. She is supposed to be watching over him, taking care of him. She can do neither now.

Without realizing it, she begins to rock. *Just let me wake up*, she thinks. *Let this be a nightmare.*

Then she realizes that while she isn't asleep, a nightmare is exactly what this is.

———————

BRANDON ASH PUTS a hand against the cut on his cheek.

He got it while he ran behind Mr. Hayes. It stings but it's not too deep.

"We'll wash it out once we get some water," Mr. Hayes whispers.

Brandon nods. Water or no water, he'll be fine.

He wonders how far they've gone into the woods. It can't be too far. He can still hear the thumping of the helicopter, and thinks he can hear the crackling of the fire, too. He can't, but it doesn't matter.

They'd seen the blaze for a few minutes while they hid near the edge of the forest. Two blazes, really, because both the Lodge and the dormitory are on fire. Brandon worries the flames will reach the Bunker where his sister and the others are. More than once, Mr. Hayes tells him it's impossible.

He hopes Mr. Hayes is right.

THE COMING STORM has moved ashore on Yanok Island. Both wind and snow are fighting for dominance, though neither can claim victory.

Captain Daniel Ash knows nothing about the storm at this moment, but even if he does, he wouldn't care. His focus is on the woman at the other side of the room.

Their eyes are locked. He knows what she is going to do. He wishes there were another way he could stop her, but there isn't.

There is only one thing he can do. As he makes this decision, he sees in her eyes that she's made hers, too.

Her finger is already in motion when he pulls the trigger.

Anxious to know what happens next?
Look for Book Three of the Project Eden Thrillers in
Spring 2012.

ACKNOWLEDGMENTS

First, a thank you to all of you for embracing the Project Eden books, and urging me to "write faster." I'm trying, oh Lord, am I trying!

As with *Sick* and my Logan Harper books, I'm blessed to be working with the very talented Jeroen ten Berge on the design of my covers. He does a bang-up job, and I couldn't be happier.

Probably the most important member of my team these days is someone I can definitely not do without. She keeps me from making a fool of myself, and constantly makes my work better. I'm talking, of course, about my fantastic copyeditor, Elyse Dinh-McCrillis. I could not do this without her.

And, as always, there's the revolving group of folks who keep me sane: Robert Browne, Bill Cameron, Derek Rogers, Stephen Blackmoore, Ivonne Decervantes, Tasha Alexander, Nine, and my parents. (I'm sure I've missed a few, so apologies for that.)

Finally, life would not be complete without my kids, Ronan, Fiona, and Keira. They are simply wonderful.